DEADLY PARADE

The striped robes of the chanting priests seemed to be writhing like snakes, and the faces that bobbed and rose in the dance were all looking at him. Arris could not see if they were smiling or scowling.

His horse was gone. The procession seemed to have stopped. The people danced in circles around Arris, shaking their cymbals at him, raw-edged circles of beaten bronze. They were faceless, whirling like weeds blown in a windspout. Then two figures in smeared, muddy black shoved through the dancers. Even through his oddly blurred vision, Arris could see that they held long knives in light, underhand grips. . . .

Ace Books by Catherine Cooke

THE WINGED ASSASSIN
REALM OF THE GODS

CATHERINE
COOKE

REALM OF
THE GODS

ACE BOOKS, NEW YORK

To my sister Amy
with my deepest love.

This book is an Ace original edition,
and has never been previously published.

REALM OF THE GODS

An Ace Book/published by arrangement with
the author

PRINTING HISTORY
Ace edition/June 1988

ISBN: 0-441-70840-4

Ace Books are published by The Berkley Publishing Group,
200 Madison Avenue, New York, New York 10016.
The name ''ACE'' and the ''A'' logo
are trademarks belonging to Charter Communications, Inc.
PRINTED IN THE UNITED STATES OF AMERICA

10   9   8   7   6   5   4   3   2   1

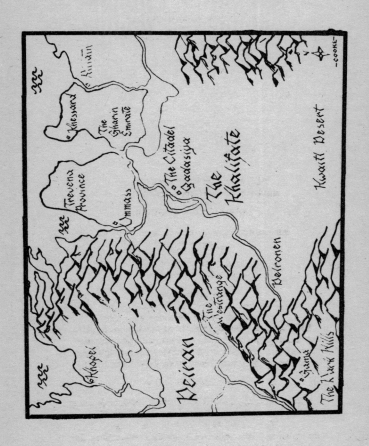

CHAPTER

1

"MY HORSE is almost spent, Terai," Arris shouted over the pounding of the animal's galloping hooves on the rocky trail, over the roaring in his own ears. His long black hair flew back behind him in the freezing wind, and the thin ceremonial tunic he wore did nothing to protect him. Sleet had begun to fall across the high ridge where they raced their stolen mounts. The saddle on Arris's horse had begun to slip, its girth loosening with the sweat that lathered the horse's flanks. Arris gripped with his knees despite the pain of blisters, and willed his numb muscles to hold out a little longer.

A short, stocky form hunched over his horse's neck, Terai rode ahead of him at a gallop. The fifty-year-old Yaighan was surely exhausted too, but he was warmer than Arris. He wore thick, woolen traveling clothes, and had boots, while Arris's feet were bare and blue with cold. There had been no time to plan this, no time to search out better equipment or fresher horses. Prince Saresha had given them this one chance to escape, and they had taken it.

"We're almost there," Terai shouted over his shoulder.

Sleet whipped Arris's face like a stinging lash, and iced his skin and hair. The horse stumbled over a stone and righted itself with a wheeze of protest. Arris leaned forward to shout encouragement to the animal. Only a little farther. Terai had said they were almost there. Wherever there was. Some safe, fortified place in the mountains, Arris supposed, but they had no weapons but a knife, and

1

no food to hold out against an assault. The soldiers and priests led by the fanatic Karillos would not give up easily.

Karillos was the high priest of the Qadasiya Temple, and this morning one of his gods had appeared to him. Sygathi Ylla, weary from his victory over the Goddess Rehoman, had commanded Karillos to kill the Goddess's creature Arris. Rehoman was sealed in her own Temple, unable to gain her freedom unless Arris returned to release her. Karillos and his god were both certain that Arris would go back to the Goddess, even though Arris had betrayed her last night when he had rescued the Crown Prince Saresha from the altar of sacrifice.

Saresha had given Arris and Terai this chance: a knife to cut their bonds, and a head start on their pursuers. He had balanced the debt he owed Arris for saving his life in the Temple. Arris could expect nothing more from Saresha. They were even, and Arris had made himself the Prince's enemy. He had killed Saresha's uncles, the Regents of the Khalifate; he had kidnapped the Prince and delivered him to the altar of the Goddess. He could not take back what he had done. Now Saresha waited with some of his Companions, guarded in a narrow valley, while Karillos led the rest of the Khalifate soldiers and priests after Arris and Terai.

"Here," Terai called. Arris squinted into the sleet to see ahead of them, and his horse stumbled into the hindquarters of Terai's mount. Arris leaned back and reined the animal to a halt, wondering if he could ever get it to run again. Both horses stood with their heads down, blowing and gasping, their sides heaving.

Terai turned around on his horse's back. Lank, graying hair blew across his flint-colored eyes with the sleet. His expression was grim and exhausted. Like Arris, he had to be suffering the aftereffects of a mind-numbing drug the Yaighan had given them yesterday afternoon. But if headaches and nausea were all that they faced today, they would be lucky.

"Dismount," Terai said. "Quickly, boy." He slid down from his saddle, holding his horse's long reins in one hand. Arris jumped down from his own horse. He landed off balance and fell, scraping his right knee on a rock. He could see the smear of blood, but he could not feel it. The cold had leached most sensation from his limbs, leaving only a general ache and stiffness.

The trail they followed stopped abruptly, looking out over a chasm that split the ridge in a deep gash as far as Arris could see. A bridge of weathered plank and rope swung in the freezing wind over the thirty-foot width of the gap. Beyond the bridge, there was another trail, little more than a goat path leading to the top of the mountain.

Arris got to his feet and gathered his horse's reins in his clumsy hands. "Can we get the horses across that?" he asked.

"Perhaps," Terai said. Then he looked sharply at Arris. "You can see the bridge?"

"The sleet isn't that thick."

"No. But our enemies will see no bridge, and no trail on the mountain beyond. They will see only a gorge, and a sheer face on the other side. It is part of the High Track, guarded by the power of the Goddess."

"Do you mean there's a shield of illusion, or is the bridge like one of the gates of Gama?" Arris could see nothing supernatural ahead of him. If it was magic, he should be as blind as any stranger who chanced across the path. He had renounced his power years ago, and last night had made him the Goddess's enemy.

"It is a part of the High Track. That is a path to many realms," Terai said. "Come."

"Karillos will see the bridge," Arris said, looking behind them at the bony hilltop. "He was able to open the gates to the city, and summon his gods. Even if this place really is guarded, it will be no barrier to him."

"Perhaps not." Terai stepped onto the bridge. The precarious structure creaked beneath his weight. "Does that mean we should stand here and wait for him?" His horse balked like a donkey, spreading its front hooves and leaning back against its reins with the bit in its teeth.

Arris slapped the animal on the rear, with no result. He shoved at it, trying to put it off balance so it would move forward.

Terai dropped the reins and looked at the horse in regret. "We haven't the time to convince them it's safe. Come, Arris, leave the horses."

It had hurt to ride, bare-legged and blistered as he was, but Arris far preferred that to walking the stony trails of the Dark Hills without shoes. He hesitated, but then he heard a shout behind him. A horse and rider were topping the rise. The man was tall and blond, one of Saresha's Companions. Perhaps it was Falcmet or Husayn. Arris's half-brothers did not care that Arris had committed his crimes out of vengeance for their murdered father. They hated Arris more, perhaps, because he was their brother and a disgrace to the family name.

"We have them!" a voice cried fiercely in the Khalifate language.

Arris abandoned his horse, pushed past Terai's mount, and ran onto the unsteady bridge. The wind battered at him, and his feet slipped with each step on the icy, wet boards. Terai ran lightly to the opposite end ahead of him. Arris was across in a few moments, breathing hard, looking back over his shoulder as more of Karillos's band appeared on the other side. There were more than twenty of them now.

"We are taken if they can cross this," Arris muttered.

"Where are they?" called the lead rider, Arris's brother Falcmet. Falcmet's loyalty was to the Prince, not to his brother, and not to the Yaighan people who had made him their ambassador to the Khalifate. Now he leaned over beside the two horses Arris and Terai had abandoned, and gathered their reins in his hands.

Karillos rode at Falcmet's right, swaying a little on his horse like a straw man bound to the saddle. The priest must surely be exhausted from his efforts to hold off Yaighan magic and summon his gods last night. Yet his pale face was fierce beneath his golden turban. He raised an arm to command attention.

"They are just ahead. I can still sense their presence. This is some illusion, some daimon's magic such as we saw in their unholy city. I will soon break through the spell." He was thirty years old, a lean and ascetic man, clean-shaven, handsome but for his narrow blue eyes. Arris feared him at this moment more than he feared the anger of any gods.

But Karillos seemed to have used up his mental strength. He cried out in frustration, startling his horse so that it pranced and whinnied. Arris saw that Terai's eyes were closed, and his face still in concentration. He guessed that his companion was adding to the power of the High Track, constructing a direct shield against Karillos. Terai had been a priest of the Goddess. He could still draw on her power. Yet Arris mistrusted and feared the magic that was protecting them. The Goddess must surely want revenge upon them both for their betrayal. They could not trust her High Track to be safe, even if they were no longer pursued by the soldiers and priests of the Khalifate.

Arris stood for a moment, watching the confusion, listening to the curses and threats of his enemies. He could not see Husayn. Perhaps the Second Ambassador of the Yaighan had had second thoughts about joining a mob to murder his brother. He had probably stayed to guard the Prince. Arris had been trying not to think about Saresha. The Prince must hate him now, and he would surely never see him again. It would be best to forget him.

"This will not stop us!" Karillos called over the chasm. His voice held harsh power that made Arris shudder. "The gods have decreed that you must die."

"We waste time and words," Falcmet said in his cool, familiar voice. "Come. We'll find a way around this. They won't get far without horses." The Companions turned with him, and the priests soon followed. Arris watched them until they vanished in the sleet.

"Can they follow us?" he asked.

Terai shrugged. He looked older than his fifty years, with deep lines in his dark face. He turned into the sleet, squinting his eyes, and began to walk up the narrow trail toward the mountaintop. The wind was full in their faces in that direction. Arris hunched his body against it, crossing his arms and nestling his hands in his armpits for what little warmth was there. He hurried to follow Terai.

• • •

The morning wore on under a frigid gray sky. The sleet came and went as Arris and Terai climbed slowly along the high ridges of the Dark Hills. The tallest mountains lay to the south, where the holy city of Gama was hidden between peaks. These were lesser hills, not as daunting as the Teeth of Gama, but still stony and unforgiving. It was nearly noon when Arris felt that he could go no farther. They had seen no sign of their pursuit since they had left them at the bridge.

Arris stopped to catch his breath at the top of a punishing rise. He had a knifing headache, and his shivering was as much from the drug he had been given yesterday as from the cold. His face felt frozen. His arms and legs might have belonged to another man, for as much as Arris could feel their presence.

Before him, he could see a daunting panorama of peaks and jagged, narrow valleys. Dark clouds moved in patches around the mountaintops. He did not know this part of the Dark Hills, but he trusted that Terai did. The older man had walked over much of the world in his years as a Yaighan courier and spy, from the Khalifate to the Kwaitl Desert and even inside the Deirani Empire. He had served his people loyally; now Terai was an outcast for helping Arris escape from the Temple. He had chosen that, for his principles, for a friendship that Arris did not think he deserved.

Arris tried to remember the mental techniques he had learned in his training as a Jai-Sohn assassin. He had been taught ways to concentrate thoughts and strength, almost as priests of the Goddess used their magical powers. If Arris could attain some level of Jai-Sohn trance, he thought, he could make himself feel the cold less. He had used the concentrating trance when he had carried out his mission for the Emperor of Deiran, killing the Regents, Nievan and Maenad, in their tower study at the Citadel. But then he had been rested, driven on by his old dreams of revenge; now he was exhausted, sick, and cold, and he could not focus his thoughts at all.

"We cannot stop here," Terai's voice said worriedly.

Arris blinked at his friend, returning from the half trance

he had created. Terai's face was bluish, his hair rimmed with ice crystals. Exhaustion sat deep in his dark eyes. Yet he still had the energy to go on. Perhaps he was drawing on his mental powers; he was a Yaighan, and had been a priest. Terai's power could not compare with that of Karillos, but he had as strong a will as the Khalifate priest.

Arris had once had power far beyond Terai's, but he had sworn never to use it, and now he no longer could. "I cannot keep walking," Arris said in a voice that sounded weak against the mountain wind. "No one is following us anymore."

"Karillos may know exactly where we are. If he has the strength remaining, he can seek out the presence of our minds." Terai shifted from one foot to the other. Even with his boots on, his feet were probably cold.

"If he knows where we are, he'll find us anyway, whether we keep moving or stop to rest." Arris was too weary to be frightened by the prospect.

"We're on the High Track, and that offers some protection. If we leave the track to find shelter, it will no longer protect us. And I cannot shield us with that drug spinning in my head."

"If the Goddess protects this path, how can you be certain we're protected? She'd have no reason to help us after what we did to her."

"She has every reason to keep you alive," Terai said. "You may be her only chance to get free of the Temple again."

The Goddess would have to find some other way, Arris thought. He wanted nothing to do with her, or her plans for him. He was free now as he had never been before. Free of the shadow of prophecy.

He had been created by the Goddess to be her Yearking at the Millennium; so he had been told, when he was twelve years old. Last night, the Goddess had wakened and called to him. Arris had felt the strength of that call, and knew the truth of what he had been told. It was his destiny. But Saresha Ilkharani had been the sacrifice upon the altar. An unwilling sacrifice, but that was not why Arris had broken the ritual to save him.

Once, Arris had plotted the Prince's death. He had pretended to be Saresha's friend, meaning to betray him all the time. But the pretense had turned on him. By the time Arris realized that he truly loved the Prince, it was too late to stop the plan he and Terai had devised. Arris had never thought he would be the one with the knife when Saresha was bound to the altar. If another Candidate for Yearking had been there, Saresha would be dead. Arris could not do it. He had faced the wakening Goddess, and Sasha bound to the standing stone, and he had made his choice.

"I have to rest." Arris hugged himself, unable to stop his furious shivering, unable to control the clacking of his teeth. "If you think we need protection, I could call the daimon. It might be willing to help."

Terai was vehement. "No. More likely it would kill us both. You promised it your soul last night in the Temple. It can have you whenever it wants. Don't tempt it."

The intermittent sleet had begun to fall again, like icy tears. Arris had not thought much yet about the pact he had made with the daimon Aghlayeshkusa. He had never meant to do it. He had summoned the daimon before. The first time, he had been ten years old, terrified and fascinated by the powerful being that had come at his call. The daimon had wanted him ever since that night.

He had had no choice in the Temple. He had resisted as well as he could, but the call of the Goddess, the power of her Messenger the Lossiran, and the massed will of the Yaighan priests and priestesses had pressed him on. The knife they had given him had a blood thirst of its own. Sasha had looked at him, his sky-blue eyes bleak with resignation, and Arris had known then that he would rather die himself than kill the Prince. He had called the daimon. He had promised it his soul, and he did not regret it.

"I cannot walk anymore," Arris repeated dully, looking away from Terai, scanning the hillsides for shelter. "You go on, if you want to."

"Damn you," Terai muttered. But he was not a fool, and he surely realized that Arris was telling the truth. He could not go any farther. It was no use to try to persuade him. "Very well. There are some shallow caves to the south, half a mile back. We'll go there. We dare not build a fire, but we'll be out of the wind. We'll rest. But no more than a few hours, understand?''

Arris nodded, grateful, wondering how he could walk the distance to the caves. But his legs obeyed him as he turned around, and he and Terai headed for shelter with the sleet at their backs.

The cave was what Terai had promised: shallow, and out of the wind. It was hidden behind a large, fallen boulder, with the threat of more rockfalls above it in a slope of shale and soft earth. The floor of the cave was uneven and sandy. It was less a cave than a cleft between rocks, and at the top it had cracks that were open to the cold. Terai and Arris built no fire, for fear that smoke through the cracks would alert their enemies. They huddled together in the back of the cave. Arris would have thought he could not have gotten to sleep when he was so cold. Instead, it was frighteningly easy to drift off, and his last waking thought was the hope that Terai's warmth would keep him from freezing to death.

He dreamed of Danae, blond-haired and green-eyed, singing to herself in her low, breathy voice as she wrote out parts to a new piece of music she had composed. She sat on a bench in a garden of the Citadel, wearing a Khalifate lady's gown and veil, and Arris wished again that they could turn their friendship into something more. He quoted a few lines from a Deirani love poem to Danae, who looked at him with one delicate eyebrow raised. She had made her position clear; she would have him to herself or not at all. Arris could not offer her that. Still, he was glad she was his friend.

The dream changed, and Danae's expression froze into one of shock and horror. She had come into the Regents' study that evening, just after Arris had killed both the rulers of the Khalifate. She had seen the bodies fallen in their blood, and had recognized Arris in his Jai-Sohn black. She almost wept with fury as she accused him. She threatened to betray him. If he was a true assassin, Arris knew, he would have killed her to be sure of her silence. Instead, he hit her over the head with the hilt of his sword, knocking her unconscious. He tied her up and left her there. As he climbed out the tower window, he felt as if he had cut off one of his limbs.

He began to dream of Saresha Ilkharani. The Prince was beautiful in his dream, smiling, his golden hair reflecting the sunlight. He laughed at Arris as they wrestled in his training room. His blue eyes were sapphires, and Arris could see through them to the skull beneath Saresha's face. No . . . he turned away from the image, and the dream obligingly turned with him.

He was sitting on a bench by a fountain, and Saresha took his hand, pulling him up. The Prince led him to look in the pool of colored water. Their faces wavered in reflection, side by side. Arris's hair and eyes were black, and Saresha was like his image reversed.

"We are the same person," Arris said to the Prince in his dream. It seemed to him that he finally understood. It had eluded his grasp for a long time, since he was a child. For a moment he was happy, gazing into the water. The two faces grew younger as he watched, until he and Saresha were nine years old again. He turned to the Prince, who spoke eagerly in a child's piping voice.

"Let's measure our shadows!"

It was a good idea. Arris stood with Sasha. Their backs were to the sun. They held hands and looked solemnly at the long, black shadows before them on the grass. Their shadows matched exactly, like two cut-out dolls joined at the hands. The two boys grinned at one another and looked again.

Arris began to feel uneasy, and then he became frightened. His shadow was changing. It grew taller. The shoulders broadened, then bulged grotesquely. It shifted into the inhuman form of the diamon he had summoned at the Temple of Rehoman. The Prince let go of his hand and took a step backward, then another. The blue eyes glared at him accusingly.

"I thought you were my friend," Saresha said in a man's voice.

"Wait," Arris said, but the child Prince had gone, and

he did not think he would ever find him again. Despair washed over him, and he sat down on the grass by the fountain and began to sob. His weeping was harsh, uncontrollable, but it was not enough for the loss he felt. The tears streamed down his face. "Oh, Sasha, I've lost you," he gasped. "I've lost you . . ."

"Arris. Arris, wake up." A rough voice broke through to him in a hissed whisper. It was Terai, and he was sitting on the floor of the cave with his arms around Arris. Arris forced his eyes open, and found to his dismay that his tears were real. He had been crying in his sleep. He twisted away from Terai and stood up unsteadily, walking to the entrance.

He stared at the underside of the boulder that shielded the opening. His breathing quieted slowly, and he regained control before he turned back around. "I'm sorry," he muttered, feeling he owed Terai something more than silence.

Terai's attempted smile was not convincing. "I woke you because I was afraid you might get louder. They could still be following you." More hesitantly the older man said, "You spoke a little in your sleep. You really . . . loved him, didn't you? Your Prince?"

"Yes," Arris whispered. "I love him." He leaned against the hard rock wall, feeling deadened by the cold of the early afternoon.

"I wonder if the Goddess meant for that to happen," Terai said, as if to himself.

"The Khalifate gods say it's a sin, for men to love other men. Saresha thinks it is. He would be horrified if he knew." Arris shrugged. "But he must hate me anyway."

Terai lay down again with his head pillowed on his hands, and spoke quietly. "To be hated by the one you love . . . I must have achieved that by now. The Lady will not forgive this, as she forgave me before."

Terai had been the Candidate for Yearking thirty years ago, when the Goddess had chosen a new priestess. Maella, the woman Terai had loved, had become the Lady. Terai had refused his calling as Yearking. He had not wanted only one year of Maella's love and then a ritual death.

Arris had tried to refuse the kingship yesterday, according to the custom. The Yaighan priests and priestesses would not accept that from him. In Terai's time, another Candidate had easily been chosen. Last night, however, the Goddess had wanted Arris only. If not for the daimon Aghlayeshkusa, she would have had him.

"We'll go on after nightfall," Terai said, little emotion now in his voice. "I know a farmhold a twelve-hour walk west of here. I've helped the family there in the past. You need clothes and shoes, and we need food. After that, it will be just a few days to the Deirani border." He sighed. "You might as well go back to sleep, if you can. If you can't, then stay alert for any signs of pursuit."

Arris sat down cross-legged at the entrance of the cave to stay on watch. He did not want to dream anymore. It seemed he might succeed in returning to Deiran. He wondered what he should tell the Emperor. He had fulfilled part of his mission. He had killed Nievan and Maenad Ilkharani. But he had not killed Saresha.

He supposed he could say that he had failed, that Karillos had rescued the Prince, that he had barely escaped with his life. He could not say that he had been willing to give up his life, that he had sold his soul, to keep Saresha alive.

CHAPTER

2

THEY HAD SLEPT until nightfall, and just after dawn the next morning they reached the farmhold Terai knew. Arris descended the hill path into the narrow valley, carefully placing his feet amid a tangled overgrowth of stickery brush. The place was poorly kept. A mountain stream ran by a sheepfold that had crumbled in places to the height of the sheep's bellies. The scrawny animals penned there had no better pasture to escape to. The hillsides were dry and barren, the garden a patch of mud and ice, the farmyard untidy, and the cottage beyond it in need of repair.

A woman sat at a loom on the cottage porch in the pale sunlight. The length of wool she was weaving was brightly dyed, but she wore layered clothes of a dull gray. She was slight, worn-looking, with black hair cut short, as if she were in mourning or had taken vows. Two small children ran with chickens in the yard.

"By the look of it, they've little aid to give," Arris muttered as he walked wearily in the path Terai's boots made. At the bottom of the hill, they reached the stream. A bridge had been built there over an old beaver dam.

Terai ran a hand through his shaggy, gray-streaked hair, pausing to look over the farmhold. "Something must be wrong. I've never known Chalin to be so careless with his work. Still, they're generous people. They'll find something to spare for us." He raised his voice as he strode across the bridge. "Goddess's blessing on this place and those who dwell in it!"

The woman rose from her stool with a startled cry. The

two children ran to the porch to clutch at her skirts, but she brushed them aside and hurried down the steps and across the yard toward the two men. If she had been surprised by Terai's hail, she was certainly not frightened.

"Ravil, it's Terai," the older man said as he went to meet her. Arris trailed behind Terai, too weary to make the effort of courtesy.

Ravil halted before them and made an awkward bow. She was young, Arris saw. Perhaps three years older than he, no more. Her face was thin and pinched-looking beneath her badly cut black hair. "My lord Terai," she said breathlessly, "the Goddess surely sent you here, so far out of season. I thought no one would come until the spring."

"Ravil, what has happened?" Terai took her hands between his. "Your husband . . ."

"Chalin is dead. Dead this past month, of a fever." She said it simply, but her grief was still raw in her eyes.

"I am sorry. There was no one here for you?"

She shook her head. "I had the fever, too. The winter set in before I recovered, or I'd have taken the girls and the sheep over the mountains to Gama. I haven't dared to go since, for fear of storms, with me the only one to keep the sheep or my daughters from straying. I thought I would wait until spring. Unless someone came through who was headed for Gama. Are you?"

"No," Terai said, almost harshly.

"We just came from there," Arris said.

"I can offer you no help, Ravil," Terai said, letting go of her hands. "I've only brought you more trouble. I will not deceive you. My friend and I are hunted men. We came here seeking shelter, rest, and food, and we're a danger to you while we're here. If you have nothing to give us, we'll go on quickly."

The young woman looked at Arris. Her gaze was probing, like a merchant's weighing a customer's purse. He had the uncomfortable sensation that she saw more than an exhausted young man in a white tunic. She was Yaighan, and most women of the race had power, whether or not they chose to become priestesses of Rehoman. Let her read what she could, Arris thought. He was too tired to care what she thought of him.

"You're welcome here, of course," she said, turning back to Terai. "Tell me who is hunting you or not, as you choose. Chalin always said that Terai was on the Lady's business, and we shouldn't question him."

Arris ventured a smile, and looked past the woman toward the cottage, where a thin stream of smoke rose to promise a warm hearth inside. Terai did not smile. He spoke in a low voice. "I'm no longer the Lady's envoy, and if she ever learns you've helped me, you may suffer for it. Don't feel bound by our friendship. If I had known you were alone here, I would not have endangered you thus."

"If I cannot be bound by friendship, then I have lost more than my husband." Ravil shrugged. "I've offered you the hospitality of my home. Refuse it if you wish, and go with my blessing. Or come with me, and I can give you food and warmer clothes."

"Both would be welcome," Arris said, with a glare at Terai. The older Yaighan still looked troubled. Well, he could skulk in the hills if he wanted to.

"Come, then," the woman said, turning to cross her farmyard again. Arris followed close behind her. After a moment he heard a sigh, and the sound of footsteps following.

The two little girls had hidden behind the doorframe of the cottage. They peered out like mice at a knothole, encouraged by a smile from their mother. One looked to be three years old, the other five. The five-year-old girl recognized Terai, and came to him demanding a kiss. He went on one knee and kissed her hand. She giggled and pulled away again. The younger girl stared at Arris with her dark eyes wide, apparently fascinated. He wondered what she was thinking. He had never spent much time with small children.

"What is your name?" the little girl demanded as he entered the cottage. "I'm Calla."

"My name is Arris." He did not pay much attention to her. The single room of the cottage was small and warm.

The floor was covered with woven rugs of bright wool, and the walls were hung with weaving as well. The fire in the hearth burned behind an iron grate. There was a wooden bench before the hearth. A table with four stools, and a large bed piled with sheepskin coverlets, were all the rest of the furniture. Arris had lived in two palaces, and this seemed as fine as my room he had seen.

"Calla, Seri, don't bother our guests," Ravil said gently. "Go back outside while the sun is shining. Take Prinn and Granna with you." The last two were dolls, made of brown wool cloth with shearling hair. The two girls picked the dolls up from the bed and ran out of the door laughing. Their mother closed the door behind them, shutting off the morning light. The hearthfire cast flickering shadows over the darkened room.

"Seri is almost old enough for the school in Gama," Terai said. "She's your daughter. She'll need some training if she has the Sight."

Ravil nodded. "Yes, I know." She seemed troubled, but it was not about her child. She watched Arris as openly as her youngest daughter had done. "I know who you are," she said. "You should be Yearking. You're wearing the Candidate's robe, and Winter Festival was two nights ago."

Arris did not know how to answer her. He edged past her and sat down on the bench before the fire. He stretched his scratched and aching feet toward the warmth. Terai spoke from behind him. "You can still turn us away, Ravil."

"No." She went to the table and picked up a basket filled with hanks of dyed yarn. "I want to know what has happened, but your tale can wait. There is bread and cheese by the hearth from our breakfast, if you would like to eat before you sleep. You're welcome to the bed. I'll be making a stew this afternoon, but I'll be quiet, and it is a warm enough day for the girls to stay outside until you wake. The Goddess grant you peaceful rest." She left them alone in the cottage.

Arris slept beside Terai in the soft, warm bed. His body

ached, and his dreams were vivid and frightening. Confused images swarmed around him. The only clear pictures were the face of the Lady, the vulture form of the Lossiran, and the daimon Aghlayeshkusa who had come to his aid on Winter Festival night. Arris was half convinced that the daimon was there in the cottage, when he woke to the smell of mutton stew and cornbread.

But Ravil greeted him softly when he sat up, and he saw her at the hearth, kneeling by the stewpot. Terai still slept peacefully on his side of the bed. Arris eased out from beneath the worn sheepskins, and found a pile of folded clothes on the rug awaiting him.

They must have belonged to Ravil's husband. There was a thick, scratchy woolen jerkin to go over Arris's white tunic; a pair of stiff, leather breeches; knitted stockings; and soft, well-worn boots. The boots fit well. Chalin must have had small feet. The rest of the clothes were too large, but they would do. When Arris reached Deiran, he would find something else to wear to court.

"Thank you for these," he said. "I'd like to wash before I eat. Where should I do that?"

She sent him outside and around to the back of the cottage. The air had grown colder as evening approached, and there was a thin layer of ice on the water in a stone cistern. Arris could hear the girls' voices from near the sheepfold, but he did not see them. He broke the ice and scrubbed some of the grime from his face and hands. His long hair was tangled into mats like felted wool. He combed it out with his fingers as well as he could. He had seen no mirror in the cottage, but he was sure he showed no signs of the beauty that had captivated the Emperor of Deiran and the Goddess Rehoman.

When he returned to the cottage, Ravil beckoned to him from the hearth bench. "Come sit with me." Arris joined her. The bread and cheese he had eaten that morning had been little to counteract two days without food. The stew and the cornbread smelled wonderful, and he could see that the bread was almost done.

He smiled warmly at Ravil. "I am in your debt."

She looked away from his eyes, and leaned to stir the

mutton stew, like a cat who could not bear his gaze and suddenly chose to wash its paw. "You will have to leave here soon."

"We cannot stay long, anyway," Arris said. "A day or two is all."

"Terai said that you bring danger with you, and he was right. I felt it while you slept, and it has been growing. There are powers seeking you that I would rather did not find you here."

Arris still felt a trace of unease from his dreams of the daimon. He shivered. "I'm grateful for what you've done already. You could have turned us away."

"Yes, I could have," she said. Her thin face was thoughtful as she gazed at the fire. "And if I had not owed Terai something for old favors, or if you had come here alone, I probably would have sent you on your way. You carry a darkness with you, and I think it is nothing from the Goddess."

Her words echoed his own thoughts. Arris shifted uncomfortably on the bench. "I mean no harm to you."

"Yet you have caused much harm, I think. Those who hunt you have good reason for it. You have killed men."

She was no simple farmwife, Arris thought. He felt compelled to defend himself. "I killed Nievan and Maenad, the Regents of the Khalifate. I avenged my father. Or the man I called my father. His true sons would not do it. They made peace with the Khalifate long ago, and ride as Companions to the Ilkharani Prince."

"You could have made your own peace with your enemies. Then you would not be where you are now, outcast and hunted. No one would wish your death."

"You cannot understand," Arris whispered. The air in the cottage seemed heavy, oppressive. He glanced back to see Terai still sleeping, a gray-headed mound beneath the sheepskins. He had the feeling that he was being watched, that something was looking over his shoulder. He supposed it was simple fear, because he was a fugitive.

"Perhaps I can be made to understand," she said, neither friendly nor condemning. "Tell me what has brought

you to this. Why are you not the Yearking, when you were
chosen by the Goddess before you were born?''

He did not know this woman, and thought he would
surely never see her again, and yet he wanted to explain to
her. Feeling that she heard more than he told her, Arris
began with the reason why he had killed the Regents, and
why he had refused the Goddess's choosing. He told her
how Nievan and Maenad had falsely accused the Lord
Areyta of having murdered the old Khalif, Rasul Ilkharani.
Areyta had been arrested and tortured to death, and his
family driven into exile in the Dark Hills. Arris had been
brought to Gama, to train to be a priest, and eventually
to become Yearking. But he had vowed to avenge his
father's death one day.

His teachers in Gama had promised that he would learn
to use his power, that his vengeance would release Areyta's
ghost from the Wheel of the world. Then Arris had learned
that they had lied. He could not release the Lord Areyta's
restless spirit, because Areyta was not his father. His
mother had betrayed her lord, commanded by the Goddess
to lie with a stranger at the fires of Spring Festival, so that
Arris would be conceived. The Goddess had arranged for
Arris's birth. It was likely that she had played a part in
Areyta's death as well, to get Arris away from him and
into the Dark Hills with his mother's people. When Arris
had learned these things, he told Ravil, he had renounced
the power and the destiny that Rehoman had planned for
him. He did not want to be Yearking. He had decided that
when he was thirteen years old.

''There is much you have not told me,'' Ravil said when
he had finished. She was looking into the flames that
burned beneath her kettle on the hearth. ''You have shed
innocent blood. That I can see. You have killed without
remorse. Darkness follows you, and you cannot blame that
on the Goddess.''

''I can,'' Arris said bitterly. ''She sent the Lossiran to
me in the Citadel when I was a child.'' He still remembered the terror he had felt when the vulture spirit had
come to him. The Goddess's Messenger. It was black and
rotting and cold, and it had given him a curse of prophecy

that had led to the Lord Areyta's death. "Darkness follows me, you say? It has haunted me. Forced me along the path the Goddess chose. It would have forced me to be Yearking, if I had not summoned Aghlayeshkusa."

The Yaighan woman flinched at the sound of that name, and hissed a long breath out through her teeth. "A daimon, a spirit of earth. The enemy of the Goddess. You summoned such? It is of your own making, that much is sure. Your own seeking. You have abandoned the Goddess in her need, in her greatest need." Her voice had gone very quiet. "You are a traitor to your own people and to many who trusted you. You have betrayed friendship. You have offended great powers, and they seek your death. I wonder if you did not seek your own death, to search out the dark as you have done."

"I saw no choice," Arris said angrily, standing up from the bench to stalk away from her. "When did I ever have a choice? Whether right or wrong, it is done."

Terai had been roused by their voices. He sat up slowly, stretching his arms with a grimace. "I'm getting too old for night journeys," he said. "My bones ache. It will take me days to recover."

"Some stew might help," said Ravil in her quiet voice. She stood up to fetch bowls and spoons from the table. Arris stepped out of her way when she passed him. She did not look at him. Ravil dished the stew into five bowls and set them back in their places. Then she put on fire mitts and turned the cornbread out of its pan onto the center of the table. "It's ready."

"We won't have days to rest," Arris said as Terai got out of the bed. "We aren't staying here."

"What do you mean?" Terai glanced over at the young woman, who had paused at the cottage door.

"You bring danger with you, old friend," Ravil said sadly. "And a darkness that I do not want under my roof."

She stepped outside to call her daughters in. Arris sat at the table, trying to master his anger. He broke off a chunk of the cornbread and began to eat, but Terai's calm, questioning look made him speak. "You said it yourself,

Terai. It's dangerous for her to offer us shelter. She has her children to think of."

"She has a right to be careful," the older man said. Arris wondered how much he had heard of the conversation by the hearth. "I suppose we can leave tonight. I feel better for the sleep. At least the headaches have finally stopped."

Arris's appetite was none the worse for his annoyance with their hostess. He wolfed the mutton stew, burning his mouth, ignoring the manners he had learned as a slave in the Sapphire Palace and a courtier in the Citadel. Terai joined him at the table, saying nothing further.

Suddenly Ravil burst back through the doorway with one child tucked beneath her arm. She was breathing hard, and her face was ashen. Her younger daughter Calla was crying, fighting to get free of her mother, holding onto her doll Prinn with a precarious grip of two fingers. She dropped the doll as Ravil set her down and pushed her toward the bed.

"Stay there," Ravil said harshly. "Wait for me. Don't go anywhere near the door, Calla. Do you understand? Promise Mama."

Calla wailed, too frightened to speak the words. Ravil left her daughter where she had put her and turned on the two men sitting at the table. "You. Come with me. The Goddess damn you both, if she hasn't already."

"What's wrong?" Arris asked as he rose to his feet. Terai loosened the ivory-hilted knife in his belt, the knife the Prince had given them for their escape. "Where is the other child?"

"See for yourself." Ravil pushed him ahead of her out the doorway, onto the cottage porch. Arris's eyes slowly adjusted to the dim twilight. The sun had set behind the Dark Hills to the west, and night was drawing in swiftly. Already the stream below the yard was in shadow. Arris could not make out the trail from the eastern ridge where he had walked that morning.

He saw two silhouettes against the grayness, seated on the low wall of the sheepfold. One was the child Seri. He could hear her talking softly and laughing. The other figure was tall, man-shaped, but no one could have mistaken it for a man.

"Aghlayeshkusa," Arris breathed.

"The daimon you summoned," Ravil said in a deadly fury. "Now go down there and make it give me back my child." Arris could see the killing light in her eyes, and knew she would gladly slay him if her daughter was harmed.

Arris did not think the daimon meant any harm to little Seri. Aghlayeshkusa was using her as bait, for some reason of its own. It could simply have appeared to Arris inside the cottage if all it wanted was to talk to him. Arris felt the cold of deep fear as he stepped off the porch and began to walk slowly toward the sheepfold. He had promised the daimon his soul. When he died, Aghlayeshkusa would consume him utterly, taking whatever strength and life he had to feed its dark power. The daimon had probably decided not to wait any longer for its promised feast.

A steady step sounded behind Arris. Terai was following him at a slight distance. Arris had no fear to spare for the danger his friend was courting. He felt as he sometimes had felt in dreams, his legs so weak and unsteady that soon he might topple over and be unable to move or speak. Yet he kept walking. There was no way to flee from this confrontation. The daimon could not be thrown off the trail as Karillos had been. Ravil had accused him of seeking his death. Arris had never been so certain that he was walking toward it.

The sheepfold was empty, except for the unmarked carcass of a dead ewe. The rest of the flock had fled at the daimon's approach, knowing a fear that seemed not to touch Ravil's daughter. Seri swung her legs against the piled stones, holding her doll Granna and chattering up at the stolen face of the daimon. Aghlayeshkusa wore the form of the warrior god Myrdethreshi, whom it had seen at the battle in the Temple two nights before. It enjoyed taking on new shapes, refining them as it learned what humans found pleasing or terrifying. Aghlayeshkusa looked like a handsome, blond warrior in archaic armor, except that it had not achieved the right proportions yet, and to

Arris's eyes it was monstrous. It had modulated its usual hollow voice to a soft tone that would not frighten a child.

The daimon still bled from wounds it had received at the Temple. It had fought with the Mother of Vultures, matching the Lossiran with claws and with power, giving Arris the time in which to escape. Arris had paid for the favor, though. He owed the daimon nothing.

"What do you want?" Arris demanded.

Seri looked up in surprise and smiled at him. Aghlayesh-kusa turned slowly to gaze at Arris. Its eyes were beacons of shifting colors, crimson and purple and orange by turns, mesmermizing and uncanny. Arris did not meet them. "My boy, how pleasant to see you once again," the daimon said in a cultured, reasonable voice that tightened the muscles in Arris's back and neck.

"Let the child go," Arris said. "You don't need her. You have me."

"Do I?" the daimon said less cheerfully. "I begin to wonder. I had thought to come here and take your soul. I must have new power if I am to heal these wounds and regain my strength. I intended to come to you and drain you like a baby at a teat, until you were no more than a husk lying in that bed, and your companion would wake to think that you had died of exhaustion and exposure from your journey."

"I dreamed that you were there," Arris said. He held out a hand to Seri, whose round face had grown somber as she listened to the daimon's words. The little girl tucked her doll under her arm, as her mother had done with her sister, and jumped off the sheepfold wall to take Arris's hand.

"You don't have to be afraid of him," Seri said to Arris. "He can't hurt you. He couldn't hurt me, even though he wanted to. He killed the ewe instead. He shouldn't have done that. Mama killed a yearling three days ago, and we have plenty of meat. He doesn't even want to eat it."

The daimon had eaten the sheep's soul in preference to its flesh. "Seri, you go back to the house. Your mother wants you," Arris said.

"She is right," said Aghlayeshkusa in a rueful tone. Its hands stroked the stones absently. "I could not harm her, and I did intend to when I found I did not have the strength to kill you."

The child looked back in fascination at the daimon, unafraid. She had probably been scolding it for killing the ewe. Arris spoke sharply. "Seri, you heard me."

"All right." She pouted as she turned and walked away from them.

Terai stood a few paces behind Arris, a silent, grim figure with his feet planted on the path. His face showed no fear, though he surely knew that even his trained priest powers could not overmatch a being of this one's dark strength.

"She is protected by the Goddess," Terai said. "You must have realized that, daimon. Ravil has the Goddess's favor, and she consecrated her daughters to Rehoman at birth."

"That explains why I could not harm the child. Her soul was already promised," the daimon said. "But why could I not kill young Arris? He is promised to me. I should be able to snuff out his life at a whim, and take him into me. Yet he is guarded as well as that little creature is."

"He is still the Goddess's," Terai said. "I wonder if he has the authority to promise you his soul. It may not be his to give."

"That is nonsense," Arris said. "I make my own choices. I did bind myself to you, daimon. But I value my life as well. I think it is my own power that guards me, even though I cannot use it consciously."

Aghlayeshkusa stood up, stretching its full height beside the mountain stream. Its shadow blocked the last light of the vanished day. "So I must believe, since I cannot slay you. I will have to seek healing another way. I shall petition for entrance into the God's Realm. There I may rest and recover from these wounds. I do not think they will deny me entrance." It smiled suddenly. "I will also seek there for the way to release your power to your control. If it keeps me from killing you now, you might be using it to grow stronger. As you grow stronger, so shall I, and when I finally take you I will be great.''

"I don't want my power back," Arris said. He had renounced it after he had killed the girl Onira, on that terrible Spring Festival night when he had learned Areyta was not his father. Nothing that had happened since, not slavery or exile, had convinced him otherwise. The Goddess-given talents he had been born with were a burden he did not intend to carry.

"You are going to need it," Terai said, stepping up beside him. "You'll need it when the Brothers Ylla come after you. They are gods, Arris. You cannot ignore them. They want you dead. They will not stop hunting you."

"You will need it," Aghlayeshkusa repeated, pleased to find support from an unexpected source. "I will regain it for you."

A freezing wind began to swirl in the farmyard, picking up dust into a choking cloud. The earth rumbled and shook as the daimon Aghlayeshkusa grinned at Arris through a dissolving face. On the porch of the cottage, Ravil cried out in fury as a chunk of thatch was blown free of her roof. The distant bleats of sheep came from the hills downstream.

The daimon reached out a heavy, cold hand to Arris's shoulder and laughed when he jerked back from the touch. An illusory cloak blew across Aghlayeshkusa's body, and the daimon was gone. A section of the sheepfold collapsed into a sudden sinkhole in the earth, and the world was still again in the winter twilight.

"It was an idiot thing to do, promising that creature your soul," Terai said in the silence. "But it is done. You need the help it offers, now that you've made the Brothers Ylla your enemies."

"They can't attack me, not directly," Arris said. "Sygathi ordered Karillos to kill me for him. They may be gods, but they have limits."

"They have no lack of willing followers who will kill you at a command. We'll have to watch our backs in Deiran."

"You still mean to come with me?"

"Of course."

"You'd be safer alone. The Khalifate gods aren't hunting you."

The older man gazed past Arris at the western hills. "The Yaighan will hunt me, I think. But they will not follow me across the Deirani border."

"Then go to Deiran. But not with me. If I brought danger with me into this valley, I'll surely bring it there."

"I'll stay with you," Terai said. "I heard you promise Saresha that you'd get Danae's family out of Deiran. I intend to see that you keep that promise."

"The Emperor owes me a favor. I hope he'll agree to let them go." The musicians had been virtual prisoners in the Sapphire Palace for years, not allowed to return to the Khalifate because they knew too much about the Deirani preparations for war. Danae had made a daring escape last year to join Arris in the Citadel, but she had left her father, brother, and sister behind.

"You owe the girl that much at least, for what you've done to her," Terai said.

Arris scowled. "I never meant to hurt Danae."

"Perhaps not," Terai said. "As you never meant to hurt these people." He turned to look at Ravil on the cottage porch. She held her daughter Seri close, and watched them in anger that had not abated with the daimon's disappearance. "I doubt that Ravil will let us back under her roof. But perhaps she'll give us food and some of her weaving for cloaks. We'll ask her, then go. Before our presence calls down something worse than the daimon into this place."

"My presence," Arris corrected him.

"Aye," Terai said, walking away to talk to the woman who had been his friend.

CHAPTER
3

THE BORDER between the Khalifate and Deiran was naturally fortified, a curving range of mountains that stretched from the Deadly Horns in the north all the way through the Dark Hills of the Yaighan in the south. The Deadly Horns thrust out into the ocean in treacherous cliffs and shoals and fogbound islets, discouraging any sea trade between the two kingdoms. The Dark Hills were another kind of barrier, since neither Deirani nor Khalifate people were welcome there. Between the two extremes was the Westrange, or so the people of the Khalifate called it. The mountains were not so high or so frightening there. They were older, more rounded, fertile enough to be good pasture. Shepherds and hill farmers made their homes there for most of the year, and merchants traveled back and forth through the less difficult passes, except when war threatened.

The hills Arris and Terai crossed on their way north and west were deserted. There were no animals but the wild goats, and no people to inhabit the crude, old huts that guarded empty pastures. Arris supposed that life in the hills must have been hard for some years now. He remembered General Iyon returning victorious from raids across the Khalifate border; the people he had robbed and slain had had little worth taking. The raids had been meant to annoy the Regents, to try to provoke them to action.

The army of Deiran had little doubt that it would win when the war came. Its soldiers were highly trained and loyal to their Emperor, and they were eager to invade and take Khalifate land. They were promised farms and homes of their own when they were victorious. Deiran was a crowded Empire, and it needed to expand. The Khalifate was complacent and soft under its pious Temple, its bureaucracy, its corrupt Regents. Now the Regents were dead and the Prince was still two years too young to take the throne. There would be nothing to rally the people. The Deirani expected little resistance.

Arris and Terai had been walking for five days since leaving Ravil's valley. They had moved fairly slowly, regaining their strength, wary of more bad weather. The days had been cold, but there were no storms, and they easily found shelter at night in the abandoned shepherds' huts. Ravil had given them food and thick lengths of woven wool to use as cloaks; she had been willing to do that much to make them leave her and her daughters in peace. Arris and Terai grew less weary day by day, and as they walked farther from Gama, the weight of what they had left behind began to lessen.

There were no signs of pursuit, either human or supernatural. Still, they stayed off the trails, and stood watches at night. Terai occasionally sat alone to reach behind them with his power, seeking anything that might wish them harm. Nothing revealed itself to him. Still, Arris would not feel completely free until he was across the Deirani border. The city of Khopei had a thousand gods of its own, and had no need to import stern deities like the Brothers Ylla who would deny any other worship. Arris did not think that Sygathi Ylla or his Brothers would be able to reach him there.

It was evening on the fifth day of their journey when Arris saw a Deirani hill-fort in the distance. The border was still some miles to the west; this was a new outpost. Arris stood by a lone tree on a ridgetop and shaded his eyes against the sunset. He could make out the wooden palisade above the rings of banks and ditches. A narrow earthen causeway led to the hilltop. The Deirani loved grace and symmetry in their buildings, but this fort was crudely functional. Its walls were planted stakes atop a thick earth berm, and the structures inside the walls were little more than tents over wooden frameworks.

A stream ran below the lowest bank, and a stone-lined trench was being built to divert it and make a moat of one of the ditches. Men were busy everywhere, more than Arris could count from this distance. He saw corrals of horses on the hillsides below the central fort, and rough barracks spilling down into the valley. They were ready for war. Arris wanted to be well away from the border when the invasion finally came. He had no desire to be caught up in the coming conflict. He had contributed enough to it already.

"We'll take a wide path around this," Arris said as Terai hiked up to join him on the ridge. "No one there will know me, or believe I've been on a mission for the Emperor."

Terai looked at the hillfort for a moment, his face hard. "The Deirani are suspicious of foreigners even when they are not about to begin a war. Yes, we'd do well to avoid these border garrisons. We're likely to be shot as Yaighan spies if we're seen. Come down from here, lad, before they spot us against the skyline."

Arris followed the older Yaighan back the way they had come. They walked along the shadowed side of the hills, headed north to make a wide circuit around the outpost. The hill grasses and brush were winter dry, and the occasional groves of trees were leafless and offered no cover. Dusk was gathering, and neither Arris nor Terai knew this part of the Westrange. They could not continue traveling after dark as they could have done in the Dark Hills. They moved at a fast pace now, wanting to be far from the Deirani hillfort when they stopped for the night.

Arris had taken the lead, and had begun to climb down a rocky slope into a narrow ravine. His boots slid in the soft earth between the rocks, and he went carefully, keeping one hand on the harsh stones. He could hear Terai's breathing growing labored behind him, and the patter of smaller rocks dislodged by their descent. The night was closing in, so that Arris could barely see the far end of the ravine, where a gentler slope led up over a bank and down

below the hillside again. The air was chill, but dry, and he
thought that they could get by without a fire tonight.

He heard a fall of rock from ahead, and then a muffled
sound of hoofbeats. He froze, one hand on a waist-high
boulder, his boots sinking a little in the red earth. A
horseman appeared on the ridgetop above them, followed
by four others. They were Deirani sentries patrolling the
outer defensive perimeter, and Arris and Terai probably
had been walking along their nightly route. Arris could see
them only as silhouettes in the dusk; they wore black
leather and ringmail, and their faces were shadowed by the
brims of their helmets. For a moment, Arris thought that if
he and Terai could remain still and silent, they would not
be seen.

But the Deirani were looking for them, scanning the
rocky slopes from the vantage of horseback. One of the
sentries stood in his stirrups and pointed straight at Arris.
Two others unslung large bows and fitted long arrows to
their bowstrings. At a sharp command, they let fly. One of
the bolts struck quivering in the earth just at Arris's feet.
He stared at its wicked point, half a man's hand in size.
Arris knew Deirani archers. He had watched companies
demonstrating their skills for the Emperor at the palace. If
he had been the target, he would be dead. The other arrow
had hit near Terai. Arris heard him swearing softly in
Yaigan.

"Throw down your weapons and come forward!" cried
the Deirani who had given the order to shoot. The Deirani
language was a lilting, musical one, but his voice was
harsh nonetheless.

"We are unarmed," Arris called out in the same language. Except for Saresha's knife that Terai still carried, it
was the truth. "Let us pass. We are peaceful travelers."

An archer set another arrow to the string and shot it off.
Arris lunged to one side, as the arrow struck where he had
been, bouncing off a rock. "Come here," said the patrol
leader, "or you'll be killed."

Arris thought that he might be able to run, and escape
over the rocky slope where the horses could not go. But he
did not know if there were other patrols nearby, and he

feared an arrow in the back before he got far. He glanced at Terai. Looking resigned, the older man stopped over one of the Deirani arrows and came to join Arris. Together, they walked slowly across the slope toward the Deirani horsemen.

Two of the sentries had long javelins in their hands, and the bowmen stared at them over poised arrows. The leader had drawn his sword. He walked his horse forward a little as Arris and Terai approached. "On your knees," he said fiercely. "Hands behind your backs."

Arris moved close enough to see the man's face before he obeyed. The soldier was young. His ivory-skinned face was smooth except for the beginnings of a mustache. His dark eyes were hooded in slanted folds, and his fine, wavy black hair was braided to one side. He was very handsome. He had the accent of the upper castes, perhaps the nobility, but he wore no jewelry or house badge that Arris could see. The others of his patrol had the look of Deirani peasants in uniform: darker skin, broader features, heavier builds. None was older than twenty-two.

"Chol, Wesu, bind them," said the patrol leader. "Search them for weapons."

The two soldiers with javelins dismounted. One was younger than Arris, and he moved clumsily, not yet comfortable with his height and strength. The other was a few years older, with a broken nose and a nervous look in his brown eyes. He came toward Arris with his javelin pointed at Arris's chest.

"We will come with you peacefully," Terai said in slow, careful Deirani. His accent was good, but it was obvious he had not spoken the language in years. Arris wondered again when Terai had been in the Empire, and why. "You have no need to bind our hands."

"Silence," said the bigger, younger soldier. He prodded Terai in the back with the point of his weapon. "Do not move."

Arris offered no resistance as his wrists were tied with harsh ropes, knotted so tightly that he thought his arms would soon go numb. A noose was tied around his neck, on a long rope that was attached to the soldier's saddle. He would not choke as long as he kept up with the horse's pace. The soldier with the broken nose hauled him to his feet and shoved him toward the horse. Terai was taken to the other man's mount.

"This is a mistake, Lieutenant," Arris said, finally identifying the insignia on the leader's helmet. "We are envoys of the Sacred Emperor, returning from a mission in the Khalifate lands . . ."

He was doubled over suddenly by a hard blow to his stomach. His captor hit him again, then jerked up on the rope around Arris's neck to pull him straight. Arris gasped for the air that had been driven from his lungs, choked by the noose.

"Enough, Wesu," said the Deirani lieutenant, but he glared at Arris. "You will not speak. A moment ago you said you were peaceful travelers, and now you are spies of the Emperor? I think you are spies, but you are not ours. You are Yaighan, that is obvious, and you are many miles from your Dark Hills. You can have no good reason to be here, or to speak our language."

"If you will not let us explain ourselves . . ." Terai began. A sharp jerk on his neck harness silenced him.

"You will have your chance to talk to the Commander," said the Lieutenant. "I imagine you'll tell him more than you wish to. Chol, Wesu, I said to search them for weapons."

"Yes, my lord," said Wesu from behind Arris. He did a quick and thorough job, his hands seeking over and under Arris's clothing, finding nothing. He emptied the food bag Ravil had given Arris, and the last dry half loaf and piece of mutton sausage rolled down the slope between the rocks. "Nothing here, Lieutenant Ebreyu. As he said, he is unarmed."

The other soldier had found Terai's knife in his belt. He handed it hilt first to the officer. "A simple farmer's knife, would you say, Chol?" Ebreyu looked at the weapon's hilt. It was ivory and malachite, simply carved, but expensive. One of Saresha's Companions had given it to the Prince when he was rescued from the Temple, and the Prince had used it to help Arris and Terai escape. "I'm sure the Commander will learn something useful from the two of you. Pakali, Avo, continue the patrol. The rest of us will take the prisoners in.'' The archers saluted and rode on.

Arris and Terai were led at a pace just fast enough to force them to run alongside the horses. Perhaps a quarter hour passed before they climbed the newly built causeway. The three soldiers dismounted before the torchlit gate. Chol and Wesu detached the captives' leading ropes from their saddles, and coiled them up to a shorter length. Like dogs on leashes, the prisoners were trotted into the fort, with Lieutenant Ebreyu walking before them, looking well pleased with his achievement. Curious glances followed them, though the disciplined gate guards stayed stiffly at their posts.

The inner courtyard was clean and well ordered, since barracks and stables were all outside the walls. The disassembled wheels and bodies of more chariots than Arris could count were stacked beneath sheltering awnings; they could not cross the Westrange, but once the army was in the Khalifate there were better roads. Blacksmith tents stood in a row near the central cluster of makeshift buildings, where smiths had been busy making and mending weapons. It must have been a task to haul a dozen forges up from the lowlands, Arris thought.

He could smell cooking meat as he and Terai were led past kitchen sheds, and he remembered that they had not stopped for supper before they were taken. His stomach ached with hunger, as well as from his new bruises. They were taken past a granary, and past the doors of three newly dug root cellars. The fourth cellar door was thick and bound with iron. Lieutenant Ebreyu opened it, and his men shoved Arris and Terai inside.

Arris could not keep his feet on the slope of the dugout, and ducked his head as he fell. He rolled ten or fifteen feet and struck the rear wall in a shower of badly packed earth. Terai landed near him, and the cellar door was closed, leaving them in darkness.

"Well, lad, we've made it to Deiran," Terai said dryly.

Arris squirmed against the wall until he got his feet
under him and was able to sit up. "Surely I can convince
their commander to send a message to the Emperor or to
General Iyon, to investigate my claims."

"Before or after he tortures us?" Terai muttered.

"He'll be in deep trouble if he kills me before I get my
report to Hareku. He'll get a public execution, no doubt
painful and slow."

"Not very gratifying to us, if we're already dead."

"Unless he's a fool, he'll keep us safe until he has word
on who we are and what to do with us."

"Then I pray he is a wise commander."

Time passed, immeasurable. When the door of the cellar
finally creaked open, Arris saw that it was long after
moonrise. Past time for dinner, he thought sourly. He had
been trying to loosen the bonds on his wrists by flexing
and relaxing his muscles. The effort was exhausting, and
the knots would not give way.

A burly soldier with a round moon-face peered in at the
two captives, a torch in one hand. "One of you, the
Commander wants. He doesn't care which is first."

Arris glanced at Terai, who shrugged slightly. "I'll
go," Arris said, struggling to his knees and then to his
feet. He walked up the dugout slope to the doorway. The
soldier grasped the rope from Arris's neck and pulled him
out. He closed the door again on Terai.

The Deirani led Arris back past the dark kitchen sheds
to one of the central tentlike buildings. There were a few
soldiers lounging nearby. Arris steeled himself to face
taunting or worse from them, but they merely watched him
pass, and muttered to one another about the Yaighan spies.
A guard at the doorway of one of the buildings dipped his
spear in acknowledgment as the soldier led Arris across the
threshold.

The room held only a few objects, but those were
enough. A brazier burning with hot coals, with a dozen
irons heating over it; a wooden slab, waist-high and the
length of a man, with restraints for hands and feet at each
corner; racks of knives, clamps, and pincers; a sturdy

wooden post on a heavy base, with an assortment of whips on a table beside it.

"Wait," Arris said. The soldier forced him to his knees at the base of the whipping post. "I'll talk to your commander without all this. There's no need . . ."

The burly soldier wrapped the halter rope around Arris's neck, effectively choking off his words. He untied Arris's hands, and tied them again to an iron ring in the post. Then he unclasped Arris's cloak and let it fall. He used a knife to slit the sleeves of the jerkin Ravil had given him. The white tunic beneath the jerkin ripped easily. Arris was bared to the waist. The air was warm against his skin.

"You'll have some new patterns on your back to go with those tattoos," said the soldier with a soft laugh. He left Arris, and went to put on a pair of leather gloves to protect his hands. He chose a single-thonged bullwhip with an iron tip from the table. There were other whips that would cause pain, but less injury. This one would cut, and cut deeply.

Maybe the whip would destroy Arris's blue and gold wing tattoos completely. Assuming he survived, Arris would not be sorry to have them gone. They were a reminder of the Goddess and her power that he had forsworn. He had been granted them years ago, for his ability to summon the Lossiran and understand its prophecies. He was the only living Winged Yaighan; the honor meant little to him now.

Arris heard the door open, and footsteps sounded behind him. He could not turn his head far enough to see who had come in. The Deirani soldier saluted, and stepped back behind Arris with his whip. "My lord Commander," the soldier said. "The Yaighan spy is ready."

There was a long moment of silence, and then a soft voice spoke in the accents of the court. "Corporal Berisi, did no one ask this prisoner his name, or his reasons for traveling toward Deiran?"

"My lord?" The corporal sounded confused. "You have had Lieutenant Ebreyu's report. He is a Yaighan spy, that's obvious."

The Commander's voice was familiar. "You may go,"

he said in apparent irritation. "I'll speak with Ebreyu later."

"What is wrong, my lord?" the corporal said, putting the whip down on the table again and taking off the gloves.

"You are dismissed."

Arris knew him now. It was General Iyon, who had been his Jai-Sohn teacher in the Sapphire Palace, and before that an abusive and demanding client when Arris had been the Emperor's slave. Relief and fury warred within Arris. He would not be tortured or killed, but for Iyon to see him like this, bound and helpless, made him feel unclean. There was a black well of cruelty beneath the General's charm, and Arris knew it better than most.

The door closed behind the retreating Corporal Berisi. General Iyon walked forward to where Arris could see his face. He was lean and graceful, handsome as a panther in his black uniform. His cold eyes were half-angry and half-amused. He was almost thirty years old now, still a young man for the power and influence he wielded.

Iyon merely looked for a long moment. Then he spoke sternly. "I trained you myself as a Jai-Sohn, and look at you. Captured by your own side and facing torture. If not for those pretty patterns on your back, I'd have had you flayed before I realized my mistake."

Arris glared up at him. "I tried to tell your Lieutenant Ebreyu that I was on a mission for the Emperor. He wouldn't believe me."

"My dear boy," said Iyon in his courtier's voice, "have you faced a mirror recently? You look like the lowest sort of Yaighan barbarian. My men have orders to detain any foreigner they find. Ebreyu was doing his duty. And if I hadn't seen those tattoos, I wouldn't have recognized you myself. You're badly dressed, covered with dirt, and you need to shave. Besides, you're two years older, and at your age that makes a difference."

"Untie me, damn you," Arris said. "And send someone to get my friend Terai out of your dungeon."

"No one knows you're here," Iyon remarked, smiling a little as if at some private joke. "I could do anything with you that I wished, make you do anything, perhaps in return for your friend's safety, or in return for food . . ."

Arris was chilled, and he did not know if he could take the General seriously. "I'm the Emperor's man, Iyon. I have a report to make to him."

Iyon nodded slowly. "A few years ago, I would have seen only fear in you. Now I see that you'd try to kill me if you had the chance. Your training was not wasted." He bent over Arris to untie his hands from the ring. "I'm sorry. You are tired, and you've been badly treated. Come. I'll make amends if I can, and then I'll hear your report from the Khalifate. I trust your mission was a success."

Arris stood up. He ripped the remnants of his jerkin and tunic away, then picked up his cloak and pulled it around his shoulders. "I killed the Regents. Nievan and Maenad Ilkharani."

"And the Prince, Saresha?"

"He still lives."

Iyon raised one eyebrow. "Your elaborate scheme with the Yaighan failed."

"It came very close to succeeding."

"You'll make a full report to me later," Iyon said. "You did well to kill the two Regents. It should leave the Khalifate badly weakened. The Prince will not be old enough to take the throne for two more years. The time has come for war. We'll take the Citadel and kill the prince ourselves long before he reaches his twenty-first year."

Arris followed Iyon out the door of the interrogation building, ignoring the stares of the guard and the soldiers in the yard. He did not want Iyon's plan to succeed. Saresha was well guarded, by Karillos and the Companions, and there might be enough strength left in the Khalifate to repel the Deirani invasion. Arris was glad he was finished with his part of the war. He followed Iyon to the General's office, in another canvas-roofed structure, and waited there while an aide was sent to get Terai out of the dugout prison.

All Terai knew of General Iyon was that he had been

Arris's Jai-Sohn master, and that his was the name to whom Arris had sent his spying reports from the Citadel. Terai had no reason to dislike Iyon. It had been Arris's own choice not to tell his friend about the rest of his relationship with the General. Still, Arris was startled and annoyed when the two men seemed to take an immediate liking to one another.

After providing them with a bath and clean Deirani uniforms, the General had invited his two erstwhile prisoners to a late dinner in his quarters. The tent was small but clean, and the table was laden with fresh roasted game, bread and butter, and wine that had been stored in one of the cellars. Iyon was in a cheerful mood, probably because Arris's news meant he could launch the invasion at last.

"The Khalifate will fall," Iyon said. "I have no doubt of that. The Ilkharani dynasty has ended." He grinned at Terai, and raised his glass. "Perhaps the Empire and your Yaighan people can reach some sort of understanding. We have a common enemy. I was pleased to hear from Arris that you were working with him in the Citadel."

Terai nodded, finishing a mouthful of venison. "My lord, if the Yaighan had anything to compare with your Jai-Sohn assassins, we would have sent one after the Ilkharani long ago. I was glad to see Rasul Ilkharani's brothers killed. The old Khalif took more than half of the ancient Yaighan lands to add to his Khalifate."

"It is a shame that his son did not die as well," Iyon said. "Arris sent me a report almost a year ago that described a bizarre scheme he had worked out with you to kill the Prince. Something to do with a ritual of sacrifice that the Yaighan perform in secret. Obviously it did not succeed. Was the plan discovered? It might have been better to have simply killed Saresha Ilkharani as you did his uncles."

Arris took a breath and began his story. "My lord, we kidnapped the Prince and brought him to Gama as I told you we would. We had him on the altar himself, ready for the sacrifice. But we did not know we had been followed south by some of the Prince's Companions and a group of

Khalifate priests. The Qadasiya high priest, Karillos, led the rescue of the Prince.''

"Karillos." Iyon looked thoughtful. His angular face was softly shadowed in the candlelight. "I recall the name from your dispatches. He was your enemy in the Citadel court. He suspected you from the beginning, but could never find any proof that would convince Saresha Ilkharani to dismiss you from his company.

"He was right. I was a danger to the Prince."

"Yet how could he have known that?" Iyon frowned, drumming fingers on the tabletop. "You were careful. If anyone else had suspected you, they would have had you watched. You would never have gotten so much military information for us. So why this one man, this priest?"

Terai spoke soberly. "He's likely to be leading the Khalifate against you, General. You had better know this, whether or not you believe it. The man has powers of the mind. He has the favor of his gods, and his gods are real. Their favor gives Karillos a strength that will be hard to assail."

"Gods?" Iyon repeated, amused. "Perhaps I should bring along a legion of priests. One for each of the thousand gods of Khopei. They can battle with this Karillos, and my men and I will handle the Khalifate army."

"It would not be a bad strategy," Terai said, undisturbed by the young general's sarcasm.

The night dragged on. Arris answered Iyon's occasional question about the military readiness of the Khalifate. Terai discussed the discipline of Iyon's troops and the well-situated design of the hill-fort. Iyon and Terai were soon lost in talk of strategy, of troop strength, and the best paths across the Westrange. The elegant young nobleman and the gruff, weathered spy seemed to have much the same ideas on the best methods of warfare, and their respect for one another had grown quickly in the few hours they had been talking.

Iyon decided to send Arris and Terai with letters for the Emperor and the garrison commanders between the border and Khopei. They would ride at courier speed, resting for only a few hours each night, changing mounts at each stop.

For an escort, he gave them Lieutenant Ebreyu and the two soldiers who had brought them in, saying they deserved a long ride with little rest.

In Khopei, at least, Arris would be far from the General. He did not deny that Iyon was intelligent and competent, and that he could be charming when it suited him. But Arris still trusted Iyon no more then he liked him. He would not fully relax until he was well distant from here, and on his way to the Sapphire Palace and the Emperor.

CHAPTER
4

IT WAS RAINING as the five riders forded a shallow stream near the border of Deiran. It was a sorrowing rain, bending the bare branches of young trees, falling straight and heavy with a wintry chill. The tears of the goddess Turuan, such a rain was called in Deiran; but few remembered who the goddess might have been, or what cause she had to grieve so at midwinter. Arris had sat for many idle hours in the harem of the Emperor, listening to the concubines sing tales of some of Khopei's better-known gods. None of them had been able to tell him of Turuan, though all agreed that she was the cause of the dense winter rains.

A few hours' journey that morning had brought them down out of the hills, following the rutted tracks that army wagons had made leading up to the hill-fort. They had kept a swift pace, loping their horses with only brief intervals to walk them. The rain had begun as they neared the lowlands, and now at midday the trails were slick and deep with mud, and the clouds close overhead were the color of the dark brown earth. The rain washed inside the hood of Arris's heavy, wet cloak, and found its way past the leather of his borrowed Deirani uniform to chill his skin.

The horses struggled up the bank on the opposite side of the stream, blowing and shivering. Arris hoped the next garrison would be soon. They would need fresh mounts to keep up this pace, and he longed for warmth and a chance for conversation. Terai rode silently at Arris's side, behind the three Deirani soldiers who had been assigned as their escort. The wet, sucking noises made by the horses' hooves in the mud, the protesting rhythm of the animals' breathing, and the creak of wet leather saddles were all that sounded over the endless sheeting of the rain. Twice, Arris had heard muttered grumbling from the two peasant soldiers, Chol and Wesu, cursing the rain and the unwanted journey. Each time, Lieutenant Ebreyu silenced them with a sharp command. They obeyed him, nervous of his temper after his conversation with Iyon that morning.

Ebreyu, it turned out, was one of the General's personal aides, and the commander of a cavalry wing. Iyon had spoken with the young officer privately, but Arris had seen Ebreyu's stiff, tight-lipped expression afterward. Arris had no reason to like the Lieutenant. Ebreyu's treatment of him was the reason for Iyon's anger. But the Lieutenant had only been doing his duty. Arris thought that it was unfair to punish Ebreyu for it.

The journey was certainly a punishment. The pace alone would exhaust them all soon, and the miserable weather only made it harder. Searching for something cheerful to think about, Arris told himself that at least the Khalifate sun-gods who were his enemies would not be watching him today. He could not imagine the Five Brothers manifesting in this grayness.

"We're almost to the border," Ebreyu called back unexpectedly. "There will be a road. We should be able to make up the time we've lost in this mud."

"Good," Arris said, feeling he should say something. A few more miles passed, and they rode through boggy meadows that still held remnants of a farmer's fall harvest. The land near the mountains was far less fertile than most of the Empire, but the expanding population had driven families from the river-laced plains. Even so, this farm would produce more in a season than a Yaighan farmer of the Dark Hills might see in ten years.

"Arris," Terai said in a voice as cold as the grieving rain. "Look." He jerked his head sideways, indicating a slight rise at the eastern edge of the meadow.

An altar stood there, low and rounded with age, overgrown with lichen and climbing vines. Any carvings that might have shown what god it had once served had crumbled away with time and neglect. Arris turned his head away, not wanting to believe what he saw. Upon the altar, a small bird lay dead, freshly killed; over it crouched a vulture. But the vulture was not eating the bird. It stared at Arris, with its head lowered and its dark feathers flat to its skull from the rain.

It was not the Lossiran. Arris told himself that firmly, trying to stop his shivering, trying to slow the pulse that thudded in his head. It was not the Messenger of the Goddess. The Lossiran was huge, ancient, an undead creature of darkness and power. This was an ordinary carrion bird. Ugly and unpleasant, but nothing to fear. It had killed a sparrow and carried it to a stone to eat it.

It was feeding on the altar of a nameless god. Perhaps not a Deirani god. The altar was very old, and the Yaighan had once ranged this far west and north. It could be an altar of the Goddess. Arris forced himself not to look back at it. Terai was watching him, waiting for him to say something, ready to pronounce a sober warning. He would remind Arris that he would never be free of the Goddess, or say that this showed that Arris would need his Goddess-given power to protect himself.

Arris did not want to hear it. He let the dread he had felt wash away from him with the rain, and he found the strength to lean forward and press his knees against his horse's flanks. The animal was willing enough to pick up its feet and break into a slow canter. Arris rode ahead of Terai and past the two sullen Deirani soldiers to join Lieutenant Ebreyu at the edge of the meadow.

The Deirani officer had not seen the vulture, or if he had, it had meant nothing to him. Ebreyu nodded to Arris as their horses came abreast of each other. "We're almost to the first milepost," Ebreyu said. "The Khitain garrison is five miles from there."

"We'll get new mounts there?"

"Aye, if we can talk the Commander into giving them to us. General Iyon had no time to send a message ahead to tell them we were coming."

"I have letters for the garrison commanders," Arris said. "We should have no trouble."

"If they believe the letters are from General Iyon," Ebreyu said. "And if they believe Iyon would send a foreign boy as his courier."

Arris was almost twenty years old, but he had always looked younger than his true age. He was shorter than most Deirani, and his looks were still boyish. Ebreyu was not much older, but the handsome officer had a man's stern face, a man's voice. Arris answered him after a short silence. "The General thought they might not believe me. That is why you're my escort. If anyone questions us, you can explain it to them."

"I can tell them what little I know. The General did not explain it to me, except to say that he had trained you himself, and that I should have let you tell me who you were. What is Yaighan doing as a spy for the Emperor, anyway?" said the Deirani irritably.

Arris did not want to tell Ebreyu that he had been the Emperor's slave. Ebreyu was from a noble family, obviously, and a freed slave would be less in his eyes than even a Yaighan. "I . . . spent some years in Deiran," Arris said. "I was General Iyon's student. I owe no loyalty to Gama, and so . . ." He shrugged slightly.

The rain was lessening a little. He could see the milepost, a five-foot obelisk set in a polished base, nothing like the standing stones of the Dark Hills. It bore no markings that might give directions to an enemy, but the road it stood beside led only one way: west, into the Empire.

"And so you chose to be loyal to our Emperor. He is known as a generous man," Ebreyu said. "I suppose you are well paid for whatever you do."

"I have not been paid yet. Perhaps the Sacred Emperor will be generous," Arris said carefully. It was common for soldiers to dislike and mistrust spies, and Ebreyu had more reason than most. He had incurred his commander's anger because of Arris.

"Let us hope so. Whatever you may have done in the Khalifate, you'll deserve something for this journey. I know I'll be half-dead when we reach Khopei, if we do it in three days as the General ordered.'' Ebreyu smiled wryly. ''Unless you are much more used to this than I am, you will be in no better condition.''

The road was built up from the meadowlands on a bed of stone slabs. The surface was dirt, but the mud was only a few inches deep over gravel. The tired horses were glad of the change, and their strides lengthened. Flanked by low stone fences and farmers' hedges, the five men rode toward the garrison of Khitain. The rain and the pace of the horses discouraged more conversation, but Arris did not drop back to ride beside Terai again. He did not want to think about the vulture they both had seen, and he certainly did not want to talk about it. He was through with the Goddess, through with all his past life, and he was ready to begin anew in Deiran.

Khitain and the two garrisons that came after it on the couriers' road were small village forts that were crowded with newly posted invasion troops. Where twenty men might have been billeted, five hundred were assigned. During the day, the soldiers trained in farmers' fields, the hooves of their horses and the wheels of their chariots packing down the wet earth. Plowing would be difficult when spring came. The garrison stewards requisitioned food and livestock from the local landowners, who got it from their peasants. They would all be glad to see the army move on when the order to invade the Khalifate came through. Arris brought word that it would be soon. Once he got past the initial suspicions of the commanders, they were glad of his message, and gave him and his escort good horses for the next leg of their journey.

By midnight of the first day, they had reached the city gates of Buval. Less a city than a cluster of dwellings around an agricultural market, Buval had no need for massive walls. These were no more than eight feet high, decorated with scalloped brickwork that would be easier to climb than a scaling ladder. The gates were wrought of iron, and Arris could see through them into the quiet street beyond. Still, the gates were guarded by five black-armored soldiers of the Emperor, and Ebreyu had to use his most arrogant and commanding voice to convince them to let his party pass inside.

The house of the City Overlord stood overlooking the northern square of the marketplace. Like the stalls and booths of the market, the house was tightly shuttered and bolted against the night and the rain. Three stories tall, built of rose-colored stone, it had gutters at each corner of its fluted roof. The rain was channeled down through the teeth of sculpted lions' heads, to land in deep stone basins for the household's water supply. The basins were full, and their overflow ran along the edges of the market streets.

Arris dismounted with the others, and let his weary horse drink a little from the fast-running streams. The muscles in his legs and back were so tight and sore that he could scarcely walk. The couriers' orders allowed them only five hours' rest before they rode out again. When he got to the Sapphire Palace, Arris thought, the Emperor would have to excuse him from the usual deep prostration. He might manage a simple bow, but that was all.

Lieutenant Ebreyu pulled back his hood and took off his helmet as he stepped onto the dry porch of the Overlord's house. His face was smeared with mud, and the braid of dark hair at one side was matted with it. He used a hanging mallet to strike a small brass gong at the side of the door. The shimmering ring was not loud over the wash of rain from the roof gutters.

There was no response from within the house. The Deirani officer struck the gong three times in succession. At last, a screen over a peephole was drawn back, and an eye and half a wrinkled forehead showed behind it.

"Couriers from the noble General Iyon, with messages for your master and the Emperor," Ebreyu said loudly.

"This is a peaceful house," said the voice of the old man behind the door. "We have no business with generals, or soldiers who demand entrance in the middle of the night."

Ebreyu scowled. "The City Overlord of Buval commands the local levies, does he not? The message is for him, and it is for him to say whether he will receive it."

"We have ridden far today," Terai said in his careful Deirani, stepping forward to join Ebreyu. "We require shelter and rest, and these horses must be tended to. Rouse the household, steward, on the Emperor's authority."

"More of the same," the old man said in a voice that probably was not intended to carry to the outside. "More of the same. Next they will be requisitioning the very plates off our tables, the robes off the Overlord's back." He went away from the door, leaving the couriers to wait in the rain.

"That servant could bear a whipping, despite his years," Ebreyu said in irritation. "The Emperor's name deserves a better reception." He turned to the two soldiers from his command. "Take the horses and find the stables. See that they are well tended, whether or not servants of this house come out to help you. And report back to me if there are five good mounts to replace them."

"Yes, my lord," said Wesu, the one with the battered face. He took the reins of Arris's horse, not looking at Arris. He had given Arris his bruises when he was captured, and he had not said a word to him on the journey so far. His younger fellow, Chol, was equally ill at ease and resentful. He gathered the other three horses and led them after Wesu around the corner of the Overlord's house.

The door opened at last, half an hour after Ebreyu had first struck the gong. The old steward bowed slightly and waved Arris, Terai, and the Lieutenant inside. Behind him, an oil lamp had been lit in a wall sconce, illuminating the short corridor before the door and casting a few feeble rays into a shadowed expanse beyond, probably the house's main hall. A sleepy-looking, balding man wearing a silk gown and slippers walked toward them.

"Are you the City Overlord of Buval?" Arris stepped forward. His cloak dripped muddy water on the inlaid mosaic tiles of the entryway. He could see no other lights in the house, and he heard no noises that might indicate the household was being wakened as Terai had ordered.

"I am the Kurontai Lettendu," said the middle-aged man in an accent that was meant to resemble that of the court.

Arris bowed, not too deeply. He drew out one of the letters he carried, and handed it to Lettendu. "From the noble General Iyon."

"So Falam told me," the Overlord muttered. He slit the seal with a long fingernail and held the parchment up to the light of the single lamp. He read the hasty characters of Iyon's scribe with some difficulty. "These couriers bear news of great importance that must reach our Sacred Emperor with the utmost speed . . . You are directed to offer any necessary aid and comfort . . . Five post horses to be returned at the earliest opportunity . . ." Lettendu folded the letter. "I appreciate your need, sir officers, but this will be difficult to achieve."

"You refuse to obey us?" Ebreyu said, ready to flash into anger that had been fueled by the slowness of the steward and the wait in the rain.

The Overlord spoke quickly. "By no means, gentle sir. By no means. In all other matters I am at your service, but in this matter of horses I cannot help you at all. What animals I had, horses, mules, all are gone. Commandeered by the Sacred Emperor's army, as were all the mounts and packbeasts in the city. General Iyon should know this. The men who took my people's animals were headed for his fort in the mountains."

Terai's eyes narrowed. "The army would have left mounts for couriers. There will be many messengers coming through as the war begins."

The old steward, Falam, laughed softly. "The army did not think of that. They were shortsighted."

"Hush, Falam," Lettendu said. He spread his hands in apology. "Forgive me, good officers, but there are no horses."

"We can continue on the mounts we brought here," Terai said. "Our pace will be a little slower, but we'll reach the next garrison. The horses will have the same amount of rest we do. It may be enough. Kurontai Lettendu, see that your grooms tend our horses well. They should be fed with warmed grain, and rubbed with good linament. Their hooves should be well scraped of mud, and they should stand in clean straw."

"Alas," the Overlord said with an almost comical look of dismay. "The army took my grooms with them, to tend the horses."

"And you will not find a measure of oats or wheat in all of Buval," said Falam. "Perhaps the horses can eat rice."

"We are about to be at war," Ebreyu said. "The fighting will be in the Khalifate, but we will need strong cities at our backs, not people weakened by hunger. This was foolishly done."

"I have sent petitioners to the Emperor for aid," said Lettendu. "Perhaps the Sacred One will choose to help us."

"Write a letter tonight," Arris said. "Explain the situation to the Emperor. I'll give it to him myself. But we truly must reach him as soon as possible, and we need to rest now. Can you give us somewhere to sleep?"

"The house is quite empty. Most of my clerks and servants were conscripted. Aye, there are rooms enough for you all. Falam will show you where you may sleep. I have your word then, gentle sir? You will urge the Sacred Emperor to help my city?"

"I have said so." Arris was too tired to feel much sympathy.

"The gods will favor you for it, I am sure. Falam, attend our guests. I will be in my chambers writing to the Emperor." The sleepy nobleman hurried away through the dark hall, his slippers sounding soft against the tiles.

"The horses can eat rice," Terai said to the steward. "If it is prepared in a warm mash, with meat gravy. Can your kitchen manage that?"

"I will see to it myself," said the old man sullenly. "Come with me." He took the oil lamp from the wall to light their way.

"Is there a bath in the house?" Arris asked. "I would rather not sleep covered with mud."

"Of course there is a bath. This is a noble house. The water runs fresh, and the fires are kept burning at all times."

"Ah." Ebreyu's scowl softened. "Then lead us there, before you tend to the horses' feed."

Terai pulled his hood up over his head again. "I'll come to bathe later. I'm going to the stables to help Chol and Wesu with the horses. They don't know we'll have to use the same animals tomorrow." He turned and went back out the front door, leaving Arris and Ebreyu to follow the old steward.

"Come, then," Falam said. He led them through the dark hall and past a door at the side. A long corridor lined with ornate doors led toward the back of the large house. The bathhouse was attached to the main building, a civilized feature that was one of the things Arris had missed when he had left Deiran.

The bath was warm, as promised. Steam rose from the pool, which was twelve feet square. The rain sounded on glass windows set high in the walls. The steward lit a pair of lamps near the door. He opened a chest beside a wooden bench, and drew out two thick, white robes with sashes. "You may wear these when you are finished," he said. "Though I fear you will have to put your muddy uniforms back on in the morning. Back down the hall, and the second door to the left, you'll find me in the kitchen making a rice mash for your horses. Come there when you wish for me to show you to your beds." He left them there, closing the thick wooden door behind him.

Arris breathed in deep, letting the steam fill his dusty lungs. Ebreyu still looked annoyed. "They are not eager to treat us with honor," the Lieutenant said, unbuckling his cloak and sword belt and setting them aside. "Even if they feel they have been ill used, we are still the Emperor's men. They owe us respect."

"I am too tired to be offended," Arris said, undressing rapidly. "All I want to think about is a bath and bed."

"I suppose a spy encounters less courteous receptions than this," Ebreyu said. "I am not accustomed to being spoken to in that way, and by a servant . . ." He paused, and looked at Arris in some embarrassment. "I did not show you much respect when I captured you, did I? You must have been very angry. The General certainly was."

Arris slipped off his last undergarment and began to ease himself into the bath. His feet had been cold all day, and they burned and tingled in the heat of the water. It hurt, but it felt marvelous. He sighed, and looked up at Ebreyu again. "You were only doing your duty. I would have been surprised if you had not suspected me and Terai."

The young Deirani nodded. "That's what I told General Iyon. He said that it is an officer's duty to interpret orders according to the situation. I should have realized you and Terai could be who you said you were. I should have treated you as if what you said was true, at least until I learned otherwise. The General was right." He spoke formally. "I am sorry for the way my men and I treated you. I hope you were not much hurt, and that you will accept my apology."

Arris summoned as much dignity as he could, standing naked in a pool of hot water up to his chest. "Whatever disrespect you showed me, you act with honor now. Perhaps we can forget how we met."

Ebreyu looked relieved. "It was unworthy of my rank to behave as I did."

"So you've already said, my lord," Arris told him. "Now, if you want to get any sleep at all tonight, you had better stop talking and get into the bath." He splashed over to the side, took a handful of soap from a basin, and began to work it into a lather on his grimy skin.

Ebreyu laughed, and pulled his undertunic over his head. In the shadows of the lamplight, his scarred soldier's muscles looked as smooth and flawless as a sculptor's marble. Arris caught himself staring and had to look away. In a moment, Ebreyu began to lower himself slowly into the pool.

"It's hopeless," Arris said, scrubbing fiercely at the ingrained dirt on his arms and hands. "We'll be just as dirty by this time tomorrow."

"I suppose so." The ivory-skinned man sank deeply into the water, trying to rinse the mud from his braided hair.

"Well, at least the old steward won't be annoyed by filthy sheets on his beds."

Smiling widely, Ebreyu said, "I care little whether Falam is annoyed."

Ebreyu took himself too seriously, and he had a short temper, but Arris wished they had met under different circumstances. He liked the Lieutenant's smile, his skin the color of old parchment, the graceful line of his lean body. This was Deiran. Even if he was uninterested in men, Ebreyu was unlikely to be offended by a compliment coming from an attractive youth. But the Lieutenant had made it clear what he thought of spies.

Arris turned away again, not wanting to be caught staring in open admiration. It was a shame, but there would be other opportunities. He would not have to pretend in Deiran. He would not have to wall off the greater part of himself, as he had done in the Khalifate. And he was no longer a slave; he could choose his lovers for himself. He would not feel for any of them what he felt for Saresha. That was certain. But he need not be lonely, either.

The heat of the water relaxed his sore muscles, and banished the bone-deep chill of the rains. Arris worked soap into his scalp. It was not worth taking the time to unbraid his hair and really wash it, but this much at least would stop his head from itching. He sank down into the pool to rinse. When he emerged, he found Ebreyu watching him with a troubled half smile.

"I had never seen a Yaighan before I met you," the young soldier said. "I don't know what I expected. I had heard they were a dark people, and small . . . but I had heard nothing about their beauty."

Startled, but pleased, Arris met Ebreyu's gaze and smiled at him. "My friend Terai would be surprised to hear anyone call him beautiful."

"I was not speaking of Terai." Ebreyu chuckled. The water was not dirty enough yet to hide that he was aroused. Arris wanted to laugh at his earlier thoughts. Yet he made no move toward Ebreyu, still acutely conscious of the other's rank and pride. It was the soldier's decision, to pursue this or not.

"The Deirani have their share of handsome men," Arris said.

Ebreyu walked over to him in the bath and put a hesitant hand on Arris's shoulder. "I . . . do not know your customs. If I offend you . . ."

"You need not worry about that." Arris ran a wet hand lightly down Ebreyu's chest, feeling him shudder. "I think our customs are the same."

Then they both heard footsteps in the corridor, and Chol and Wesu's grumbling voices. Terai called out to the steward that the horses were hungry.

"The water is relaxing, but I think I am clean enough," Ebreyu said. He bent and kissed Arris roughly, a soldier's kiss. "Come with me, and we can ask Falam to find us someplace to sleep."

"I'd like that." Arris let Ebreyu help him out of the pool, and they dried themselves and put on the robes. Their three companions entered the bathhouse, dripping wet and muddy. Arris bade them good night. He and Ebreyu left the bathhouse together to go and find the steward. Both were tired from their journey, but Arris did not think they would get much sleep that night. He did not care. The journey to Khopei had suddenly become much more pleasant.

CHAPTER
5

THE CITY OF Buval was not unique in its experience with the soldiers of the Deirani army. Due to the lack of fresh horses, Arris and his companions made the journey to Khopei in four days rather than the three Iyon had wanted. It was a long road, and the rain did not let up as they traveled from the border provinces through the fertile, low-lying lands of the central Empire. The countless rivers that webbed the countryside were swollen with rain, but few minded that the rice shallows were flooded a little deeper than usual. The rice farmers would be planting soon. They were confident that the water would drop in time. Meanwhile, the river deposited layers of rich silt on the already dark, boggy earth.

The road cut through farms and villages, bending around the scattered cities. Arris regretted passing by the high, smooth walls of the cities. He would have liked to have seen them. He knew Khopei too well for the prospect of going there to seem exciting. Khopei and the Sapphire Palace were all he really knew of Deiran. He had been brought there as a frightened, newly captured slave of thirteen years, and when he left, his mission to spy in the Khalifate had kept him from exploring the Empire.

There were slave markets in the villages they rode past. Arris looked uneasily at the half-naked, miserable men and women who were sold there. He could have ended up as one of them, sold to a farmer to work the rice shallows, fed a bowl of rice a day, beaten when he did not work quickly enough. But the slaver who had brought him to Deiran had seen beauty in him, and had decided he belonged to the Emperor's harem. Arris thought that he could have done much worse. He had been ill-treated only rarely, when he was sent to entertain men like General Iyon. The Emperor had claimed to love him. Perhaps he really had. No, it had not been a terrible life.

If Arris had felt humiliated or degraded, it was only because he was a slave, not because of the duties of his slavery. Yet Arris did not want to tell Lieutenant Ebreyu how he had come to be in the Emperor's service. The Lieutenant would not understand. Arris did not think that Terai understood how he could have sworn loyalty to the Emperor after he had been given his freedom.

Arris and Terai had never spoken about Arris's life in the Sapphire Palace. Arris suspected that the thought of it made Terai very uncomfortable. No doubt the palace would seem a very strange place for the Yaighan warrior. For Arris, it was the only home he had left anymore. He had ruined his chances of any other life. Deiran was his only choice, and he was determined to be pleased with it.

So he rode toward the high arch of the eastern city gate of Khopei, at midday on the fourth day of his journey from the hill-fort. Khopei sprawled, many-layered and teeming, around the River Vaclav and its natural and man-made canals, curving around the rivermouth harbor under the terraced hills of the Sapphire Palace. It was the largest city in Deiran. It was overcrowded and alive, spangled with temples and shrines to its countless gods. The presence of thousands of the Emperor's soldiers went scarcely noticed amid the press of the crowds in the streets and the bazaars. The city had a distinctive scent, a smell compounded of river-damp, incense, spices, and humanity. Arris felt envigorated by the air itself.

The gate guards passed them through when Ebreyu shouted his name up at them. Riding at Arris's side, Ebreyu was more talkative now that the end of the road was near. He was more cheerful this morning than in all of the past days and nights.

"When this mission is over, perhaps I'll be granted a few days' leave before I'm sent back to the border," Ebreyu said now, as their horses forced a way through the market-day crowd near the gate. "I should go and visit my family. It has been months since I've seen them."

Arris knew something of Ebreyu's background now. He was the fourth son of a retired general, due to inherit little but his father's pride in his choice of the military as his career. Ebreyu had been raised away from court, with his mother and five sisters, in a country villa thirty miles downriver from Khopei.

"I'll ask the Emperor to grant you a couple of weeks leave," Arris said, feeling generous. He smiled and shook his head at a group of children who tried to cluster around the horses, holding up baskets of dried fruit.

"Perhaps you'd like to come along, to visit my family?" Ebreyu suggested. "Unless the Emperor will be sending you out on another mission right away."

They were free of the eager fruit-sellers, and Arris was able to bring his mount to a trot as they turned along one of the main east-west roads of the city. "I've had enough of spying, and I want nothing more to do with the war," Arris said. "I'd like to go with you, very much." He was startled by the invitation. Though they had become lovers, there was a gulf between them, felt keenly by both men. Arris had told Ebreyu nothing about himself, but the Deirani nobleman surely assumed that Arris was far below him in social rank. A noble might take a commoner as a lover, but to present him to his family as a friend—that was more than anyone would expect.

"We have a task in Khopei first," Terai said from behind them. He urged his horse up beside Arris's mount. Of them all, he seemed the least exhausted by the relentless pace, the continual mud and rain of the journey. His back was as straight as it had been the first day.

The two young Deirani soldiers were trailing farther behind, slumped disconsolately in their saddles, as they had done throughout the journey. Their grumbling had been a low, monotonous accompaniment to the long ride.

Arris nodded impatiently. "Of course. I have to give the Emperor my report." He could no longer see the layered tile roofs of the Sapphire Palace; the narrow streets closed in around them, and the royal hills to the west of the city were not high.

"And you have to fulfill your promise to Danae."

Arris had forgotten that. He had promised to help Danae's family get out of Deiran. Terai had said that was the reason he had come along, to be certain it was done. "That may take only a few moments," Arris said guiltily. "I mean to ask it as a favor from the Emperor."

"I would not count on his good will," Terai said darkly.

They drew up rein at a cross street before one of the Vaclav bridges. A procession was swaying down the avenue. Men and women filled the street, dancing and clashing rough cymbals together, chanting the praises of some obscure god. Arris did not recognize the striped robes of the priests who led the crowd, or the statues that were carried on the shoulders of worshipers.

There truly were a thousand shrines in Khopei. Every village of the Empire seemed to have its own gods, with their own names and attributes and customs of worship. Many of the deities were merely more or less powerful versions of the gods of neighboring villages, but the people were jealous in their refusal to accept another name or aspect for their patron gods. Khopei, as it grew, had gathered people from all parts of the Empire, and with them had come their gods.

The clamor of chanting and shouting and the scree of the music was upsetting the tired horses. Arris took a firm grip on his reins as his mount shook its head back and forth and pranced, seeking to turn around and go back the way they had come. The procession of worshipers thronged before them, completely blocking access to the river bridge. The noise and movement were too much for Arris's weary senses. His head had begun to ache, as the simple, haunting melody the people were chanting began to sound as harsh as the cries of the Lossiran.

"How do we get around this?" he shouted. Ebreyu

shrugged, busy trying to control his own horse. Terai sat
very still, his mount quiet under his firm hands, a frown
creasing his brow beneath the rim of his Deirani helmet.
Chol and Wesu shifted in their saddles to see over the
gathering crowd, apparently interested in the spectacle.

"The next bridge is a half mile to the north," said a
woman who had halted nearby. She held a small boy on
her shoulders, whose feet drummed against his mother's
breasts in excitement. "You'll do best to wait for them to
pass, as we all must do."

"Who are they?" Terai asked in an urgent tone. His
strange accent made the woman look at him in sudden
suspicion. She clutched her child tighter, scowling up at
his dark, foreign face, and did not answer.

"They are the followers of the god Anoguri," an old
man said. Near Ebreyu's horse, he turned to call up at the
soldiers. "They say their god spoke in his temple yesterday. The priests were as amazed as the people were. Such
a thing to happen!" He laughed dryly.

"One of the Thousand appearing in his shrine?" said a
man mockingly.

"Is the river running upstream?" shouted a girl from a
group of ragged children who clustered on the porch of a
shop. Her friends clapped her on the back and roared with
laughter. It was an old Deirani saying, Arris remembered.
When the Thousand Gods appear in their shrines, and the
River Vaclav runs upstream . . . it was a way of saying
that a thing was impossible.

"We can go through them." Arris felt a vast impatience. "We have no time to waste here." He urged his
horse forward in the press.

"No." Terai spoke in Yaighan. He leaned forward to
grasp Arris's rein and stop him. The horse snorted and
kicked. "Do not draw their attention, lad."

"What do you mean?"

"It will do you no good to be noticed by any god, even
a Deirani one." The older Yaighan spoke swiftly in his
native language. Ebreyu was frowning now, wondering
what was said. "I can sense power in these worshipers of

Anoguri, whoever he is. And until your daimon finds a way to free your own power, you must be very careful."

"I'm in no danger in Khopei," Arris said. He returned to the Deirani language. "We are couriers of the Emperor. We cannot be delayed for the convenience of these people. It has already taken us a day too long to get here. I am not going to wait." He twitched his reins from Terai's fingers and kneed his horse.

Already nervous, the animal sprang forward in a prancing trot, forcing its way into the twisting line of the priests and dancing worshipers. The chanting and the clashing instruments rose up to engulf Arris, and he felt a crawling sensation on his skin as he tried to guide the horse across the path of the procession. Faces glared at him, and voices shouted. Hands reached toward his horse's reins to turn it aside, but the horse flashed its teeth and made its own way.

The chipped-glass eyes of the god's effigy were momentarily on a level with Arris's. The statue was carried on a man's shoulders. Its roughly carven face seemed to quicken to life briefly, long enough to give Arris an intense, probing look. He felt a chill sensation, and then the statue was gone, swept away in the flood of people.

The street seemed endlessly wide. Arris could no longer see the bridge. He could not see the rooftops beyond the River Vaclav. His heart began to race with the quickening time of the drums, and he had the urge to dismount and dance along with the people of the god. He was growing dizzy, and his hands shook. His horse had turned when he was not paying attention, and now it walked along with the procession, in a bright tunnel that closed around them both. Arris shook his head. No, he could not join them. He had to get to the Emperor. He was late already.

He leaned down to gather the horse's reins. Somehow he had dropped them. The knotted ends trailed in the dust. He could not reach them. Then, as if the horse had knelt down in the middle of the street, Arris felt a lurching drop. He slid off the animal's back sideways to land unhurt on the cobblestones. He blinked his eyes rapidly, trying to clear them of a bright fog that blurred everything. The striped robes of the chanting priests seemed to be writhing like snakes, and the faces that bobbed and rose in the dance were all looking at him. Arris could not see if they were smiling or scowling.

His horse was gone. The procession seemed to have stopped. The people danced in circles around Arris, shaking their cymbals at him, raw-edged circles of beaten bronze. They were faceless, whirling like weeds blown in a windspout. Then two figures in smeared, muddy black shoved through the dancers. Even through his oddly blurred vision, Arris could see that they held long knives in light, underhand grips.

These two had faces, and hooded, dark eyes that glowed with lunatic pleasure. One was tall and awkward, and the other had a broken nose. Chol and Wesu, his grumbling companions along the couriers' road.

The worshipers of Anoguri sang louder and danced more wildly as the soldiers walked toward him. Arris had no doubt that they meant to kill him. He stumbled to his feet, feeling that something was very wrong. He could not see or think clearly. It was as if he had wandered on stage, drunk, in the climactic scene of a play he did not know, and yet his was the central role. He remembered that there had been a warning he had refused to heed.

He had no weapons. He was a messenger, under the protection of the Emperor's soldiers. Now two men from his escort stalked him, circling, laughing, chanting confused phrases from the priest's song. Arris reached back in his memory for a shielding, focusing spell he had learned in training at Gama. He lacked the power to complete it, but the effort of concentration finally cleared his vision and lessened his drugged feeling.

Arris backed up slowly, looking around for an opening where he could get out of the crowd. The people danced around one another in tight patterns. There were no holes. Two of the effigies of the god swayed back and forth on men's shoulders. A prancing child was playing a shrill flute, her bright eyes fixed on Arris.

"So be it," he muttered in Yaighan. He unbuckled his heavy cloak and wrapped it partway around his left arm, letting the weighted hem swing free in an arc, brushing the cobblestones of the street. There was nothing of Khopei around him but those worn paving stones. He could not see past the colorful sway of the dancers, and he heard only a rising skirl of music that had grown fierce and hungry, and he smelled a sharp scent of burning herbs that made his eyes water.

Chol and Wesu had been moving like men in a dream, but now they shouted suddenly and charged at Arris with their knives held low. Arris swung his cloak and hit Chol in the face. He sprang between them, turning. Wesu lashed out viciously with a high kick that caught Arris just above his right hip and knocked him off his feet.

Chol dropped heavily on top of Arris, thrusting with his knife as Arris rolled out from under him. The blade caught Arris in the back, glancing off his shoulder blade and slashing down in a burning line. Arris cried out at the pain, but even as the knife cut him he had gotten free, and had his feet under him.

He fell back toward the dancers, who pushed him forward again. They scarcely seemed to notice him, but their worship had taken on a frenzied edge, and cymbals and drums sounded wildly, without rhythm. Arris turned to one of the musicians, an old man, and punched him hard below the ribs. Without a cry, the man doubled over, and dropped the cymbals he had been playing.

Arris picked up one of the cymbals, cutting his hand slightly on the ragged edge. Chol and Wesu were coming at him, full of confidence now that they had drawn blood. They were still laughing like idiots.

Arris leapt to the left of the bigger youth, Chol, and in a smooth movement like a slinger, he swung the cymbal around and brought it edge-first across Chol's throat. It dragged across the soft flesh, leaving a thick track of blood. Chol dropped his knife and clutched at his neck.

Wesu lunged for Arris's back and got one arm around Arris's neck. Arris twisted like one of the whirling dancers, and felt the soldier's knife graze his right side. He kicked backward and connected with one of Wesu's knee-caps. The soldier groaned, but held on, and tried to thrust again. Arris caught the arm with the knife against his body, grasped the hand and elbow in two hands, and threw Wesu to the ground over his hip. He kept a tight hold of Wesu's arm, and felt the crack as both forearm bones broke. The knife fell from nerveless fingers. Arris let go and stepped back.

There was a rushing noise like a great wind, and the dancers resumed their procession, eddying around Arris like river water around a bridge pylon. Their music was plaintive and haunting once more, no longer the rending noise that had risen when Chol and Wesu had attacked. A man trotted by with a child on his shoulders, not an effigy of Anoguri; she was a pretty little girl, with a flute in one hand. She smiled at Arris, showing two missing teeth.

Whimpering softly, Wesu cradled his broken arm. Chol held his hands to his throat. Blood dripped over them, but it did not spurt. The cymbal had not cut into the artery. Arris stood there gasping for breath, with a headache that was worse than the pain from the cut across his upper back. The procession was gone. It had left them alone in the middle of the street, between the riverside porches and the graceful, arched bridge.

"Arris!" Terai shouted. He and Ebreyu dismounted and ran toward him. The city people who had been watching the procession were nowhere to be seen. Arris's riderless horse stood beside Terai's mount, with the horses that Chol and Wesu had been riding.

"What happened?" Ebreyu demanded. His face was more than usually pale. "We could see nothing. We couldn't move forward into the street to look for you. Your horse came back, and Chol and Wesu leapt off their mounts when all the people went to join the dancers."

"They tried to kill me," Arris said. He was overwhelmingly dizzy. He clung to Terai to keep from falling.

"Goddess defend us," Terai muttered in Yaighan. "I sensed nothing from them. No danger. Nothing but two conscript soldiers unhappy with their lot. You're bleeding, lad.'' He turned Arris around, and carefully pulled back the edges of torn cloth and leather where the knife had gone through his uniform. "It's a long cut, but not too deep."

"That doesn't look bad," Ebreyu said worriedly. "Can you wait until we get to the palace to have it tended, or should we stop at a healer's?"

"I can wait for the palace," Arris said. He watched as Terai bound Chol's throat with a strip of cloth torn from the soldier's cloak. Ebreyu put a makeshift sling on Wesu. Arris thought that he should have killed them outright. Their deaths now would not be so easy. The justice of the Emperor was harsh.

"Why did you do this thing?" Ebreyu asked fiercely, helping Wesu onto his horse.

Arris pulled himself into his saddle, listening with a dim curiosity. He did not know what had happened. How had he fallen off his horse; how had the city faded away around him, leaving only the music and the whirling dancers? He felt confused and clouded again. The concentration had achieved when he was attacked was gone.

Wesu answered after a long silence, as the five men rode across the Vaclav bridge. "My lord, I do not know." His voice was oddly flat. "I can remember doing it, but I do not know why."

"Were you possessed by your god?" Terai asked.

Wesu made a sound that was something between a sob and a laugh. "My god? I do not know this Anoguri. I do not worship him. And I have no quarrel with your friend."

"I think you are lying," Ebreyu said. "The Emperor's questioners will learn the truth."

"I wonder," Terai said.

The palace of Deiran's Sacred Emperor was an interweaving of graceful buildings with fluted roofs, gardens of a hundred varieties, fountains, and parade grounds, all encircled by a series of low walls. For defense against thieves or uninvited commoners, the walls were guarded by countless black-armored soldiers with pikes. No armed enemy had gotten anywhere near the place in all of its history, and no one had seen a need for siege defenses.

Under the reign of the Emperor Hareku, the court of Deiran was an elegant and vital place. No nobleman or woman of the realm would stay away from it for long if they could help it. To be sent to a provincial post, like that of the Buval City Overlord, was like being exiled from the heart of the world. At the Emperor's court, those who were serious about their roles as noble advisors to their lord could make themselves heard; those who wished to seek favor could scheme and bribe and present lavish entertainments; those who enjoyed beauty in artwork, gardens, music, and slaves would find what they sought.

After almost two years, Arris felt more like a stranger than a returning denizen of the palace. Before, he had been one of the graceful, jeweled creatures that old men pointed to when they complained about the decadence of the court. Now he was an exhausted soldier in a muddy black uniform.

Chol and Wesu were sent off under armed guard. Grooms took the horses to one of the stables. A page was sent to the Chamberlain's office with word that couriers had arrived and sought an audience with the Emperor. A litter was procured, and Arris, Terai, and Ebreyu rode in curtained state through the palace grounds to Ebreyu's family apartments.

The early afternoon was cool, but the rain had stopped. The palace fountains played their colored and scented waters amid the winter gardens of delicately trimmed evergreens and flowering shrubs. The beauty of the terraced paths seemed unreal to Arris after what had happened in Khopei. He closed his eyes, feeling nauseated with the rocking of the litter. He hoped the Emperor would not insist on granting them an audience soon.

Lieutenant Ebreyu dismissed the litter bearers when they reached one of the long, low wooden buildings that housed the noble families' suits. Arris and Terai followed the young officer through a low gate in a garden wall. A raked gravel path wound between empty flower beds and gnarled dwarf trees that were carefully twisted and trimmed. A few simple benches were placed where they would be shaded from summer heat. One looked over a small goldfish pond, also empty for the season. It was a pleasant place.

Ebreyu rapped on the doorpost of his family apartments. A modest crest was painted on the door-screen, a trout leaping over the crossed swords of a military house. The fish seemed alive to Arris's bleary gaze. It shimmered and swam before his eyes. Terai looked at him in concern, and took his arm in a steadying grip.

A plump, pretty young woman folded back the door-screen at last. She wore no face paint, and her brown hair waved back naturally from her high forehead. It took Arris a moment to recognize Tibi, a courtesan who had been one of the most requested jewels of the Emperor's harem. She knew him, and stared at him wide-eyed before turning to Ebreyu.

"My lord! You've come back. You've taken sick, or been wounded?"

Ebreyu shook his head. "No, Tibi. I came back as a courier, under General Iyon's orders. These two gentlemen are under my protection, and they'll be staying with us." He waved Arris and Terai inside. Tibi stepped back and bowed as they passed.

Arris was waiting for her to say something that would betray him, something that would tell Ebreyu he had been one of the Emperor's slaves. Tibi only led them into the front room of the apartments. She moved with her old bouncy, swaying walk, but the simple robe she wore did not have the effect of the harem silks.

The front room was very clean, decorated with dried flowers and fresh cedar branches in tall vases. A fresco of a school of pale fish was painted into the plaster of one wall. Arris recognized the stylized lines. He heard his voice ask as if from a great distance, "Is that a piece by Qwerin?"

Ebreyu shrugged. Tibi smiled at Arris. "It is. Painted last spring as a gift for the master when he retired from the army.'' Qwerin was a common-born artist who enjoyed the rare favor of the Emperor. It was unusual to see his work in a private chamber. He was known for his outdoor frescoes, large and ambitious works that were the more renowned for their temporary nature. One might last five winters. This delicate school of fish was likely to be around much longer, though few would see it.

''Your master is fortunate to be surrounded by beauty,'' Arris said, before the room began to close in on him like a dark hand. He felt his knees giving way, and Terai's strong arms caught him as he fainted.

CHAPTER
6

ARRIS WOKE TO WARMTH and the tart smell of lemon-scented water. Steam hovered in the cool air. He could hear the sounds of splashing, and a woman's low voice. He opened his eyes and found himself lying on his side on a bench, looking at the patterned tiles of a bath-chamber wall. His head ached. The cut on his back throbbed in time with his heartbeat.

He began to turn over, and Terai's hands caught his shoulders to help him sit up. "You're awake, then," said the Yaighan, who had been sitting on a stool beside him. His voice was gruff with relief. "I was beginning to worry."

"I fainted, didn't I?" Arris sat still, fighting dizziness. The bath chamber held a large pool. Ebreyu was bathing with the help of Tibi, who knelt at the side of the bath and poured a pitcherful of scented water over him to rinse out his long hair. Terai wore a short, clean robe, and Arris was dressed the same way. He moved his left shoulder carefully, and felt the soft friction of a tight bandage.

"You hadn't lost that much blood." Terai frowned at him. "I'm not sure it was because of your wound. You were attacked with something stronger than knives, back there in the street."

"It felt unreal then, and the memory doesn't make it any different. I should apologize, Terai. You warned me I was in danger."

"And then I let you go anyway." The older man spoke in Yaighan. "When the attack came, I couldn't even move forward to look for you. If you had not been able to save yourself . . . it was my failure. I sensed power there, and did nothing to protect you.''

Arris nodded slowly, watching Ebreyu's handsome body in the pool, not looking at Terai. ''That's why you came with me to Deiran. To protect me.''

''To keep you from getting yourself killed. Yes.''

''I didn't ask for your protection.''

''I know that.''

Arris stood up carefully. ''I don't understand why you're doing this. But I'll probably listen to you the next time you warn me of danger.'' His dizziness was lessening.

''Arris?'' Ebreyu's voice showed his concern. ''How do you feel? The Emperor has summoned us for an audience in an hour, but I didn't know if you'd be well enough to attend.'' He was wringing out his hair, and Tibi had turned to look coolly at Arris. She looked so different in the dress of a household slave. She had a new dignity, a calmness that was apparent even as she knelt with a pitcher in her hands, her gown soaked at the knees with splashed water.

''I'll be all right. You'll have to lend me something to wear. I have nothing but the uniform, and it's torn.''

''Anything you like,'' Ebreyu said more cheerfully. ''All my robes will be too long for you, though.'' He pulled himself up out of the pool, and stood while Tibi dried him and wrapped the drying cloth around his waist. ''You have time to bathe, and Tibi will wash your hair for you. Terai, if you'll come with me, we'll choose something of my father's for you to wear to the audience.'' Terai glanced at Arris, who nodded that he would be all right alone. The two men left the chamber together and closed the door behind them.

''Well.'' The plump young woman laughed softly. ''You're a mess, Arris. I hardly would have known you.''

''You're as pretty as ever, Tibi.'' He walked over to her, and suddenly was wrapped in a wet embrace. Arris grinned at the ex-courtesan as she pushed him away and held him at arm's length.

''So are you, love. More so, to my taste, though you'd be too old for the Emperor now. You've added an inch or two, and your shoulders are wider. Once we wash the mud off you and comb your hair, you'll turn more heads than Ebreyu's." Tibi giggled. "However did you manage it? I haven't seen him so infatuated. And he isn't usually attracted to pretty boys."

Arris shrugged, and winced as the movement pulled at his wound. "It just happened. I like him."

"Sit down," she said sternly. "Here at the edge. The water is so hot you'd probably faint again if you went in. And you shouldn't get the bandage wet."

She helped him remove his robe. Arris was not embarrassed to be naked in front of Tibi. She had been one of his less formal trainers in the arts of the Dance when he had first come to the Emperor's harem. She had been sixteen then, and noblemen came to blows over her favors and begged the Emperor to allow them to purchase her. Since the Emperor had no interest in the women among his concubines, Tibi had never been jealous of Arris's position. They had been friends, or as near friends as was possible amid the intrigue and boredom of the harem.

Arris sat in front of her, letting his feet soak in the pool. "What are you doing here, Tibi? Are you really Ebreyu's slave now?"

"A gift from his father on his twenty-first birthday, last year." She sounded indifferent. "I was getting too old for the harem, and I was tired of it all, so I made the keepers accept the General's offer. It's easy work here. I take care of the suite, and the garden in the summer. Ebreyu isn't often here. The rest of his family never comes to court at all."

She began to sponge his back, kneading his sore muscles with practiced fingers. Arris closed his eyes and tried to forget his weariness. "Are you happy here?"

Her hands paused for a moment, then continued around to the front. "Ebreyu is a strong man, a good soldier . . . and not like General Iyon. He never tries to hurt me, though sometimes he seems not to know I'm there. You know what they're like."

Arris did know. Many of the noblemen and women the Emperor had sent him to entertain had treated him that way, as a mindless creature whose only function was their pleasure. But he had almost liked that better than the patrons who had wanted to talk to him as if he were a man, and then expected him to perform like a trained animal. "It hasn't been like that, with Ebreyu and me."

"He doesn't know who you are, does he?" Tibi asked quietly. She worked her fingers through his hair, undoing his braids, and then poured water over his head. "He wasn't often at court when you were here. He doesn't know you were a slave, and the Emperor's boy. If you want to keep his friendship, Arris . . . be sure he never finds out."

Arris turned a little to look at her, blinking through the water that dripped over his eyes. "Does it matter that much? It will be impossible to keep it a secret if we stay at the palace for long."

"Lean your head back." Tibi massaged soap into his hair. The scent of lemons was pleasant, not overpowering or sweet. "You're right, people will remember you. The Emperor hasn't taken another favorite since you left. Oh, he sends for boys, and sometimes keeps one for a few nights. But for two years, he has not allowed any slave to get as close to him as you were. People still talk about you. Arris the beautiful dancer, the one they couldn't bribe, the slave Hareku freed for saving his life. No one knew where you went when you left. Everyone thinks the Emperor is still pining away for you."

"I can't see Hareku pining for anything," Arris said lightly, but Tibi's words troubled him.

"The slaves wonder what sorcery you used to make him love you. You started a brief fashion among the seraglio boys. Some of them had themselves tattooed, until the Emperor forbade it. And they all pretended to be acrobats, dancers, singers. They pester the lyrists to teach them to play." She rinsed his hair, and began to rub it dry with a thick cloth.

"You make me almost afraid to see him again," Arris said.

"Afraid he'll declare you never were free, and take you back to his bed?" Tibi shook her head. "I think he'll look

at you, and smile in memory, and be glad he let you go."
She took his hand and helped him rise to his feet. Momentarily the room went dark before Arris's eyes, but then it cleared as he stood still. "I'm not worried about the Emperor," Tibi said. "I'm worried about Ebreyu. It's going to hurt him to learn the truth. He has great pride, in his position, in his noble family. He'll be angry with you for not telling him."

"If I had told him in the beginning, he never would have spoken to me, much less slept with me." Arris wrapped the cloth around his waist.

Tibi nodded. "You may be right. Come. We have little time to make you ready to appear before the Emperor."

An hour later, Arris, Ebreyu, and Terai followed a woman from the Chamberlain's office across the palace grounds to the central complex. They entered at a side door, where two pikemen saluted with their weapons and let them pass. The ceiling of the breezy corridor was arched and scalloped above them, painted in an intricate pattern of pale blue and yellow and white. The floor was carpeted in desert-colored stripes, rich weaving that might have paid a year's wage to ten laborers. The traces of delicate perfumes vied with the scented oil of the wall lamps, but the effect was not the close, stuffy smell that permeated the Citadel. Windows and door-screens were open to let in the air, and the palace was honeycombed with open courtyards.

The woman who was their guide led them to the guarded door of a small reception chamber, where the Emperor would grant them a private audience. Arris was pleased to be able to bypass the ceremony of the great Audience Hall, and the tension of the chamber where petitioners waited to see the Emperor. He, Terai, and Ebreyu would have made enemies simply by being passed through quickly to their audience, while most supplicants had to wait more than half a day if they were seen at all.

"How do you wish to be announced?" asked the official.

"The noble Lieutenant Ebreyu of the Army of the Empire, Terai of the Yaighan, and Arris, in the service of the

Sacred Emperor," Arris said. She bowed slightly, opened the door a little, and slipped through.

Arris still felt weakened, and his wound pained him. He smoothed his robe over the belt that kept it from dragging on the ground, and wondered if he had chosen well to dress his hair simply in a long tail and wear only a small pair of gold earrings as jewelry. He wanted to face the Emperor as a changed person, a grown man who had just completed a dangerous mission. He did not want to remind Hareku of the boy he had been.

Ebreyu looked the part of a Deirani nobleman, with two necklaces, arm cuffs, and jewels on his sash. Ebreyu had also lined his dark eyes a little with kohl, common among men and women at the court. Terai had refused any kind of ornament. He had chosen dark green robes, and looked solemn and grave, like the priest he had once been.

The woman returned after a few moments, and bowed once more. "Your presence is requested by the Most Sacred Emperor Hareku."

"May the gods attend him," Arris and Ebreyu said automatically, in unison. The protocol of the court had been such a part of Arris that he did not think he could ever forget the most minor point.

Before she opened the door again, the woman drew Arris aside and spoke to him too softly for the others to hear, "I have been charged to bring you to another audience after this one, sir. The Royal Princess Kakima was with her father when I announced you. She wishes to see you alone later."

So Kakima was a Royal Princess still, and not the wife of any of the Emperor's great lords. She would be twenty-two years old. "I will be honored to attend Her Highness at her convenience," Arris said.

"I will await you here."

Arris turned to his companions. Even Terai looked nervous. Ebreyu was holding himself more erect than any soldier at attention Arris had ever seen, and licking dry lips. Arris gave them each a brief smile of reassurance, and stepped to the door to open it.

The room was narrow, but the ceilings were high and

decorated with bright patterns. Banners hung on the walls, rippling a little in the breeze from open windows near the ceiling. The Emperor Hareku sat on a heavy wooden chair on a shallow dais with two steps. His graying hair was cropped short in a soldier's cut, and the sword he bore today was not a ceremonial saber, but a curved scimitar with a worn grip. He was forty-five years old, with the hard, muscular body of a much younger man, and a proud, handsome face that showed the effects of years and responsibility.

Arris had never known if he really had loved the Emperor. He still did not know, but he felt a thrill of pleasure and pride in looking at him. Hareku was a powerful man, a god by the standards of his people, and Arris had won his love.

Terai and Ebreyu flanked Arris on either side, as the door closed behind them. The Emperor's iron-gray eyes were fixed on Arris in an intense, unwavering gaze. Arris stepped forward a few paces and knelt, prostrating himself in the full ceremonial bow. Behind him, Ebreyu did the same, and Terai followed their example only a little slowly.

"Rise, gentlemen," the Emperor said. "Lieutenant Ebreyu, you did well to escort these men to me. Terai of the Yaighan, you are welcome to my court. And Arris—I had heard that you were wounded, attacked in the streets of Khopei by men wearing my uniform. You do not look much hurt."

"It was a minor wound," Arris said. He found himself smiling widely, against all protocol, as if the Emperor were simply an old friend he had not seen for a long time.

"It was my fault, Sacred One," Ebreyu said quickly, at attention again. "Chol and Wesu were under my command. General Iyon assigned them with me to protect Arris."

Hareku leaned forward in his throne, and there was a faint smile on his face as well. "Arris is a Jai-Sohn, and should be able to protect himself. I will hear the confession of the soldiers later, but I do not think you will be held responsible, Lieutenant."

Arris drew a rolled letter from his belt. Iyon's seal hung

on the ribbon that bound it. "I reported to General Iyon first, at the border. He is eager to hear your word, Sacred One." He stepped up onto the first level of the dais and handed the scroll to Hareku.

The warrior's voice was low. "There are proverbs about the loyalty of freed slaves. I ignored them, and placed my trust in you, for no better reason than love. I hope you are here to prove me right, Arris."

Arris could not help glancing at Ebreyu. The young lieutenant was pale and tight-lipped, and did not meet his eyes. He had not known Arris was a Jai-Sohn assassin, and he had not known he was a slave. The secret had not lasted long.

"Sacred One, I am honored by your trust," Arris said, putting aside his wistful thoughts. "I did my best to uphold it. The Regents of the Khalifate, Nievan and Maenad, are dead. But I failed to kill the Ilkharani Prince. He was rescued by the high priest Karillos, and is back in the Citadel by now. I barely escaped with my life. That is yours now, if it is your will, for my failure."

It was part of the Jai-Sohn Way that an assassin could be killed in the place of his intended victim, if he survived an unsuccessful attempt. Arris waited with his head bowed, not looking at the Emperor's face. He thought that Hareku would be merciful; yet he had been known to be capricious before, and some called him cruel.

The wooden throne creaked a little, as Hareku settled back into it with a soft curse. "Do you think I would have you killed, boy? Gods preserve me from such tyranny. You did well. I am disappointed that Saresha Ilkharani lives. But you have eliminated my most important enemies, and the Prince is still underage. You have mortally wounded the Khalifate, ripped out its heart. We will merely be desecrating the corpse. And the time for that has come, at long last."

Lieutenant Ebreyu took a step forward. "Most Sacred Emperor, if it is your will . . . I would be glad to swear to you never to reveal what I have heard here today. That you . . . that you sent an assassin against the rulers of the Khalifate."

"You disapprove?" Hareku looked with interest at the young officer. "And you believe, perhaps, that my court and my army would also disapprove?" At Ebreyu's uneasy nod, the Emperor's voice became harsh. "Know this, my noble Lieutenant. In war there are no laws. And this war was joined long ago. The Ilkharani sent an assassin against me four years ago."

Alarmed, Ebreyu looked up. "You need not justify your actions to me, my Emperor."

"No." Hareku glanced at Arris, a thoughtful, measuring look. "I am not angry, Lieutenant. You are young. One day, perhaps, you may discuss this question with your father, the Kurontai Tikendi. You may be interested to know that he was trained as a Jai-Sohn as a young man, and he carried out missions as a Black Sword. Nothing as vital as what Arris has done for me, though." He took a dagger from his belt, and slit the seal of Iyon's letter. His big hands unfolded the parchment on his lap, and he began to read.

Ebreyu looked as if he had been slapped. His jaw was trembling. No doubt he thought the Emperor was lying. His father was a respected general, and could not have been a Jai-Sohn. Soldiers in the army despised assassins more than they did spies. Arris suspected Hareku had told Ebreyu the truth. But if the Emperor had meant to calm Ebreyu, he had not succeeded.

When he was done, Hareku was grinning like a leopard over a kill. "I will draw up the proclamation of war this afternoon, and have a hundred couriers on the road by sunset. Iyon's forces will cross the Khalifate border within three days, and I will follow with the rest of my army when I can gather the western garrisons. Lieutenant Ebreyu, take a few days' leave if you wish, but then you must return to General Iyon. He'll be in the Khalifate by that time. But you'll be no good to him if I send you back today, exhausted from your journey."

"Thank you, Sacred One," the soldier said. He bowed low.

Hareku turned again to Arris, and the touch of his gray eyes was like a caress. "I hope you will continue to serve me, my hawk. I mean to reward you for your mission with a good sum of gold, but I also offer you a commission in my army. As a lieutenant of the reconnaissance wing. I cannot spare General Iyon to teach spying to my soldiers, and he has said you were the best Jai-Sohn he ever taught. Much of the Shadowed Way is as useful to scouts as it is to assassins.''

"My lord, I . . ." Arris began again. "Sacred One, I cannot accept a commission. I do not wish to be involved any further in this war.''

The Emperor was silent for a long moment. He hated to have a gift refused, Arris remembered, and what he had offered was no small reward for Arris's work. A commissioned officer in the army had the privileges of a minor nobleman, and the opportunity of gaining land and even a title in time. Finally the Emperor sighed and nodded. "As you wish. The gold will still be yours. I will have the Treasury approve it by tonight. What else may I do for you? You have done me a great service.''

Arris saw Terai's dark, impatient glare, and remembered what he was supposed to ask. "Sacred One, if you would grant me another favor, let it be this. Do you remember the family of musicians from the Khalifate who were my friends? Senna, Van, and Vaessa are their names. Allow them to return to their homeland. Do not keep them imprisoned here any longer. They will be your subjects in the Khalifate too, soon enough.''

The Emperor shook his head. "I cannot give you that. Those musicians were sold as slaves after the youngest of them made her escape. I might have had them killed, if you had not written me that the girl Danae was helping you in the Citadel. But they could not go unpunished.''

"Slaves? My lord, they are artists! You had no . . .''

"I had no right to do it?" Hareku said in a still, quiet tone. "Take care, boy.''

Arris swallowed hard and looked at the carpeted floor. "Forgive me. I had not expected this. Can you tell me where they are now?''

"There would be records somewhere. You have enough gold to purchase their freedom if you find them. You have my permission to do that, if that is how you wish to spend your reward. But hear me, Arris. They are not to leave Khopei. If I learn that you have somehow gotten them out of the country, I will consider it an act of treason.''

"I understand," Arris whispered.

"Good. Well, I had not intended to be angry with you," Hareku said with a weary smile. "Truly, I am most grateful for what you have done. If you change your mind about the commission, my offer still stands. And you, Terai, are also offered my favor if you will serve me in this war. General Iyon speaks highly of you in his letter, as a man experienced in warfare. And knowledgeable in strategy, especially in reconnaissance.''

Terai bowed deeply. "I have my own loyalties, Sacred Emperor. But I thank you for the offer.''

Arris stepped back to stand with his friends. The breeze had died in the room, and the banners hung straight and unwavering overhead. He could hear the chink of armor as the guards outside the door paced back and forth. The Emperor shifted position again on his throne, crossing his legs. He was not a man who could be still for long. Arris knew his restlessness and his impatience well; his quicksilver moods, his occasional acts of great kindness or great cruelty. There was something in Arris that longed to serve this Emperor again, in any way that he desired. But Hareku was making ready for war at last, and Arris did not want to kill again, or train men to kill.

"My daughter asked for you," Hareku said. "Will you go to her, before you chase after your musician friends? She would be most pleased.''

"I will be glad to see her again." Arris smiled affectionately at the man on the carven throne.

"I have much to do," the Emperor said abruptly, getting to his feet with Iyon's letter in his hand. "When I have leisure, I will send for you again, Arris. I would like to hear your thoughts about the Ilkharani court, and the men who will lead their army against me. I have your reports, but there must be more you can tell me.''

"I am at your command, Sacred One.''

"Yes. You may go now." He nodded politely as the

three men bowed, but he seemed distracted. He glanced down at the letter again as Arris turned and led Ebreyu and Terai from the room.

Outside in the corridor, Arris was glad to see the woman from the Chamberlain's office waiting impatiently for him. He went with her, before there was time to talk to Terai about the problem of Danae's family, and before he had to face Ebreyu's reaction to what the Emperor had revealed. Neither conversation was likely to be pleasant. Seeing Kakima again promised to be more enjoyable.

CHAPTER

7

THE PRINCESS KAKIMA waited for Arris on the balcony of
her apartments, overlooking the subtle music of the fountains. The Water Gardens played a winter variation, less
boisterous and bright than its summer splashing. Arris's
guide left him at the open screen that led to the balcony.
He walked slowly out onto the flagstone paving. The sun
was hidden behind pale gray clouds, and the air was
growing cooler. Kakima sat in a wicker chair, with no
attendants but a bored-looking boy of about ten years. The
boy was perched on the balcony railing, swinging his
slippered feet against an embroidered hanging that screened
the open spaces between the rails.

Arris bowed very low, with a graceful flourish that
pulled painfully at his bandaged shoulder. He held his
position, hearing a silken rustle as the young woman rose
from her chair. Kakima walked forward to him, took his
hands between hers, and wordlessly bade him straighten.
Arris obeyed her, answering her smile with one of his
own.

"You are well?" Kakima asked. She was a woman
now, but she still had the look of a shy and sheltered girl.
Her skin was very pale, and her hair was plaited simply
down her back. Her hands in Arris's were soft and without
character, like a baby's. "I have been so afraid for you. I
knew what you were sent to do, and I was sure you would
be captured and killed. How could a boy be given such a
mission? But here you are, safe returned. But much
changed."

"You have only grown more beautiful, Princess," Arris said as she took his arm to lead him to the railing. The young boy who sat there watched them with a blank expression. "But . . . what did you know about my mission?"

"You were sent to kill the Ilkharani, of course," she said. "I made General Iyon tell me. He will do almost anything for me. He wants to marry me, but Father won't let him even ask me until the war is over."

"You mustn't marry Iyon," Arris said. It was a matter they had discussed before. "You must have other suitors. Almost anyone would be better, Princess."

She looked sidelong at him, unconcerned. "Iyon may die in battle. Then I shall probably marry the Kurontai Roka. But the Emperor in his wisdom will not let me marry anyone before the end of his precious war." She laughed softly, but her dark eyes were bitter. "I have been so bored while you were away. I want you to tell me everything you did, and everything you saw. That young musician followed you there, didn't she? That was brave of her. Was she much disappointed when she found out you weren't in love with her?"

"She didn't expect me to be. That wasn't the reason she left Deiran." Arris was growing more and more uncomfortable. The Princess clung to his arm, imitating the manner of one of the court's jaded noblewomen, talking in a chirping tone that was belied by the tension Arris could feel in her grip. It was chilly out on the balcony, but that was not why Kakima was trembling.

"Is the Ilkharani court much different from this one?" she asked. "I have heard that the women are veiled, the property of the men, even the ones who are not slaves or princesses."

"They manage to make their presence known, and their opinions heard," Arris said warily. The boy on the railing gazed at him steadily. The child was slender, with a plain face and unruly black hair. He was dressed in expensive silks, which might mean that he was one of the Emperor's concubines or one of Kakima's brothers. Arris guessed the latter. The boy was over-young for Hareku's tastes, and he was not pretty.

Kakima saw that she had lost Arris's attention. She turned to the boy. "Ekani," she said in a wheedling tone, "you can see that I am quite safe with Arris. Will you give up this idea of being my bodyguard, and leave us alone for a while? We are old friends with much to discuss."

Arris bowed again as the boy jumped down to the balcony floor. Ekani was the Emperor's only son, the heir to the throne. The boy's mother had much disliked the youths in Hareku's seraglio, blaming them for her husband's indifference to her. She had been careful to keep Ekani away from Arris when he was younger. This was the first time Arris had been close enough to the Crown Prince to make out his features.

"Royal Prince, forgive me for not greeting you properly. I did not know who you were," Arris said.

"I did not greet you at all, even though I knew very well who you were," the boy said in a cool voice. "So we are even, I think. Good afternoon." He turned and left them. They could hear his quick footsteps fade as he left his sister's apartments.

So Ekani's mother had taught him her dislike of Hareku's favorites. Arris resolved to be wary of the Prince in the future. He could be a dangerous enemy.

"Father will be leaving now to lead his army," Kakima said, letting go of Arris's arm to lean on the railing overlooking the fountains. "He refuses to trust this war to his generals. Will you go with him, Arris?"

"No."

"Will you stay at court, then? Say that you will, for my sake. I am very lonely here." The artifice was gone now from her voice; it was as fragile and vulnerable as her delicate features.

"I can't stay at court," Arris said. "I have no place here now."

"Then I will not wait to ask you," the Princess said. She stood up straight. She was a little taller than Arris in her flat court slippers, and he had to look up to meet her brown eyes. When Kakima spoke again, her voice was

husky with emotion. "The war may last for years. I know
that. It may be even longer before I am allowed to marry
and leave this place. Arris . . . I want to know what it is
like."

"I don't understand."

"I want you to make love to me."

Arris stared at her, dismayed. When he did not immediately take her into an embrace, Kakima swallowed hard
and looked at her feet.

"I . . . I have heard old women say that if a woman is a
virgin for too long, it will hurt a lot when she finally takes
a husband. And so I have decided I no longer want to be a
virgin."

"I'm not a slave anymore, to perform at a command,"
Arris said, turning away from her. She did not realize what
she was asking, he told himself.

"I wouldn't have asked you if you were," Kakima said
in confusion. "We are friends. I wouldn't be frightened
with you, and I know you would not hurt me."

She had not meant to insult him. Arris wondered if he
could say anything that would not hurt her feelings. "Princess . . . Kakima, I am honored that you would ask this of
me. But I cannot."

"You don't want me." Her voice was shaky.

"Shadow take it, you're a lovely woman," Arris said in
frustration. "We might both enjoy it very much. But there
are no secrets in the palace. You know that. Someone
would find out, and I would be arrested and killed, and
you would be dishonored." It was as sure a death as that
faced by the Yearking of the Goddess, and Kakima was no
Lady of the Yaighan with beauty powerful enough to
compel a man to choose death. Arris had been able to
resist the Goddess. He could certainly refuse the Princess.

"You are afraid," she accused. "General Iyon would
not fear what might happen if someone found out. He
would do anything to please me."

"Then ask him. But I won't help you do something this
foolish. You have your duty . . ."

"Why should I have to stay a child forever?" The
young woman gripped the back of the wicker chair, rock-

ing it with her hands. "My father should have let me begin my life years ago. I am dead inside, Arris. I go from day to day like a little girl, led by my attendants, with slaves ready to answer any request I have. But no one will give me what I need." She looked at him with the trapped, pleading eyes of a chained pet.

Arris went to her and put his hands on her shoulders, leaning to kiss her lightly on the cheek. He could not keep pity from his voice. "Oh, Kakima. Do you think one night with me would change any of that? The next day would be the same as all the days before. You would have no more freedom. Your life would be no different."

She pulled away from him and kicked the wicker chair. It fell onto its side and slid a little on the flagstones. She kicked it again. "I would know that it was different! I would have done something, at least." She turned to glare at Arris, and her voice became brittle. "It must be a great distinction, to be refused by you. You, who have been with almost everyone in the court, from Iyon to the Kurontai Roka to my lady-in-waiting Shichal to my father. I should feel very special."

Now she was trying to cut him, and it stung. Arris thought he had better leave before he said something really foolish. "I am sorry if I have offended you. With your permission, Royal Princess . . ."

"Yes, go," she said in a fury. "Leave me to my boredom, if you will do nothing to relieve it."

She would be contrite tomorrow, Arris thought. She would probably send him a gift in apology. But this mood would return. As he turned away and left her balcony, Arris wondered how long it would be before the Princess was the scandal of the court. How long would it be before she found someone to give her what she thought she wanted? He guessed she would be quickly bored of that as well.

Arris hurried away, hoping he would not regret this choice. One of the experienced women of the court, rejected by someone she desired, would have many weapons with which to repay the slight. An accusation of rape, for instance, would give Kakima some of the excitement she craved. Arris hoped that she was still too much a child to think of it.

Returning to Ebreyu's family apartments, Arris was relieved to find Tibi and Terai alone, eating an evening meal of delicate green-rolls and rice. The Lieutenant was not there. They sat at a low table in a room that was obviously a study; rolls of parchment were scattered over a large desk and filed in neatly tied volumes in a rack against one wall. Inkstands and quivers of quill pens stood on the desk. One pen lay where it was set down when the writer was interrupted.

That was another difference in Tibi; there were inkstains on her fingers as she handed Arris a rice bowl and three of the little fried rolls. Arris would never have guessed that she was educated enough to write.

"Your work?" he asked, sitting down on a cushion beside her.

"I am writing an epic on the gods of Khopei," she said proudly.

"She showed me some of it after Ebreyu left," Terai said. "I thought it was very good. But I am no judge of Deirani poetry."

"Don't look so surprised, Arris," she chided him. "We were taught all the arts of the Dance in the harem. I wrote hundreds of love poems."

"But this is different," Arris said. "An epic on the gods of Khopei? If you mention each one, it will take you thirty years to write." He ate quickly, enjoying the simple food.

"I have those years ahead of me. You can read it, if you like. Though I'm sure you are no judge of poetry either."

"Like you, I was schooled in many arts," he said with a smile. In truth, he had read much of the best Deirani poetry, and had recited it to patrons for hours, accompanying himself on the lyre. Some of the nobles had truly enjoyed it, and others felt that they should, and insisted on having him perform even when it bored him.

"And you mastered a few of them." The young woman laughed.

"Where is Ebreyu?" Arris asked, thinking of what Tibi had said about how her master would take it when he learned Arris had been a harem slave.

"He went to attend the questioning of Chol and Wesu," Terai said. "They will not tell the torturers anything. It may last all night." He shook his head sadly. "You should have killed them outright, Arris. It would have been cleaner."

Tibi looked sharply at them both. Arris ignored her, and spoke in Yaighan. "I will give no souls to Aghlayeshkusa, if I can keep from it."

"Aye. I understand."

"Are you well enough to go into the city tomorrow?" Tibi said impatiently. She stood in a graceful motion and began to stack their bowls, empty now. "I know where you can find your friends the minstrels. Terai said you wanted to buy their freedom."

"They are old friends." Arris realized how that must sound, and he said impulsively, "I'll buy yours as well, if you want."

"Oh." Her breath caught, and she fumbled with the bowls. "That's . . . a kind offer, Arris. But the musicians will be expensive enough. And Ebreyu would not sell me."

"I'll ask him." Arris grinned at her, feeling much more cheerful. He had done some harsh and violent things in his life, and he had hurt many people who had trusted him. Maybe now he could redeem himself a little.

"The City Overlord bought Senna and his children," Terai said. "The Kurontai Roka. Tibi tells me they probably haven't been ill-treated."

Tibi nodded. "Roka is not a harsh man. I've heard he made the pretty girl his concubine. Vaessa, isn't it? But they've been allowed to work at their music. He does not make them do other labor."

Terai swore. "You did not say he had forced Vaessa to his bed."

The young woman shrugged. "A pretty slave usually has to sleep with people she does not choose for herself. It is nothing unusual. And Roka would be gentle. I've attended him in the past, and so has Arris."

Embarrassed, Arris avoided Terai's sharp gaze. "We'll go tomorrow morning and get my reward money from the Treasury. Then we can visit the palace of the City Overlord." He yawned widely. "Tibi, will you show me where I'm to sleep?"

"Down the corridor, the fourth room to the left," she said, going off in another direction with the supper dishes. "Good night."

Rough hands on Arris's shoulders woke him out of a heavy, dreamless sleep. Ebreyu crouched over him, breathing harshly, smelling of wine. Ebreyu was naked, and aroused, but the glare in his eyes was not the look of a tender lover. It took Arris a moment to become fully awake. He was cold without the blankets over him, despite the winter nightshirt he wore.

The small bedroom was lit by a candle that had almost burned down. In the candlelight, Ebreyu cast a hulking shadow against the woven hangings at the foot of the bed. It was very late. The darkness was complete outside the latticed window, and the only sound Arris could hear was Ebreyu's hoarse breathing. The soldier's long hair obscured his fierce-looking face. He knelt heavily on Arris's legs.

"Get off of me," Arris said quietly, not wanting to wake Terai in the next room. He tried to twist away from Ebreyu, but the Deirani clamped his legs around Arris's waist and gripped his wrists with bruising fingers.

"Pretty harem boy," Ebreyu said in a hissing whisper, his voice slurred with drink. "The Emperor's whore. You were General Iyon's whore, too, weren't you? That's why he was so angry with me for capturing you."

"Ebreyu, let me go," Arris said angrily. "You're drunk. Go sleep it off."

"You won't refuse me. You wouldn't dare, little slave." Handling Arris with a wrestler's practiced skill, he turned him facedown in the flower-scented sheets.

Arris began to struggle in earnest. He kicked and fought, his hands pinioned behind his back, as Ebreyu used one hand to push his nightshirt up around his waist. "The

Goddess damn you, stop it!'' he said. "I'm not a slave anymore. You have no right . . ."

"You liked it better the other way, when you did the seducing," Ebreyu said, pressing against him. "You knew plenty of tricks, harem boy, and you used them on me. I had never slept with a man before, but you made me want to."

"I don't believe that. You knew what you were doing." Arris scissored his legs upward suddenly, and jolted Ebreyu between the legs. The soldier cursed. His grip on Arris loosened. Arris arched his back like a cat and heaved his body up to the side. Both men fell off the narrow bed onto the woven straw carpet. Ebreyu could not keep hold of Arris.

Arris rolled away from him and came to his feet, furious almost to the point of tears. Ebreyu sat where he had landed on the floor. Arris went to the pile of clothes the Deirani officer had discarded near the door. He picked them up and threw them into Ebreyu's lap.

"Get out."

"I'll go." Ebreyu stood up. "It's all true, isn't it?" he said bitterly. "You were a slave, and a Jai-Sohn assassin. You have dishonored me."

"How? But not letting you rape me?" Arris demanded.

"By not telling me. By letting me think you were from some noble Yaighan family. So that I would sleep with you."

"I never told you that."

"You never told me otherwise. I would not have imagined that a slave would pretend to be my equal."

Arris was trembling now, more in hurt than anger. He had liked Ebreyu. He still found him very attractive, though he probably should fear him. "And I . . . I would not have imagined that a man of honor would treat anyone the way you have treated me tonight."

The door to the bedroom was only a screen, and now it opened slightly. Terai stepped through into the candlelight, wearing a loosely tied night robe. He had been listening for at least a little while, because he turned to Ebreyu and spoke with deadly scorn. "It may ease your honor to know that Arris is highborn among the Yaighan. Of an older family than you can claim, Deirani.''

Ebreyu made a stiff little bow, and stalked past Terai into the corridor, carrying his clothes. After a moment, Arris heard him rap on another door. ''Tibi, attend me.'' So she would have to deal with his angry desire tonight.

Arris could not look at Terai. He sat down at the end of the bed and stared at the woven patterns of straw on the floor.

''I heard noises from your room,'' Terai said. ''My first thought was that the power that attacked you in the streets of Khopei had come back.''

''No,'' Arris muttered.

''He was drunk.''

Arris shook his head. ''He was angry. He thinks I dishonored him. If he had been sober, he might not have tried what he did. But he won't be sorry.''

Terai's voice was hesitant. He had to be more embarrassed than Arris was. ''Perhaps we should rent a room in Khopei tomorrow.''

''Yes.''

''We'll buy new clothes, and send these borrowed ones back here.'' He put a hand on Arris's shoulder. ''Will you be able to sleep all right?''

''Don't worry about me. Good night, Terai.'' Arris pulled away from him and climbed back beneath his blankets. After a moment, Terai left the room and pulled the screen closed again.

He wondered if he should have fought with Ebreyu. He could have pretended to enjoy it. But Ebreyu had not meant to make love to him. He had meant to hurt him, to punish him. Like General Iyon. Every time with Iyon, Arris had thought he knew what to expect, and every time Iyon had found some new way to frighten him, humiliate him, make him helpless. Arris had promised himself when he had gained his freedom that he would never let anyone do that to him again.

He heard Tibi cry out softly in the night. She could not refuse, could not fight, for fear of a whipping or worse. Arris pulled a pillow over his ears so he would hear nothing more. The long ride, his fight for his life in Khopei, the interviews with the Emperor and Kakima, and now the struggle with Ebreyu all weighed on him. He was too exhausted to hold it all in his mind any longer. In a haze of anger and bitterness, he fell back into a deep sleep.

When Arris came out of his bedroom warily at dawn, he found that Ebreyu and Tibi were still asleep. He went to the bath chamber. The fires in the passage below the pool had gone out. Arris let the cold water wake him up, careful not to disturb the bandage on his shoulder. When he was clean and clear-headed, he dressed in the robes he had worn the day before, and went to look for Terai.

The sun was rising, but the morning was still heavy with winter mist. Like one of the bent trees brought to life, Terai was in the garden, slowly moving through a sequence of meditative exercises with a short sword he must have found somewhere in the apartments. His thick muscles corded with the strain of each controlled posture, but still he had grace that a court dancer would have admired.

"We'll buy swords in the city," Arris said. "You can leave that one for Ebreyu."

"With a note of thanks for his hospitality?" Terai lunged into the last movement of the cycle, and then straightened to stand still for a moment.

"It may be the coward's way," Arris said, shrugging. "But I would rather not have to talk to him." He would send a messenger later with his offer to buy Tibi.

Terai went back inside the suite for a short time. When he returned, he was dressed in the dark green robe like a Yaighan priest's. He and Arris walked out of the garden gate and headed for the Palace Treasury in the hushed stillness of the early morning.

CHAPTER
8

WALKING THROUGH THE NARROW, muddy streets of Khopei near the rivermouth harbor, Arris thought that the city was much changed. There had been garrisons of soldiers stationed here two years ago, but now the squadrons of half a dozen different divisions crowded the streets and the markets, at a sword's edge of tension with the knowledge that they were about to ride to war. The black raven banner of the Feng garrisons flew from rooftops at inns they had commandeered; they had left few soldiers in their western city, and were to leave Khopei in a few days to join General Iyon's army. Four-wheeled chariots with low walls of overlapping shields bore slim charioteers and proud officers behind spirited teams. Groups of plainsmen from the far western provinces, with red-dyed braids and armor of overlapping leather scales, rode half-wild horses with bells plaited into their manes.

Near the docks, warships had been built and sea-walls fortified, probably as a result of reports Arris had sent the Emperor. The Khalifate had been building ships that were supposed to be able to sail around the Deadly Horns to attack Deiran by sea. It was a standing argument in the Citadel councils whether the vessels were even seaworthy, much less if they could survive that journey. But Deiran would be ready, if the Khalifate warships appeared in the bay.

The people of Khopei were quick to step aside to let the soldiers pass, but they seemed preoccupied. In the squares and the bazaars, in the public houses where Arris and

Terai inquired about rooms, the talk was of marvels and signs. Different people reacted in varying degrees of belief and skepticism, but all repeated the stories. Miracles were seen daily. Statues moved and spoke, and sacrifices were being consumed by the gods instead of feeding the priests. The Just God, Chiou-Ro, had always been a popular deity in Khopei. Now the god himself seemed to possess his priests, inspiring them to give brilliant sermons on the value of order and law, and to perform charitable acts that were far out of character.

Arris was interested, and would have liked to have seen some of these marvels. Terai steered him firmly away from the temple streets and made him cross the street on the other side from any shrines they passed. Arris argued that they knew of only one Deirani god who wished him harm, and they could easily avoid temples of Anoguri. But Terai would not be swayed.

It began to rain by late morning, a heavy, dark winter rain that brought a numbing chill. By then, Arris and Terai had found rooms in an inn called the Riverbranch that perched beside a shallow, silted canal. Flat pole-boats clustered beneath the inn's docks, pulled in because of the weather. It was a merchant's inn, in a district of leather and ceramic workers. Dressed in new tunics of heavy linen cloth, trousers, high boots, and thick woolen cloaks, with round caps on their heads and short swords at their belts, the two Yaighan excited no suspicion.

Arris sent messengers from the inn to Lieutenant Ebreyu and the Kurontai Roka. To Ebreyu, he sent back the borrowed court robes, and an offer to buy Tibi's freedom at a fair price. To the City Overlord, he wrote a respectful letter that mentioned past friendship and proposed a handsome price for the three Khalifate musicians.

Shortly after the noon meal, he received his replies. From Ebreyu, a curt refusal to sell a gift from his father. From Roka, an invitation to a private dinner next week, and a higher figure for the slaves, due to his sentimental attachment to the young woman Vaessa. If Arris agreed to this price, he was to deposit it in gold at a jeweler's shop near the Overlord's palace, and come with receipt in hand to take the slaves at dusk.

The Kurontai Roka was an intelligent, ambitious man whose rise in the Emperor's favor had partly come about because of a gift he had presented Hareku: a wild, barbarian slave boy with wing tattoos. Arris had not spoken any Deirani when Roka had bought him from the slave trader who had captured him. Later, he had come to know the young nobleman as a rare courtier who took his duty seriously as the Emperor's counselor. Arris had come to like his reserve and his gentleness. Even after Hareku had freed him, Arris had sometimes accepted Roka's evening invitations, and he had worn the gifts of jewelry and clothing the Kurontai had given him. He felt no urge to renew the relationship, but the memories were pleasant.

Arris and Terai took the gold to the jeweler as Roka had requested. The Emperor's reward would have been enough to live on comfortably for two years in Khopei, or enough to buy a very small farm, or a city apartment. Now two-thirds of that total was gone. Slaves who were also artists were very valuable to noblemen who meant to impress the court with their cultural taste; and a pretty, exotic woman like Vaessa was worth three plain minstrels. In truth, the Kurontai Roka had not named as high a price as he could have.

The jeweler was an old woman, whose shop on the third floor of a guarded building displayed an array of beautifully mounted stones and worked gold. She had already been sent an authorization from Roka, and she had one of her three burly sons weigh Arris's gold, while another wrote out a receipt in a careful hand, and the third watched Arris and Terai as if they might try to steal back their own wealth.

At last the transaction was done, and they were back in the rainy street. Arris spent a small coin to hire a covered cart and driver. The evening was cold and gloomy as they 'their way slowly through the cobblestone streets in the rich district on the western bank of the River Vaclav. Tall houses showed windowless faces, miniature fortresses that curved around elaborate inner courtyards and apartments. The Overlord's Palace covered the top of a low hill, with a view of the river, the harbor, and the higher roofs of the Sapphire Palace beyond the city.

The Kurontai Roka had gone to court in answer to the Emperor's general summons, presumably to hear the declaration of war. His gate guards would not admit Arris and Terai inside the courtyard. Arris gave them his papers and waited in the rain. After some fifteen minutes, the gates were opened, and three people and five large instrument cases were deposited outside. The guard handed Arris his papers again, bowed, and vanished behind the gates.

Terai stepped forward with an angry oath when he saw his old friends. Not looking him full in the face, with no apparent recognition and no reaction but fear, the aging minstrel Senna put a protective arm around his daughter Vaessa. His son Van stared at the ground. They were wearing short, dark robes and sandals, with no protection from the rain.

Senna's heavy belly strained against the belt of his robe, but his pale face above his beard looked thin and lined. Vaessa's blond hair was unbound, and her green eyes were harder than Arris remembered. Van was a big man, going soft in the middle in imitation of his father. Arris felt little but pity, seeing them here. He had never been a close friend to any of the family but Danae, though Senna had been kind to him as a child.

"You're our new master?" Van said to Terai with a challenging note in his deep voice. His Deirani had a singer's sureness of accent and pitch. "Why did you buy us from the Overlord?"

"My friends, don't you know me?" Terai said in the Khalifate language. "Four years is not that long."

More than a head taller than he, Senna looked down at him uncertainly. His eyes suddenly widened. "Terai. The gods have answered me."

Arris held out his papers, Roka's offer, and the jeweler's receipt. "These are yours. You're free. If we can, we're going to get you out of Deiran."

"You," Van said, recognizing him without pleasure.

"You're the Emperor's slave, the one Danae followed when she ran away. We were sold because of what Danae did, and it's your fault."

"Danae . . . how is she?" Vaessa asked, taking the papers from Arris and putting them into the breast of her robe.

"She is well," Terai said. "She lives at the Citadel, under the patronage of Prince Saresha. Her reputation as a composer is growing. Players vie with one another to perform her works."

"Aye, that's welcome news," Senna said with a deep sigh. He put an arm around Terai's shoulders. "How you came to Deiran I won't ask, but you surely know what a great thing you have done for us today."

"Arris bought your freedom," Terai said. "You can thank him."

"I promised Danae I'd help you." Arris picked up the two largest instrument cases, and felt a painful tug in his cut shoulder. He carried the heavy, awkward cases to the back of the hired cart and set them down quickly. One was the long stringed bass that Senna would play, seated cross-legged on the ground droning out the backbone of the music. The other was Van's two-necked lute, that few men ever mastered. The stubborn, irritable young man was a brilliant player. Vaessa had a pleasing singing voice, though she lacked any genius. But the heart of the family's performances had been Danae's compositions. It would be a worthy task, to bring them all together again. Arris was sorry he would not be able to hear them once more.

"We can never repay you, young man," Senna said gravely. "Danae is fortunate to have such a friend." He had never made the connection between the frightened boy he had helped escape from the Khalifate ten years ago, and the Emperor's favorite who had befriended his family in the Sapphire Palace. It did not matter. Arris smiled at him and climbed into the cart after Vaessa, while Van loaded the flutes and the drum in with the other instruments. With Senna and Terai sharing the driver's board, the carter urged his mules forward, and they started down the hill toward the distant Riverbranch Inn.

•   •   •

A cold wind blew with the rain outside the shuttered windows of the inn. Dripping wet and miserable, Arris sat with the others in one of the rooms they had rented, watching as Terai tried again to light the damp, green wood the innkeeper had supplied for them. "We could go as traders," Terai said, leaning over the hearth. "Selling food to people in the border provinces, where the army has been. It should be fairly easy to slip away and cross the mountains to the Khalifate side without being noticed. Then Arris and I will leave you there, with packhorses to carry your instruments, and we'll go back to Deiran and make our way slowly back to Khopei."

"It's too dangerous," Vaessa said decisively. Her voice was very unlike her old whining way. "You told the Emperor you were going to buy our freedom. He knows you want to try to get us out of Deiran."

"She's right, lad," her father said. "The Emperor forbade you to try. He said he'd consider it treason."

"He is a tyrant," Van muttered. "A savage."

"He is about to launch a war, and he believes you would be able to tell the Khalifate generals too much about his armies," Terai said. He finally succeeded in starting a smoky flame. He fanned it intently as fire-shadows flickered across his dark face.

"I will tell them everything I know," Van said. "Your Emperor is right about that."

"It will be dangerous," Arris said, meeting Vaessa's cold green eyes. "But it would be more dangerous for you to stay in Khopei now. You may be considered enemy spies. You won't have the protection of being slaves."

"Surely we'll be suspected even more the closer we get to the border." Vaessa got up and knelt on the floor with her back to the fire. Her blond hair and her pointed features were much like Danae's. She had always been prettier than her younger sister, even now, with the anger and bitterness of her slavery around her like a thin, hard shell.

"You'd have to dye your hair and darken your skin. But your Deirani accents are good enough now to pass as

Khopei merchants in the east." Arris yawned, and realized how tired he was. "I think it can be done without the Emperor knowing. Terai has experience with this sort of thing. So do I."

Senna looked at him narrowly. "You were spying for the Emperor at the Citadel, weren't you? I hope you didn't get Danae involved in that, and endanger her position there."

"She can take care of herself," Terai said, getting to his feet. "Senna, I can't promise you that we'll succeed in getting you out safely. I'd like to attempt it. But it is your decision. You could stay in Khopei and wait until the war is over."

"One more day in this filthy place and I will go mad." Van leaned forward in his chair. "I say we risk it."

"We should think about it seriously, Papa," Vaessa said with a frown. "A few days one way or the other won't hurt."

"We should discuss it alone," Senna turned to Arris and Terai. "Will you leave us until morning?"

Terai bowed slightly. "As you wish. Our room is across the hall, if you need us. Otherwise, we'll meet you for breakfast in the common room downstairs."

Arris followed Terai to their room, which was as large as the other, big enough for two comfortable beds and with space for chairs around the hearth. A tall window looked out on a balcony with a view of the rain-swollen canal. The hearth was cold. Arris sat for a while and watched Terai coaxing another fire, but he was still weak from the journey and his wound, and they had walked more than a few miles that day. He stripped off his sober tradesman's clothes and went to bed. He was soon deeply asleep.

Arris could not escape from a dream of the Lossiran. He felt smothered, buried alive, and the wing tattoos on his back beat in an urgent, uneven rhythm that was the rhythm of his heart. The Mother of Vultures was in the room, trying to speak to him. Only he was no longer in his bed, no longer in the traders' inn at all, and this did not seem to be his dream. He was someone else, a woman, ancient and bitter, filled with a towering frustration.

It was a vast, high-arched, pillared place that glittered with gold, and she was trapped there. Nothing she did made any difference. No one heard her furious cries, and she could not pound on the splintered doors or the cold stone walls because she had no hands. She had no substance at all. The body that had been hers for a little while was dead, from terror and starvation. It lay curled up in the shadow of the standing stone altar, nothing but skin over long bones, the face that had been proud and beautiful ruined under a veil of reddish-brown hair.

They had bound her here after they had fought her to stalemate. She could still see the bright, arrogant faces, the armor and figured cloaks that clothed the man-shapes they wore. They should never have been able to break through her world-gate to enter the Temple of Rehoman. If she had only been granted the sacrifice, they would never have come this close to victory over her. Even as she had been, deprived of her full strength, she had saved herself from destruction. She could still break free, if only her traitor Yearking would come back to her. She had sent the Lossiran, but it too was weakened by her bonds, and had little power to compel.

Arris suddenly knew himself, still in his dream, and he fled from the consciousness of the Goddess Rehoman in terror. He found himself flying on the wings he had been granted for summoning the Lossiran. Every wingbeat pained him, like a band of flame across his back. He looked down and saw the pitiful body of the abandoned Lady of the Yaighan, and remembered that she was Maella, the woman Terai had loved. She had been trapped in the Temple, possessed by the Goddess, when all her people had fled from the battle with the Brothers Ylla. Arris had loved her, in awe and fear, like all her subjects, when he had been a student at Gama. He grieved for the waste of her strength and beauty, even if she had been his enemy in trying to force him to play his part in the Goddess's schemes.

He could feel the Goddess trying to touch him, trying to plead with him, but he could not hear her words, and the

Lossiran could not speak to him either. He was falling away from that terrible gilded prison, falling in the grip of sudden, overwhelming pain that burned across his chest. He curled into a ball, his blue and gold wings cramped into uselessness. He screamed and thrashed out with arms and legs, trying to slow his fall, but he could not escape the pain.

Arris woke, and knew he was not dreaming anymore. He heard Terai cursing, and the crashing noises of a struggle. Oh, gods, it hurt. Arris opened his eyes, panicked, his breathing growing shallow and rapid. He heard a groan, and saw the silhouette of a man fall to the floor in the darkened room, run through by the short sword Terai had bought in the bazaar that day. The window lattice had been broken, and the oiled paper shade blew inward with the rain.

The line of pain on Arris's chest had begun to spread, pulsing with the beat of his heart, gripping him with reaching fingers. He gasped for air. There was blood on the sheet that covered him. Arris tried to move his hand to pull the covering away and see how badly he was wounded. The effort made the muscles in his arm cramp in agony, as his dream-wings had done when he had begun to fall.

Terai was at his side now, wearing only a long shirt that hung past his knees. He had dropped the sword. He pulled the sheet away and looked at Arris's bleeding chest. Then he sighed with relief, and said, "I wasn't long asleep. He was quiet, I'll give him that, but I woke to see him bending over you. I knocked him away before he could finish his thrust. It's only a scratch, boy. Shorter and less deep than the one on your back. Get up now. We have to get rid of him. The inn should be well asleep. We can dump him in the canal, I suppose." His voice sounded farther and farther away.

Arris shook his head. It cost him a great effort. "I can't . . . move, Terai. It hurts. Like fire." The pain had spread all through him now. His muscles drew in as if they were wound into coils, forcing him to curl up on his side. He could scarcely breathe past an iron band that was closing around his chest. The pain washed over him in waves. He moaned and closed his eyes.

"Arris!" Terai touched his face. "You're burning. The blade must have been poisoned."

"The Lossiran," Arris gasped. "The Goddess tried to warn me." He could not speak anymore. He could feel Terai's hands at his breast, probing the wound. It was a distant, dull hurt that meant little compared to the sea of pain that was drowning him. The waves beat at him like a storm against a foundering ship, and he felt himself falling away from the pain into unconsciousness.

Terai shouted at him, telling him to breathe, cursing him for a coward and a weakling. Arris fought through the blackness, but could not reach the surface. He felt the pain clutch at his heart, trying to still its beating. He could not let that happen. All his concentration went into the rhythm of his heartbeat. The thick little muscle contracted and released, contracted and released, but it would stop if he let it. He had to tell it each time, force it to work through the pain. He was growing weaker.

Goddess, he thought clearly, Goddess, it hurts. I can't bear this much longer. I'll die. Then he realized that the Lossiran had not stayed behind in the Temple. It was fighting with him, through the tattoos on his back. He was cradled by its dead black wings, and he was not frightened of it. The poison that filled him was far darker than the Mother of Vultures.

Terai pleaded with him to fight. He washed the wound with water from the nightstand, but Arris knew that would not help. He forced himself to take in a breath. His body cramped again and again, raising the pain to a level where it no longer came in waves, but burned him with a constant flame. He would not let it destroy him. He would not.

He lost all awareness of the room, Terai, the rain through the window. He was deep inside himself, drowning in pain. But after a very long time, Arris began to reach the surface again. He felt the Lossiran withdraw from him, soundless as it was invisible, leaving him gasping for air and strength. The pain still chopped through him like waves over a boat's deck. But Arris could feel his heart beating strongly, and though his breath was ragged and uneven he did not have to fight to breathe. He lay in his bed in the room at the Riverbranch, curled up around himself, shaking uncontrollably, crying out softly at each new onslaught of pain.

"Was that the worst of it?" a deep voice whispered. "I thought for certain he was dying. Sygathi Ylla, why won't you send for a healer, Terai?" That was Senna. Arris did not know how much time had passed. He could not think very clearly, and the battle was not over. He could not spare the energy to try to speak.

Terai's voice was hoarse. "Because there is no antidote but time. It will kill him, or it will run its course and leave him alive." His breath caught. "It was only a scratch, the wound he got. Dear Goddess, if the knife had gone any deeper . . ."

"A poisoned blade," Vaessa said. "Why? Why would anyone want to kill him?"

"They'll try again if he survives," Terai said. Arris felt a rough hand on his face, cool against the heat of his forehead and cheeks. He thought of opening his eyes and smiling, trying to reassure Terai that he would live. But then the pain hit him afresh and he cried out, a weak, soft cry like a baby bird's. "Shadow take them," Terai cursed in Yaighan. "They know now that he is in Khopei. We have to leave this place. Senna, I care little whether you come with us or not, but Khopei is more dangerous than the journey to the border could be."

"We'll go with you," Vaessa said before her father could speak. "But who are these enemies, Terai? Not the Emperor's men, surely."

"I can't tell you. Arris may, if he chooses. If he lives. Senna, you and Van come with me to carry out the assassin. Watch him, Vaessa, and keep talking to him while we're gone."

"What if it gets bad again?" she asked in fear.

"There is nothing you can do," Terai said roughly. "When I get back you can get some sleep. In the morning we'll buy a wagon, some kind of trade goods, and horses.

You will all have to be disguised. I want to be gone from here by midday."

"Will Arris be well enough to travel?" Senna said doubtfully.

"No. But there is no help for it."

Arris stopped listening to their talk. He felt Vaessa sitting beside him, holding him against the cramps. He was drawn back into the black depths of the poison. It was a battle against heavy odds, and the enemy was so much stronger than he. Still, he clung to life. He had not escaped the Goddess's schemes to die as the prey of her enemy gods. Rehoman wanted him alive, but only for a year. The Brothers Ylla wanted him dead now. Arris would cheat them all if he could.

CHAPTER 9

A SOFT BED in the Khopei inn or a pallet on the floor of a covered cart, it made little difference to Arris in his desperate sickness. Terai carried him downstairs from the inn early in the afternoon. Alternating between cramped muscles and uncontrollable shaking, and between fever and chills as his body worked to fend off the poison, Arris was only dimly aware of his surroundings. He lay beneath a pile of blankets in the front section of the partitioned cart, just behind the curtains of the driver's seat. Behind him in the middle section were sacks of flour and seed, and barrels of salt fish; in the rear of the cart, fluttering and complaining in rows of cages, were three dozen hens and a few angry cocks.

Maybe it was the poison, the pain, and fever, but Arris could not believe that he was escaping from anything. The danger followed him. The darkness Ravil had sensed in him could not be left behind. If he truly cared what happened to Danae's family, he would make them go without him. Terai could get them out of the country alone. Arris was more than a burden to them now; he was a deadly beacon, and he would draw his enemies to them all.

He had muttered to Terai that morning that they should leave him at the inn, but his old friend had dismissed his words as delirium. Arris did not think Terai would willingly abandon him. For whatever reason, Terai had appointed himself Arris's protector. It was more than friendship, Arris thought. It meant more to Terai than that.

The next time the assassins might be quicker. They would not hesitate to kill Terai to get to Arris. Arris did not want that blood guilt on his soul. But for the moment, he had no choice. He was helpless as an infant, too sick to move his head, much less run away and let the darkness follow him.

Arris could feel the jolting of the cart over city cobble-stones, and hear the clatter and shouting in the streets as Senna drove them out of Khopei. Much of his money from the Emperor had been spent this morning on the long cart and the goods it carried. Two patient mules pulled in the traces, and Terai and Van rode aging, indifferently trained horses on either side of the cart. Disguised to the extent of blackened hair and tradesmen's clothes, Senna and Vaessa shared the driver's board. The musicians' instruments were buried beneath the sacks of grain in the middle part of the wagon.

If they were really merchants intending to make a profit off the border villages, they would have a true caravan instead of this single cart. Assuming the people in the border lands had any means to pay for the goods, one small town market might buy out their stock in a few hours' time. But perhaps the disguise was enough to make their story credible. It should keep any Emperor's men from suspicion. Arris did not think it would stop his enemies; not if Terai was right, and the Khalifate gods were using these Deirani fanatics to strike at him.

To think about anything beyond the pain and his utter weariness required a great effort. Arris wanted to stop fighting it, to sink deep into the pain like a man swallowed up in a bog, to let mud and moss stifle his ears and close over his head, to become oblivious. If he did, he did not think he would wake again. He could not let go, could not even allow himself to sleep. In sleep, he would be unable to battle with the poison that seized his muscles and flowed with his blood through his burning limbs. If it tried to stop his heart, to freeze his lungs, he would not be aware enough to command his body.

He would not let it kill him. He did not want to die in any case, and he certainly did not want to allow the

Brothers Ylla to claim their victory in his death. The five sun-gods had condemned him, not for any of the crimes he had committed, but for something he had rejected utterly: his place in the dreams of the Goddess. They called him the Goddess's creature. If he truly was Rehoman's creation and her slave, Arris thought, he could never have defied her as he had done on Winter Festival night. Or perhaps Rehoman had created him, but then she had given him the power of choosing his destiny. Arris had made his choice, but the Brothers Ylla did not trust him to abide by it.

There was movement through the curtains at the front of the cart, and they parted long enough for Vaessa to crawl between them to where Arris lay. Arris forced his eyes to open slightly, but the early afternoon sun burned him as it shone past the bulk of Senna's seated form. He shut his eyes, and shivered when a wet cloth was stroked across his forehead.

"You're chilled again?" Vaessa asked worriedly. "I'll put my cloak over your blankets if you like. But your skin is hot to the touch still. Can you take some water?" She slipped one hand behind his neck and raised his head slightly, putting the spout of a waterskin to his lips.

Arris was suddenly very thirsty. He drank as greedily as a sucking babe, until Vaessa took the waterskin away and lowered his head back onto the pallet. "Thank you," he whispered.

She added another layer to the heavy coverings on top of him, and said, "I don't understand Yaighan, but that doesn't matter. You can understand what I'm saying, can't you? I wish I could do more. You gave me my freedom. I don't think you'll ever know what a gift that was to me. I can't repay it." She kissed him. He felt the brush of her lips on his, cool and moist. "You did it for Danae's sake, not mine. I know that. It doesn't matter. Just don't die, Arris. If I reach the Citadel and find my sister again, I can't tell her that you're dead. Promise me you'll get better."

"I . . . promise," Arris said, trying to smile a little. Then a knifing cramp doubled him up, and he could not hear Vaessa's response. The pain receded after long, labored heartbeats. Vaessa was gone. Probably the intensity of his pain had frightened her, and she knew she could do nothing to help him through it. Arris wanted to tell her it did not matter, that she owed him nothing; he could not frame the words in his mind, in any language he knew. He had spoken to her in Yaighan, the language of his mother's people, the only tongue he had known as a small child. He was afraid that he was losing his sanity. He could not bear this much longer. He would have to give up, give in to the pain, and then he would be lost.

Vaessa could not help him. He needed strength, more than he could summon from within himself. The Goddess had tried to help him from the distant place where she was imprisoned, but she could do no more than send the Lossiran, and the Lossiran had done what it could. All the power was gone now from the blue and gold wing tattoos on Arris's back. He could seek help from only one source: the earth spirit Aghlayeshkusa. The daimon was unpredictable. It had meant to kill him at Ravil's farm, but it had fought for him like a cornered tiger in the Temple of Rehoman.

When he was ten years old, Arris had learned how to summon spirits like Aghlayeshkusa. It was a ritual that required a circle of power, a group of trained minds linked into a pattern that was poured through a living vessel. Arris had played that part, bearing the maelstrom forces and adding his own Goddess-granted power to the call. Now he had no coven of turncoat priests and priestesses. He was alone, and powerless. But he had sworn a pact with the daimon. There should be a link between them that would make Aghlayeshkusa hear his call. Arris only wondered if the daimon would answer, and how: with the help he so desperately needed, or with the smile of a cat finally seeing its prey helpless, its struggles exhausted.

The rocking motion of the cart and the human and animal noises and smells of the streets faded as Arris turned his mind inward upon itself. He did not have the power for a priest's trance, but the focusing way of the Jai-Sohn had been drilled into him by a fanatical teacher; it was ingrained so deeply that when Arris began to visualize its patterns the pain, the poison that enmeshed him, and his weariness did not matter. He felt himself sinking into the dark, mossy bog he had imagined earlier, but he descended with his eyes open. All of his senses were deadened, except for the inward voice with which he sent his call.

The name Arris intoned in his mind was not the simple syllables of "Aghlayeshkusa." That word was no more than a label the daimon had chosen, to fit the memory of the young boy Arris had been when they had first met. The true name of the earth spirit could not be pronounced in the tones of any human language. A human voice could barely encompass its range. But in his mind Arris could say it. The word rose like an oncoming storm, howling, wild, a shriek of despair or the gibbering of a madman.

With that effort made, Arris could not keep hold of his resolve. He felt the pain clutch at him, and offered it no resistance. He could see the deadly poison in his mind's eye, all through his body like a woven net or a spider's web. He could hear his heart begin an irregular, labored beat. He could not climb back out of the morass; there was nothing to cling to, no branches or stones to stop him from sinking farther and farther underneath.

Then a pull began from outside him, an irresistible force that he could not help but follow. With a shuddering, twisting sensation, he left his body behind in the mire and flew, sightless and deaf and feeling nothing but the power that pulled him in like a landed fish. He did not battle against the hook. He scarcely had the strength to wonder where he was going, and how he could have left his body beneath the blankets in the cart. He felt no curiosity, or even fear.

When Arris had eyes to open again, he felt like a fish indeed. He lay naked on his stomach, wet and gasping for air that seemed too thin to breathe, on a grassy bank by the side of a clear, shallow stream. The grass was brown, but had a summer smell, and it was soft and felt alive against his skin. The thin air was warm, and the day was bright. Arris lifted his head and looked up. A canopy of leaves and branches moved slightly in a breeze he could not feel.

He remembered his bodiless traveling, and he felt a sense of utter strangeness that only grew. He knew very well that he did not belong here, wherever he was. The air was wrong, and no shadows fell from the forest around him to dapple the grass or his bare skin. The brightness of daylight was all around, yet Arris could not discover the sun anywhere. The light came from no discernible direction. And there were no reflections in the water of the stream. Arris could see polished stones in its bed, and small, colorful fish swimming amid fronds of pale ferns. It was as if the trees were not there at all, to cast shadows or reflections; yet he smelled a sharp tang of sap, and heard the soft rustling of the leaves. The leaves were yellow, brown, and red, but they were not dry. Like the grass, they showed the winter season, yet they lived.

Arris got to his feet with slow, careful movements. He felt a distant ache, like the memory of pain, but the poison that had racked him had not come with him to this place. He ran his hand along the bark of the nearest tree trunk; it was reassuringly solid, rough and age-cracked, and sticky with sap. Its leaves were soft and cool to the touch, despite their colors. As he walked down the bank to the stream, Arris discovered that he cast no shadow either, and nothing reflected of his form or face in the running water.

He knelt by the stream, and drank from a little eddy by a rock. The water was cold, and tasted like a spring Arris had once found high upon the mountainside of one of the Teeth of Gama. He could feel the water going down his throat, and he was thirsty for it; that made him even more sure that he was not a ghost or a spirit in this place.

"There you are," said a low voice in a near whisper that startled Arris so much he almost lost his balance. He steadied himself with one hand on the bank to keep from falling in the water, and looked behind him.

A wounded soldier leaned against a tree near the edge of the forest. His face was handsome, though pale and drawn, and beneath the pieces of leather armor and the dark-stained bandages his body was perfectly sculpted, an artist's ideal of muscular grace. He had long blond hair coiled in a smooth topknot, and heavy brass earrings hung to his shoulders. His sword was archaic, long and straight in its copper-chased sheath at his belt. The details were almost perfect. He was Myrdethreshi the Warrior, the middle brother of the Five, except for his eyes. They were a cloudy shade of purple that shifted as Arris watched.

"Daimon," Arris said warily. "You heard my call."

"Not here," said Aghlayeshkusa in the same low voice as before. "Come with me." He—Arris could not call him "it" in this form, somehow—limped away toward the deep, tangled forest that began fifty yards from the river-bank on that side.

Arris hesitated. "How do I know I can trust you?"

Aghlayeshkusa glared back at him. "You summoned me to help you. That is what I am trying to do, young one." He sounded angry, and even hurt. When Arris did not respond immediately, he pointed one hand at him. "Stay where you are then, if you prefer. Your enemies will find you quicker there, where the forest canopy is broken by the water. They have a long reach even where their rule does not extend."

"My enemies? You mean the Five . . ."

"Do not name them," the daimon-soldier said hurriedly. "It was a great risk to bring you here like this. Your body is unprotected where you left it. If they learn what we have done, they will take the opportunity to finish the poison's work."

Arris felt the echo of his pain more strongly, and a tugging like the line that had pulled him here, trying to pull him back. He took a deep breath and moved against it, walking quickly across the grass to follow the daimon. Aghlayeshkusa set a swift pace despite his limp. They hurried into the thick woods, where the aged trees grew as closely together as their massive roots would allow. The branches interlocked and twisted back upon themselves overhead, and the daylight was lessened as Arris and the daimon went deeper inward.

"What is this place?" Arris asked. He was tiring quickly. The air still seemed less than it should be, and his breathing became rapid as he half ran at the daimon's shoulder beneath the roof of the forest.

"The Gods' Realm," Aghlayeshkusa said in a biting tone. "And I belong here no more than you, and am even less welcome, if that be possible. What place for even a prince of Shadow in the shadowless land?" He smiled at Arris mockingly, and Arris remembered the summerhouse of his father's estate on the eve of battle nine years ago, when a severed head had moved and spoken to him. It had had the daimon's ever-shifting eyes, with a longing in them that had made him want to clutch his soul close for safety.

"The Gods' Realm," Arris repeated in wonder. "Then they . . . my enemies . . . are here?"

"And many others besides. Most of them quite unambitious and self-satisfied, pleased when their village or two of worshipers sacrifice a particularly tasty pig." Aghlayeshkusa's well-shaped blond brows knitted scornfully. "Then there are a few pilgrims like me, seeking healing or peace or power. An assortment of lesser spirits make their homes here; your Lossiran is one, who gave me these wounds. And the great ones, your enemies, and a few others."

Arris had been too confused before to be frightened. Now he could no longer avoid it. He was running like a hedge-robber through a forest of the Gods' Realm, with no power of his own with which to defend himself, his only protection the uncertain strength and intentions of a being who probably wanted him dead as much as the Brothers Ylla did.

"Where are we going?" he asked breathlessly. Aglayeshkusa swerved off to the right around the bole of a great oak, and halted at the vine-hung entrance to a thatched bower. Arris stopped a few paces back, and his fear and awe were redoubled as he gazed past the daimon's muscular shoulders at the pair of red-eyed wolves who slouched out of the enclosure to stand guard at its door.

They were the only animals Arris had seen, besides the fish in the stream, and those had seemed merely ornamental, like the tame goldfish in pools at the Sapphire Palace. The wolves were nearly as tall as Arris at the shoulder.

Their fur was matted and rough, a light silver-gray, and their eyes were the color of fresh blood. They smelled of old meat they had eaten, and of clover they had rolled in sometime recently. There were bits of grass and clover in the thick fur on their rumps and backs. Their lips were drawn back in habitual snarls that wrinkled more when Aghlayeshkusa took a step forward and spoke.

"Lord, I have him with me."

He was not speaking to the wolves, Arris knew. Deep inside the bower, in the overgrown tangle of autumn-colored leaves and branches and living thatch, was a power that made Arris want to run out of the forest to the place where the Brothers Ylla reigned, to invite them to strike him down because it would be easier to face. The power the Goddess had granted Arris at his birth was bound deep inside him, and he could not use it. But he would have had to have been mindless, senseless, not to have known who was the master of the wolves.

"Why did you bring me here?" Arris whispered, frozen where he stood.

"I did not have the power to answer your call," the daimon said. His own fear and uncertainty were clear on his pale warrior's face. "I could not help you against the poison. My wounds still bleed, boy. I have not been granted the healing I sought. I . . . struck a bargain. I would bring you here, and then he would help both of us. He only wants to talk to you."

There was a rustling inside the bower, and the wolves raised their massive heads and whined softly in their throats. Arris backed up a few steps, but Aghlayeshkusa reached out a hand and grasped his shoulder in a bruising grip. They stood together, the young man naked and terrified, the daimon-soldier hardly less frightened, but resolute. Arris felt a touch of the breeze that moved along the high branches, and the soft black earth beneath his bare feet almost hummed with life.

A great figure half-obscured with vines appeared in the entrance to the bower. The lord of the forest bent his shaggy head so that his heavy rack of stag's antlers just brushed against the thatch of the roof, as he moved out between his two companion wolves. Fierce, indifferent beauty; the knotted strength of tree roots in the muscles of arms and calves; a musky, overwhelmingly male smell, like a lion or a stallion; skin the dark color of deep forest shadows, though there were no shadows in this world: all were contained in the shape of a stag-horned man. Arris could not meet the angry, challenging gaze of the dark green eyes. This was the Hunter, the consort of the Goddess, whom he had betrayed on Winter Festival night.

"Lord," Aghlayeshkusa whispered, "I have brought Arris, of whom we have spoken . . ."

"We know one another, he and I," said the Hunter in a rumbling voice like distant thunder. The wolves growled furiously, catching their master's mood. "Leave us until I call for you, earth spirit."

"I trust the Lord does not forget what I have been promised," the daimon said as he released Arris's shoulder and backed slowly away.

Arris would sooner trust a lightning storm than this god, this wild-hearted lover who was torn to death each year by his own beasts, the male reflection of Rehoman the Destroyer. It was not that the Hunter was treacherous in the way a daimon could be, but the honor of the forest beasts was not the honor of man, and bargains and promises were not part of his nature.

"So," said the horned god in harsh-accented Yaighan when the daimon had gone. "Where is the courage you had in the Temple, when you turned traitor and stole the sacrifice from the stone? You fear me."

"Yes," Arris said. It was hard to keep his voice steady. The huge gray wolf on his right had begun to advance on him, snarling, shoulders hunched and head lowered. "Should I not? I broke the ritual, and there is no Yearking, and the Goddess is trapped behind golden walls."

"And the Hunter escaped the wolves," said the low voice, "and did not die, and was cast out of the old Yearking with no way to be reborn. There have been cycle upon cycle of centuries, and the years are much the same, but I would remember if that had happened before."

"The sacrifice is supposed to be willing, and the Candi-

date is supposed to choose to be Yearking," Arris said
with a flash of the anger he had felt. "Saresha never
wanted to carry your horns, Hunter. And I took the choice
that should have been offered to me."

"You took a fool's choice." With a gesture of one
hand, the god called back his wolf. "You have no idea of
the damage you have done to the balance of things." Arris
felt his fury like a hot wind against his skin. "Or maybe
you do know. You speak so vehemently of choices made,
of choices denied. But you know that you are no ordinary
youth, and you were not chosen as Candidate on a whim.
When your mother lay with a man in the spring rite, she
was the Lady for that night, and her consort was the
Yearking. You are the child of the Goddess, and my child.
You are not entirely human, to demand the right of choosing your own fate."

"What you tell me . . . may be true," Arris said. He
had to fight against an urge to kneel before the Horned
One, to beg forgiveness and agree to anything he said. He
felt more than awe; something akin to love. "But it does
not change my course. I will find my own path."

"You will only find a meaningless death, at the hands
of the Goddess's enemies." The god was half again Arris's size; his wolves came up only to his waist. His hands
rested now on their necks, and his eyes were not so much
angry as puzzled. So green they were almost black, they
gazed at Arris without understanding. "If I send you back
now to where you were you will die of your poisoned wound
within the hour. It was Sygathi Ylla who convinced Anoguri
to set his worshipers against you. The Truthsayer knows
that you belong to the Goddess, and must return to her."

"If I die of that wound, I can never return to free her,"
Arris said in sudden challenge. "Send me back, without
helping me overcome the poison. I do not think the Goddess will thank you for it." The wolves moved forward
toward him, growling.

"You will free her," her Consort cried out. "You must.
And then we will join together, in one flesh, you and I, as
the Goddess intended. You cannot escape it, boy. You are
hers, body and spirit, as much as I am, as much as the

Lossiran is. Go to her. She will forgive you for your defiance. I can promise you that.''

"If I decide one day to free her, then I will do it," Arris said. "But now my choice is to live like any other man. Send me back to my body now, Lord of the Forest. Give me strength to survive the poison, if you want to keep me alive. But I promise you nothing. The Goddess has tried to control my life. She cannot control me now.''

The wind from the trees lifted Arris's hair and chilled his skin as the god's frustration grew. Arris doubted the wisdom of his challenge; the Hunter was as likely to strike him dead for his insolence as he was to keep him alive in hope for the future. The wolves snarled and snapped at him, coming to within inches of his naked body before they twisted away and circled again. The daimon Aghlayesh-kusa had come back to the bower, and stood fearfully alone off to the side. Whatever the Horned One decided, the daimon was unlikely to be offered the healing he sought, Arris suspected.

As if freshly cut, the wound across his chest opened suddenly, and agony struck through him. He fell back into the clutches of his sickness. Cramps snapped his muscles taut like twisted rope, and Arris dropped to the earth of the forest floor, doubled over on himself and sure he was about to die.

There was a roaring of fury and power; the sound echoed in Arris's ears and blocked all of his senses into stunned unawareness. He did not even feel the pulling from his body as he was sent back. He felt only the pain, fiercer than he had ever known it before, and he was back in the trader's cart beneath his blankets, left to fight as best he could, not knowing which choice the Consort of Rehoman had made for him.

CHAPTER
10

TWO DAYS LATER, Arris was well enough to sit up on the driver's board at Senna's side. The poison had left his body weakened, and the fever still sometimes returned. But he was alive, and no enemies had attacked him again since he had returned to his body from the Realm of the Gods. He supposed that the Hunter had chosen to help him, if reluctantly. He felt no trace of a return of his Goddess-given power; her Consort had loaned him strength to overcome the poison, nothing more.

He had not spoken to anyone of his strange journey or of his encounter with the god. Terai might seize on the Hunter's statement that the Goddess would forgive him, and urge Arris to return to aid her. Arris had begun to suspect the real reason why Terai had chosen to protect him; the Yaighan wanted to keep him safe, until the time he would free the Goddess and the delayed Millennium would begin. It was only a suspicion. Arris would not confront Terai with it, not unless he was forced to.

The eastward road was muddy from the winter rains, sometimes washed down to jagged gravel pavement that hurt the horses' feet. The long wagon moved slowly through clouded landscapes of fields and orchards and villages, toward the border provinces that were across the Westrange from the Khalifate city of Ummass. Terai meant to cross the border at a high pass nearly eighty miles north from the hill-fort where General Iyon had been mustering the main invasion force. That would keep them out of the soldiers' way, he hoped. But there were troops on the road, traveling in the same direction. Arris ducked into the hood of his cloak whenever a battalion rode past, but there was no trouble. The cart would pull to the side of the road, and the soldiers would trot their animals past taking little notice. Twice an officer had shouted out a question on their destination; Terai had answered with the name of a city a day's journey away, and was not challenged.

"We are going to make it out of the country, aren't we?" Vaessa said, looking up at Arris. She walked beside the cart on the grass at the side of the road, taking her turn on foot. Since Arris had left his pallet, she, Terai, and Van rode the two horses or walked. Sometimes all three walked, to give the animals a rest. They stopped every few hours in any case, to clean the packed mud and stones out of the horses' and mules' hooves, and to allow them to drink from the rain-filled ditches along the road's edge.

"It's likely," Arris said.

Vaessa smiled. She seemed to be determined to forget her slavery. Of them all, she was the most continually cheerful. It might have annoyed Arris any other time, but he was glad for her smiles when he felt his sickness returning. In a round leather cap, tunic, and trousers, Vaessa carried off her part as a young merchant woman, but her beauty shone even through the road dust on her face and the black dye in her braided hair.

"You should come with us," she said. "Back to the Khalifate."

Arris shook his head. "It's too dangerous."

"It will be dangerous for you here, if the Emperor learns that you helped us," said Senna. The spring-mounted board creaked as he shifted his heavy weight, and flicked the reins expertly to prod a slowing mule. "And people are trying to kill you in Deiran, boy. Though I haven't been told the reason."

"It would be hard to explain," Arris said. "But when you get to the Citadel you'll learn why I can't go back to the Khalifate. Danae will tell you."

"Van thinks that you hurt her somehow," Vaessa said in a low voice that could not be heard by her brother where he rode ahead of the wagon team. "And that's why you won't go back, and why you won't tell us."

A picture rose in Arris's mind, of Danae's face when she had caught him with the Regents' bodies. What had she said—that she thought she might have loved him, but now she felt nothing but hatred? It was something to that effect. "I did hurt her," Arris said after a moment. "But not in the way Van thinks. She'll be glad to forget me. But you'll find her well, and happy with her work with her musicians." He hoped that was true. The priest Karillos might accuse Danae of conspiring with him. But the widow of the Regent Nievan, Oella, liked Danae enough to defend her. Arris thought she would prevail.

"I am not worried about her," Senna said softly. "My daughter has always been able to take care of herself. But I have missed her terribly. If I can be with her again, these past two years might fade from my memory. We all bear scars . . . Van has the most obvious ones, I fear."

Vaessa scowled, her cheerful mood gone. "The Kurontai Roka was generally a reasonable man, but Van has never been tactful, and he would say what he thought to the master's face. He was whipped three times for things he said. We were afraid Roka would sell him away from us if it happened again."

They were silent then, and Arris listened to the creaking of the cart wheels and the plod of the mules' hooves in the drying mud. He thought of what Vaessa had said. He bore no scars from his five years of slavery. His skin was unmarked. Even General Iyon had been careful not to damage the Emperor's favorite when he took his pleasure. Arris had no visible reminders of the pain he had endured. He had been proud of his beauty then, glad that it set him apart from the other slaves. But Arris thought that Van had more reason to be proud. He had never truly become a slave, in the way Arris had. He had spoken his mind, he had protested the inhumanity of his position, and he had borne his punishment for it. Arris had often been angry, and often hurt, but he had buried those feelings and hidden them even from himself.

Terai had drawn aside from the road up ahead, leaning

down from his horse to speak with a farmer in a broad, conical hat. The farmer, an old man in short trousers and a loose smock, stood at the edge of a fallow field that had been trampled into flat, hard-packed earth. Stagnant pools of water were trapped in places. Arris had seen such fields before, on his courier's ride north to Khopei. Troops had exercised there, men and horses, perhaps chariots. They were not far from the border now.

Leaving the old man, Terai rode back to the wagon. Van watched him curiously, but rode at the front still. Terai's horsemanship made the old, lazy gelding he rode behave like one of the smart Yaighan hill ponies; at its cues from Terai's knees, the horse trotted smoothly in beside the wagon at Senna's elbow.

"The army has been here, hasn't it?" Arris called across to Terai.

"The local garrison was at four time its usual strength," the farmer said, until yesterday. They all rode away, straight to the east." Beneath his trader's cap, Terai's face was troubled. "The courier must have come with the Emperor's commands, but why they did not ride south to join Iyon's forces I cannot guess."

"Do you think we'll have trouble?" Senna asked.

"It's possible."

Vaessa reached up and took Arris's hand, and he pulled her up into the wagon seat beside him. It was crowded, with barely room for three. "Terai, the garrison that left . . . did it take the people's food, their animals?"

"Most likely," he said.

"Then we should stop in the town, and sell what we can while we find out about the troops. We need to know where they were headed, to know where we can safely cross."

"Aye, that's sensible," her father said. "But I worry about maintaining our disguise for more than an hour in one place. These Deirani mistrust strangers already."

"We'll watch ourselves," Terai said. "Senna, your accent is good enough, if you keep from getting into long conversations. Vaessa and Van will have to be careful. Arris and I can seek out the information we need. In these clothes, and if we're lucky, we can pass for undersize Deirani.''

"Terai can wander around the market," Arris said. "I don't have the strength to do much but sit in the common room of an inn."

"That's the best place for you," Vaessa said. She seemed eager to attempt it; her bitter mood had passed. "Van and I will stay with the wagon, and Papa can sell our goods. But not all of them. We have another day still to travel, and we have to have something to point to when soldiers ask questions."

With that decided, Senna urged the mules into a faster walk. The afternoon was graying toward evening, and they had to arrive while the town market, and the gates if there were any, were still open. Vaessa rode with Arris and her father, while Terai and Van cantered their ill-gaited mounts out of sight to search out a place in the bazaar for the wagon. Arris pulled his cloak around him for warmth, and hoped his fever would not return until they left the town. A sick man would draw attention they did not need, and it certainly would not help if he suddenly began talking in Yaighan.

If they had hoped to go unnoticed in the town of Guelan, it was futile. The merchants in the bazaar had had their stock decimated by the garrison, and within the first few minutes that Arris and his companions were there, their load was almost entirely gone. In return for the staple goods they had carried, they bargained for a load of the local striped silk and red-figured clay pots. At Vaessa's insistence, they held back a few barrels of salt fish and bags of flour. Arris went off to the inn as he had promised, leaving Van and Vaessa scrubbing the chicken smells out of the back of the cart so the bolts of silk would not be contaminated. Arris reflected that he and Terai might not be rich when they returned to Khopei with this cargo, but they would have made a profit.

The innkeeper of the Harvest Cellar was a sturdy, round-faced woman who had a quick way of moving and speaking. Her name was Ohan, she told Arris as she seated him at one end of the common board. Eight local men and women had gathered in the inn to take a meal and discuss the problem they faced. They greeted the young stranger courteously, and passed the pot of cabbage soup that was the first course.

Arris smiled, and told them he had just come into town with a load of foodstuff, which was on sale now in the bazaar. The woman Ohan immediately sent a child with a few coins to buy chickens, and the tension in the others lessened.

"Then there are no shortages in the city?" asked a well-dressed man, a magistrate or some kind of city leader by the way the others deferred to him.

"We did not know of any problems here," Arris said. "We'd thought to sell supplies to the army, but they had already gone."

"Yes," said an older woman in dark gray silks. "They left yesterday, so heavily weighted with our goods that they'll probably die of exhaustion in the mountain passes." She sighed and shook her head.

"Not if they take the southern roads," Arris said casually, spooning his soup. "Those are better for chariots, anyway."

"They had their chariots broken up and parceled out on strings of mules," said the woman. "No, they were headed straight east to the mountains. But thank the gods they're gone; while they were here they lived off of us like parasites, and now we can at least replenish our losses. Will there be caravans coming from Khopei, do you think, young man?"

Arris shrugged. "As I said, we didn't know of any shortages. But I'll be headed back that way in a few days, and I'll spread the word to the traders in the city."

"We can send wagons of our own," a meek-voiced man said from the far end of the table. "If they start tomorrow, they can be at Khopei in three days."

"But who could we send who knows enough of the city to find what we need?" said the first man who had spoken, the statesman.

Arris called for parchment and ink, and pushed his food

aside. He drew a quick sketch map of the Khopei bazaars that clustered near the harbor, where Terai had bought the goods they carried. They would be certain to find what they sought there, he said.

They were warm in their thanks, and the meal continued in much better spirits than it had begun. Arris had learned what he needed to know: The army was headed to the same passes where Terai had thought to cross the mountains. Arris wondered if Iyon might not be moving his troops north to meet them. The mercantile city of Ummass would be a good base of operations for the Deirani invasion. It was closest of all the Khalifate cities to Deiran, and if the Khalifate had no advance warning of the invasion, Iyon's army would not have too much difficulty laying siege.

The townspeople of Guelan had heard some of the rumors of miracles and visitations by the gods in Khopei. Arris repeated stories he had heard; they were disappointed that he had no news of the local chief god, a rice spirit called Fefilinai. Ohan urged him to bring his friends and spend the night at the Harvest Cellar. Arris promised to recommend it to them, and he left the inn, very tired and light-headed, wanting only to lie down and close his eyes.

In a narrow street, beside an empty stable whose horses must have been commandeered by the army, a clumsy noise of something falling made Arris turn. He had a glimpse of a thin, frightened face beneath a hood, and the glint of a knife blade in a voluminous sleeve as a man picked himself up after leaping off a wall and rushed at Arris.

Feeling his fever rising again, not so much startled as annoyed, Arris sidestepped his attacker and drew the short sword Terai had bought him in the bazaar of Khopei. The man was not a cunning assassin, or a trained soldier like Chol or Wesu; he tried to parry Arris's sword with his knife, and Arris lunged past the short blade.

The sword plunged into the weak resistance of flesh and found the man's heart. The weight of the dying man went full on the sword, and Arris put another hand to its hilt to lower the man slowly to the street. The blood welled out over the front of a thin cotton tunic, threadbare and patched, not the silk that was worn by most in Guelan. The man sank to his knees, his hands feebly attempting to staunch the blood, the knife still clutched in his fist clashing against Arris's sword. Then his movement stopped and he sagged forward.

Arris rolled him over, put a foot to his shoulder, and pulled out his sword. It scraped against a rib and was free. The smell of death rose in the cool night air. Arris cleaned his blade on the Deirani's sleeve and sheathed his sword. Then he wrapped the man in his own cloak, and lifted him to his shoulders with an effort that almost made him faint. The body made a treacherous burden, hard to balance, heavier than Arris was. Arris staggered with it into the dark stable and dropped it into an abandoned stall. He forked hay over it and left it there.

Back out in the street, he still saw no one else. He dug handfuls of gravel from the roadside and threw them over the pool of blood where the man had died. The street was muddy and rutted from the recent rainy weather. The evidence of death would not be seen easily, but no doubt a local dog would smell it out, if the army had not taken the dogs.

There was blood and dirt smeared on his tunic and his cloak. Arris took them both off and bundled them under his arm, and headed for the town market in his white linen shirt, his trousers and boots. He felt as if he were walking on shipboard; the streets tossed and heaved like a deck in choppy seas. His face felt bloodless and hot, and his hands were shaking.

Van saw him first, and put down the bolts of silk he was carrying. "Here, sit down," he said, taking Arris's arm and leading him to the rear of the cart. Two folding steps had been let down from the wagon bed for loading. Arris sat on the upper step, still holding his bundle of clothes. "You look half-dead. Are you going to be all right?" Van said.

Arris was grateful for his concern. "I'm just tired," he said. "Where is Terai?"

"Talking with my father. About the route we should

take, I think. He found out about where the army has gone."

"So did I," Arris said. "If we cross the mountains on their heels, we can set you over the border, but you'll be behind enemy lines. I don't like it."

"Well, we aren't staying here," Van said with a trace of belligerence.

"That would be impossible," Arris agreed, thinking of the body he had left in the empty stall.

"I don't care if we do end up in the middle of the war. I am going to fight in it, against the Deirani. I'll tell our generals everything I know about their troops, their weapons and training, their commanders. I learned a lot in the palace; people aren't careful of what they say around a slave."

Hareku was right in his suspicions, and he was right to forbid Arris to help Senna's family back to their own country. Arris was Deirani now, if he was anything, but he would see this through. For Danae's sake, and because Terai wanted it.

"Will you tell Terai I need to talk to him?" Arris said, awash in dizziness once more. Van's tall, soft-bellied form blurred and doubled before his eyes, but he saw him nod and hurry away.

He wanted to crawl into his little curtained space behind the driver's board and lie down, but he could not do that yet. He twisted around to look at the load in the wagon, the silks and the pots wrapped in cotton. The Guelan striped silk was not the finest, and it would not sell to the court of the Sapphire Palace, but there was certainly a market for it in Khopei. The clay pots were pretty, the red-figured ware unusual, but Arris had no idea how much they would sell for. He would have to learn those things if he was to become a merchant. At the moment, he wanted nothing more than a peaceful, harmless occupation.

"Van said you heard about the troops," Terai came around the corner, his voice low and worried. "We can't decide what to do. If we cross farther south, we're likely to run into Iyon's forces. We can't cross any farther north, unless we want to abandon the wagon and horses and climb on foot. Vaessa is willing to give up and go back to Khopei. But Senna and Van want to go on, and I don't blame them. We're so close now.''

Terai was alone, and they were camped in an open area at the rear of the dark, deserted bazaar. Arris looked up at him, forcing his unsteady eyes to focus on his old friend's dark-skinned face. "I just killed a man."

Terai turned his head quickly to see that they were unobserved. "What? I was a fool to let you go alone."

"He might have simply been a thief," Arris said. "He was poorly dressed. But he jumped off a wall just behind me, and came at me with a knife. I drew and ran him through. I didn't have time to think about it."

"Where is the body?" Terai demanded. "Were you able to hide it?"

"I covered it with hay in a stall of an empty stable." Arris leaned back against the wagon bed and closed his eyes, feeling as if he were weighted with lead. "There was blood on the street. I put dirt over it. I have blood on my clothes, too. I'll need a new jerkin and cloak."

"You weren't hurt?"

"No. It was very quick. He never even cried out."

"We can't stay here tonight," Terai said. "If the man was an assassin sent by some local god, others will know he went after you. They'll look for him, and they're likely to find him." He leaned over Arris, and Arris felt a calloused hand on his forehead.

"Yes, the fever is back," Arris muttered. "I feel terrible."

"Get into the wagon, and sleep if you can," Terai said gently. "We'll load the rest of this and be gone within the hour."

"Are you going to try the mountain pass?" Arris asked. His voice seemed to be coming from a great distance.

"I think so."

"I don't like it," Arris said as Terai helped him to his feet and half lifted him into the back of the cart. "They'll besiege Ummass. Senna will have to get through the Deirani lines."

"We don't know that for sure," Terai said irritably. "It

could be this particular garrison simply chose to cross at the nearest pass, and they'll be going south to meet with Iyon on the Khalifate side.''

''You don't really think so,'' Arris said.

''I'm trying not to think about it,'' Terai told him roughly. ''None of this is getting any easier. Now go to sleep, and stay quiet. By morning we'll be nearly to the mountains.''

CHAPTER

11

THE DEIRANI TROOPS had apparently taken a high, narrow pass, where their packhorses could climb but no wagons could go. It was a shorter and straighter route across the Westrange. Much relieved, Terai took an old wagon road ten miles farther north. There were a few old ruts in the road, but mostly it was neglected, overgrown with short mountain wildgrass. There had not been much travel between Deiran and the Khalifate in the past few years. The pass was crescent-shaped, curving up even farther north before it wound down to the uplands of the northern Khalifate. The road cut between slopes that were covered with short, dark pines and bare outcroppings of rock. The mules complained a little in the traces as they climbed the switchbacks, but the load of silks and ceramics was not too heavy for them.

Still wary, nervous of being spotted by outriders, Terai rode a mile and a half ahead of the wagon, and set Van as a rearguard the same distance behind. Arris rode in the wagon most of the first day in the mountains, feeling sick, uninterested in the scenery. He was haunted by the face of the man he had killed, by the weight sagging onto his sword. His pact with Aghlayeshkusa meant that the soul of any person Arris killed belonged to the daimon. Whatever god the would-be murderer had worshiped, whatever afterlife he had expected to find, it did not matter. His soul was lost, gone to feed the earth's spirit's hunger for power. Somehow that made this death worse than the others Arris had caused.

He lay in the cart, not listening to the cheerful conversation of Senna and Vaessa on the driver's board. Occasionally they stopped the mules to let them rest, and each time it was harder to get the wagonload moving again. In the early evening they were nearing the summit, and Arris had to get out for a few miles and walk with Vaessa, while Senna led the mules from the front. The way was steep and narrow between rocky hillsides and deep forested bowls that sloped downward from the road's edge. Vaessa walked along with long strides, chattering about the clear, cool air and the wonderful stillness until Arris's glares silenced her. Arris was dizzy and exhausted when they reached the highest point of the road. He sat on the stone cairn travelers had built to mark the spot, and waited with ringing ears and labored breath until Senna judged the mules rested enough to go on. Then Arris climbed back into the cart and tried to sleep.

That night they camped without a fire, hidden by the tall pines in one of the hollows. The next morning Arris felt stronger, and was able to sit on the driver's seat with Senna. They descended the pass slowly and cautiously. Every five miles or so Senna would stop and wait for Terai to ride back and tell them it was safe to go farther. Arris rode with his sword belt buckled on, a blanket around his shoulders in place of his bloodstained cloak. By early afternoon, though, they were over the border into the Khalifate, and they had seen no one. The day was clear and cool, and the rolling grasslands below the foothills showed traces of green in hollows and on streambanks. More than thirty miles away, the River Majeha showed as a dark, narrow line of trees along the plains. They were above its northernmost curve. From there, it flowed east into the small, sheltered harbor of the city of Ummass.

They paused on a ridgetop curve of the road, and Terai rejoined them to point out the river. "If you follow this side of the Majeha, and make a wide circuit around Ummass, you'll be most likely to avoid the army. Even if they do intend a siege."

"The river will take us all the way south to Qadasiya and the Citadel," Senna said. "This is as far as you need to go, Terai. You and Arris must go back before you're missed. Vaessa, help me get our instruments out of the cart. We'll load them on the horses, and be on our way." They were to have the two horses as pack animals, and Arris and Terai would return to Deiran with the cart and mules.

"We can go a little farther with you, surely," Arris said as Vaessa jumped off the wagon seat to help her father shift the bolts of silk that covered their instrument cases. "What if you run into a Deirani patrol? You're unarmed."

"If we run into a Deirani patrol, two swordsmen will be little help," Senna said. "You've already done more than we can repay. We can find our way from here."

In a few minutes Van had ridden up from his rearguard position to join them. Arris helped Vaessa load the horse that had been Terai's, while Van and his father arranged the heavier instruments on his mount's saddle. When they were finished, the sun had fallen a little lower, into a bank of thick white clouds. Arris went to his pallet in the cart, and pulled out a small bag of the gold the Emperor had given him. He climbed back out.

"For food and lodging on your journey," he said, handing it out to Senna. "And for new clothes, something to wear when you perform."

"We are already too much in your debt," the big man muttered, but he took the bag. "We'll repay you if we can, someday."

Van thanked Terai gravely, and nodded to Arris. He led his horse away down the sloping road. Senna took the reins of the other horse. Vaessa hesitated a moment, then came over to Arris and embraced him. She stepped back, and looked at him soberly.

"I will pray to Sygathi Ylla for your safety. Perhaps he will listen."

Arris was so startled that he almost laughed. He turned the impulse into a warm smile. "Pray for your own safe journey. And tell Danae when you see her that I wish her well."

He doubted that he would see any of them again. Arris watched Terai kiss Vaessa, then send her after her father and brother. They walked down the hill toward the distant river and the homeland they had been kept from for so long.

Arris had been trained to drive a chariot while he had been General Iyon's student; but a light, maneuverable Deirani chariot with spirited warhorses to draw it was no relation to this merchants' wagon. He felt as clumsy as a river barge pilot, trying to keep his mules on the track and his cart in midstream. The Westrange pass rose and twisted before him, as the meadows gave way once more to dark stands of pine.

He went slowly, on Terai's orders. The Yaighan ranged ahead—Arris did not know how many miles—along the forest's edge and behind rocky escarpments, watching for Deirani regiments who might be crossing into the Khalifate. It was far more dangerous to be traveling this direction, against the army's path, then it had been to travel the same way the Deirani troops were headed.

Arris was less concerned about the danger of running into soldiers than he was about other possibilities. He flinched whenever a bird called out as it crossed the road overhead; he jumped at every shadow that changed position as he passed. The enemies he feared were not the army. The Five Brothers would know by now that he had not died from his poisoned wound. If they had sent the cutthroat in Guelan, they would know that he had failed. It had been two days since the last attempt on his life, and Arris was growing restless with waiting.

The driver's seat was hard and grew more and more uncomfortable. After an hour or so, Arris stopped, crawled into the back of the wagon, and filled one of the mules' nosebags with dried fruit from the dwindling stores of food for the journey. He climbed out onto the road, and ate as he walked, leading the mules from the front. They pulled the cart along willingly enough, since he fed them bits of apricot and prune whenever they slowed their pace too much.

By evening, Arris and the mules were equally tired and footsore. They came upon Terai sitting on a fallen log by the side of the track, a dark figure in the chill shadows of the twilight pass. The sun had fallen behind the mountains ahead of them an hour before. Arris did not even wonder if the shape might be another assassin; he knew Terai's short, thick silhouette, and perhaps he had a little power left to sense his friend's presence.

"No one on the road ahead?" Arris asked as Terai stood up to walk with him.

"It's quiet. A few beasts, many birds. I saw a shepherd dog, alone on the ridgetop to the south. Without any flock, or any master near."

"The Deirani army, do you think?"

Terai shrugged. "Perhaps. Maybe the shepherd was coming down the path they took, and they killed him and took his animals. Or maybe the dog had gone wild. I whistled to it, but it wouldn't come to me."

It was growing colder. "Should we keep on? We're near the place were we camped last night."

"I'd as soon be out of this pass," Terai said. "But we'll stop. You've been ill, and you need to sleep."

"I feel all right," Arris said. To his surprise, he realized it was the truth. He was getting his strength back, and his fever was completely gone. He was tired, but no more than he should be after a long day of traveling.

Terai took off the mule's halter, and guided the team to the side of the road. The grass there showed the tracks the wagon had made that morning, coming up out of the hollow where they had camped. "You're stronger than I'd have guessed, Arris," he said. "When I knew you were poisoned, I thought you would die. If I didn't know differently, I'd say you were under the protection of some powerful god."

"I asked the daimon for help," Arris said. He would not mention the Goddess's Consort to Terai.

"I'd have thought it would have wanted to let you die."

"I don't know what it wants." Arris climbed back onto the driver's seat, and set the drag brake as they rolled down a slope into the tree-lined hollow. It was very dark beneath the pines, and the night sounds of the forest creatures had begun. They stopped the cart in the shadows, and Arris went to help unhitch the mules and lead them to water at the cold, shallow stream that was nearby.

"I wonder." Terai knelt on the bank and cupped his hands to dip into the water. His voice was deep and rough, and Arris could no longer see his face in the darkness. "I wonder if anything or anyone can kill you, Arris."

Arris laughed. "Any number of things could kill me, if they caught me by surprise, or if there were too many for me to defend myself against."

"I wonder," Terai said again, getting to his feet with a grunt of effort.

"You think the Goddess is protecting me?" Arris said in disbelief.

"I think you are part of a larger pattern. And your part has to be played out to the end."

"You mean I should go back and be Yearking, and die at next Winter Festival." Arris led his mule back up beside the wagon, and picketed it between two trees. Terai followed him. "I think that is why you came with me to Deiran. To keep me alive so I could go back."

Arris saw a faint gleam of teeth in the darkness as Terai smiled. "I didn't come with you as the Lady's agent. I swear it."

"She's dead," Arris said quietly. "The Lady Maella."

"What?"

"'I saw her lying in the Temple, in a dream. She was trapped there, alone with the Goddess, and she couldn't get out. She died of starvation. I'm sorry."

"You . . . saw this in a dream?" Terai said, his low voice growing angry.

"It was a true dream. The Lossiran came to me, tried to warn me, that night in the inn at Khopei. I had forgotten about it while I was still fighting the poison." Arris had not meant to speak of it, or of his suspicions about Terai's reasons for keeping him company. Well, it could not be unsaid. "I'm sorry, Terai."

"You killed her, then," Terai said. "And I helped you do it. If you had gone through with the sacrifice, the Goddess would have had the strength to defeat her enemies. They would not have been able to trap her there, and Maella would be alive.''

''You may be right.'' Arris walked back to the rear of the wagon and sat on one of the steps. The night was very quiet. The mules shifted on their picket ropes, nosing one another; the stream bubbled softly a few yards away; it was still winter, and there were no sounds of insects. Nothing stirred.

Terai joined him on the step after a while. They sat together without speaking until Terai finally said, ''I didn't come with you to protect you for the Goddess, or the Lady. Or for the good of the Yaighan people. I don't know if you'll believe me.''

''Then why did you?'' Arris said.

Simply, Terai said. ''I don't know.''

Arris hesitated for a moment, but it was a night for speaking what was on his mind. ''I've thought, sometimes . . . I've wondered . . . if you might be my real father.''

Terai turned in the darkness to look at him. ''Your father was the Yearking, twenty years ago at Spring Festival. I was never Yearking. If I had been, it would have been ten years before that.''

''So he's dead.''

''He died before you were born, at the next Winter Festival. I don't even remember his name. I didn't go back to Gama that year.''

Arris nodded. ''Then that isn't the reason you came with me. Or the reason you brought me to Gama in the first place, or the reason you searched for me all those years after I killed Onira.''

''I told you I don't know why,'' Terai said irritably.

''You should find some other mission in life, before you get killed trying to protect me from the Khalifate gods.''

''That would be the wisest course.'' The aging warrior stood up and stretched his arms behind his back. Arris watched him, silhouetted against the black pines. ''But I'm not afraid of death. I have lived thirty years longer than I was meant to, Arris. I should have died on the altar at the Temple when I was twenty. I've always felt that I cheated the Goddess, upset the order of things.''

"You chose your own destiny," Arris said. "As I am doing."

"Did I?" The anger had gone out of Terai's voice, and he sounded almost amused. "Perhaps I have just now reached my destiny. I seem not to have a choice anymore. I would not have chosen to help you betray the Goddess at Winter Festival, but I did it. Perhaps it was my fate to help you accomplish . . . whatever it is you're meant to do, that has kept you alive though half the Gods' Realm is calling for your death." He reached out and rested a hand briefly on Arris's shoulder. "I don't know why I stay with you, boy. Let's call it friendship, and leave it at that. Now get some sleep. I'll stand the first watch."

The next morning Arris was in no mood for further talk of destinies found or chosen. He was relieved that Terai barely spoke to him at all, helping him hitch up the mules and then trotting away on foot to go ahead of Arris as he had the day before. Arris drove the wagon up out of the hollow, and across the rough ground for a mile until he had reached the road again.

It was a cold day, damp and foggy in the high pass. It did not rain, but the clouds hovered around the hilltops and sometimes rolled like kneaded dough across the meadows and the grassy road. Arris shivered on the driver's board with two blankets around his shoulders, until he finally gave up the struggle and got out his cloak. The stains on it were dark and stiff, but they were not obviously human blood. He might have worn the cloak hunting, and not bothered to take it off while he butchered a deer. It was warm, at least.

He had been uneasy yesterday, ready to see a threat from the Brothers Ylla around every turn, beside every bush. Today he was only tired of the journey. Occupied with his thoughts, his mood as gloomy as the weather, Arris was startled when he saw Terai running over an embankment on the ridgetop. Terai half slid and half climbed down toward Arris, waving his arms in an apparent signal for Arris to get off the road. There was nowhere to go, here in the barren heights of the pass. No shallow hollows, not even rocks close enough together to hide behind. The wagon could go nowhere but straight along the road, either forward or back the way they had come.

Checking his sword in its sheath, Arris jumped down from the wagon seat and waited for Terai. The mules caught something of his fear, and stamped and snorted in their harness, rolling their eyes. The wagon had stopped on a slope, and began to roll backward. Arris climbed half up onto it again, and set the brake.

Terai did not call out to him, and that was the worst of it. It meant the danger was very near. Arris ran to meet him as the older Yaighan stumbled onto the road. Terai was gasping for breath from his running and the thin mountain air. He held his side with a grimace of pain.

"What is it? Soldiers?" Arris demanded.

Terai nodded. "More than one division, I think. A mounted force, not burdened with supplies or pack animals. They're coming up fast. We can't avoid them, lad."

"We could leave the wagon," Arris said. "Take the mules with us."

"No." Terai brushed by him, and hauled himself up onto the wagon seat. He loosed the brake and took up the reins. His breathing was getting a little slower, but he was sweating and his skin was ashen in the cold, damp air. "If they saw the wagon, they'd search for us, and there are enough of them to spread out all through these mountains. They'd find us, and we'd be in worse trouble than we were when we were captured at the hill-fort. Your General Iyon is already in the Khalifate. These men won't know you."

"What can we do?" Arris cried in frustration, his hand on the hilt of his short sword.

"Play the innocent," Terai grinned at him. "It's a challenge, boy. We're innocent traders, returning from Ummass to our home in Khopei. We know nothing of war or soldiers."

Arris unbuckled his sword and held out his hand for Terai's weapon. Reluctantly the older man handed it down. Arris went to the back of the wagon and thrust both sheathed swords into the middle of a bolt of silk so they were completely hidden. Then he joined Terai on the driver's seat. They had to cajole the unnerved mules to pull forward again.

Terai glanced sharply at him. "Get rid of that blood-stained cloak, Arris."

Arris quickly obeyed, unclasping the wool garment and rolling it up. He thrust it through the curtains behind him, and tried not to shiver in his linen shirt. He did not see how he or Terai could pass for Deirani merchants under the suspicious eyes of soldiers, despite their clothes and their command of the language. Arris's Deirani accent was learned at court, and he could not imitate the merchant's cant that he had heard so little.

The outriders of the Deirani divisions jogged their horses into view, and drew rein with a shouted challenge when they saw the wagon. Terai halted the mules and set the brake, and he and Arris waited silently in the shadow of the rocky slopes. The soldiers wore full armor, all in black, ringmail with solid breastplates and greaves. Their horses were the big, long-limbed, war-trained mounts of the heavy cavalry. One man carried a banner pole, with the Deirani hawk on a blue pennant, and the raven of the Fengian garrison, black on gold.

"They're from Feng," Arris said softly. "There won't be any conscripts here. These are veteran troops."

The outriders advanced warily, javelins set, in a line five horses deep that blocked the mountain track. Their black helmets hid their features. They were so ready for battle, Arris thought, that they might not care whether the wagon's drivers were friend or foe. It was well that the cargo of silks and pots was nothing these soldiers would need on their campaign.

The mules had started to back up in their traces, frightened witless by the advancing soldiers who seemed likely to run straight into them. Arris climbed down from his seat, keeping his hands at shoulder height, his expression carefully neutral. He went to the front of the wagon and grasped the halters of both animals, murmuring nonsense to them in Deirani. They were not happy about it, but they stood still.

A soldier demanded their names and business. Terai

answered in better Deirani than Arris had yet heard him use. He was Obren of the Caravaner's Guild in Khopei, and this young man was his son and apprentice, Jiashu. His brother ran the Riverbranch Inn near the harbormouth; perhaps they had visited there?

The soldier ordered Terai down off the wagon, and he and Arris were surrounded by mounted men with javelins as others searched their cargo briefly. Terai talked about Ummassid silks and Trevena pots. It seemed to be going well. The soldiers were inclined to be suspicious, but not unreasonable, and it was a reasonable picture Terai presented. Arris had begun to relax, though he had no difficulty looking properly frightened when one of the soldiers demanded to know why he was not in the army.

Then the vanguard of the troops rode around the bend below them, and Arris could see that there were hundreds of men following along. A group of five officers, seeing that the outriders had stopped, pressed their horses to a gallop and rode up to where the soldiers had Terai and Arris surrounded.

A sergeant of the outriders began to repeat Terai's story in a respectful tone, as one of the officers cantered around to see what was in the wagon. Then one of the newcomers pushed his helmet back and cut off the sergeant's recitation with a gesture.

"I know these men," he said.

Arris looked up sharply, and looked away in defeat. It was Lieutenant Ebreyu, being sent back to General Iyon after his few days' leave. The handsome young Deirani looked as hard and cold as he had when he had first captured Arris and Terai, a week ago and eighty miles to the south. There was a bitter new set to Ebreyu's mouth. Arris guessed that he was the cause. He expected no mercy from the man.

"Lieutenant," Terai said wearily. He looked old in that moment, older than Arris had ever seen him.

"Take them prisoner, and confiscate the wagon," Ebreyu ordered. "These are spies, and turncoat spies at that."

A captain of the Feng troops drew his sword. "We have no time for prisoners, Lieutenant. I'll kill them now."

Ebreyu urged his horse in front of the man. "No. By your leave, Captain Rais, we have to take them to General Iyon. The younger one is one of Iyon's Jai-Sohn killers. The General will want to deal with him personally."

"As you say." Rais sheathed his weapon. "I'd as soon not soil my blade on a Jai-Sohn, at that." He raised his voice. "Empty out the wagon and get it turned around. I want two men to drive it, and two in the back with the prisoners. Bind them well. I'll have the death of the soldier who lets the Jai-Sohn escape."

Arris shivered in the cold as four men dismounted and headed for him. "Lieutenant Ebreyu," he called out. "Will you let me explain what I've been doing here?"

Ebreyu nodded at the men, and they grabbed hold of Arris and threw him full length on the ground to truss his arms and legs. "You already had one story for us," said the Lieutenant, his voice very calm and his noble accent pronounced. "I imagine you'll say you were on a mission for the Emperor. But I was there in his chambers when you refused his commission, and I know what you have been doing. You've no doubt just set your friends across the mountains, the slaves you wanted to purchase. The Emperor warned you not to take them out of the country. He said it would be treason."

"They're only musicians," Arris protested from the ground. His face was bleeding, cut on a rock in the road, and they had bound him so he could move no more than his head, his fingers and toes. "They are no threat to the Emperor."

"They'd been in the country for years, I understood," Ebreyu said. "If nothing else, they can warn the Khalifate of the coming invasion. The Emperor said it would be treason, and that is what you have done, Arris. Iyon will judge you. I will leave it up to him." He reined his horse around and rode past with the other officers.

Terai had been similarly bound. He and Arris lay still, having no choice, while the outriders emptied the wagon. Then they were slung into the back onto the bare boards like two sacks of rice. Two of the outriders climbed in after them as the wagon lurched around on the narrow road to fall in with the column of Deirani soldiers. Four war-horses, belonging to the two guards and the two drivers, followed unhappily on leading ropes. The guards, no more pleased than their mounts at this change of duty, sat bracing themselves against the wagon's bouncing, holding their javelins and scowling down at Arris and Terai.

Arris did not have the heart to speak, and he suspected his captors would not allow it anyway. But he wanted to ask if Terai thought this was a part of their glorious, gods-defying destiny, to ride toward their deaths unable to move a muscle to save themselves. And it was ironic, he wanted to tell Terai, that when he was marked for death by gods, he would be sent there because of the mischance of running into a bitter, angry man who had briefly been his lover.

CHAPTER
12

THIS JOURNEY was the longest Arris had ever had to endure. He was as bruised as if he'd been beaten before half a day had passed from the endless jouncing of the wagon and the cruel, cutting edges of the ropes that bound him. He grew numb from the bindings and from the cold. He had nothing to cover him, and could not move to warm his blood. He knew he was going to be killed. He wished Terai had not been caught up in this with him, but he had known his friend would die if he stayed with him for long.

They did not stop that night, but kept on the interminable way down the pass. Arris slept fitfully, wakening whenever the wagon hit a rut and he rolled helplessly against the wooden side slats or against Terai. He thought of calling for help from the daimon or even the Horned One, but what could they do? If they pulled him into the Gods' Realm, it still would leave his body tied up and headed for General Iyon's mercies. This was not a supernatural battle they could give him strength to fight.

At lengthy intervals the column halted, and when Arris reminded his guards of the need, they lifted him and Terai out and unbound their legs long enough for them to relieve themselves by the roadside. They did not feed the prisoners at all, or give them any water. Why waste rations on men headed for certain death? It was logical, and it left very little room for hope.

It was late on the second night of their captivity when Arris and Terai were hauled into Iyon's fortified camp in the back of the wagon the Emperor's money had purchased in Khopei. They lay there as helpless as logs before the fire, while their guards left with their horses, and new guards came to stand outside at the foot of the wagon, gazing in curiously at the prisoners.

There was a cluster of arguing voices, and then Arris picked out Iyon's cultured accent. "Bring them to my tent. Lieutenant Ebreyu, I want you there."

"My lord," Ebreyu answered crisply.

The guards clambered inside and bent to cut the bonds on Arris's and Terai's legs. Arris felt the blood rushing back into his unbound limbs like liquid fire, and he could not stifle a moan of pain. Beside him, he saw that Terai had fainted. The guards slapped the older man's face to bring him to, and when his eyes opened blearily again, they hauled both men to their feet and dragged them out of the wagon.

Arris could not stand or walk. Terai was able to take a few stiff steps. Torches filled the night with drifting smoke and pale, unsteady light. Some were borne by soldiers, and others were lit on poles along the narrow streets formed by the officers' tents in the central camp. A pattern of near and distant torches spread all through a wide, bowl-shaped valley that had once been someone's farm, surrounded by forested hills that were blacker than the clouded night sky. It was cold enough to see men's breath.

The guard holding Arris cursed and kicked at him, but finally he had to hold him under the arms and drag him toward the General's tent. In not much more dignified fashion, Terai traveled alongside him. Lieutenant Ebreyu and Genera Iyon had outdistanced them quickly, and by the time Arris and Terai reached the tent, Iyon had already had a table and two chairs set up and had ordered a late supper for himself and Ebreyu.

The tent was brightly lit, with candles on the table and torches in holders on the wooden door supports. The guards awaited Iyon's command, then dragged Arris and Terai inside and sat them down on a wooden bench. Their feet were bound again, this time to the bench, and the guards were dismissed to wait outside the door.

Arris found that it took nearly all his strength to sit up and keep his eyes open. Terai looked ghastly in the light, gray-faced, his lips parched and bleeding, bruises on his cheeks and above one eye. Arris was certain he looked no better. He forced himself to meet Ebreyu's gaze, and the young lieutenant had the grace to look away in confusion, and put down the water glass he had been holding.

"Gentlemen," Iyon said, seeming at a loss as to how to begin. Arris watched him dully. The army commander showed the effects of sleepless nights and long, unpleasant days. His face was lean and wolfish, and his eyes blood-shot. He had cut his hair short to wear under his helmet. "This is a serious matter," he said. "The Lieutenant tells me that you aided slaves from the Khalifate to escape from Khopei and cross the border. He calls this treason, and says that the penalty must be death."

If Ebreyu had felt any qualms upon seeing Arris's and Terai's condition, he had lost them now. His mouth was set on a firm line, and he folded his arms to gaze at the prisoners without pity. "I would have been within my rights to kill them where I found them," he said. "But I thought you would want to judge them yourself, my lord."

Iyon nodded. "Well. Do you have anything to say?"

Arris found that he could produce a hoarse whisper. "It wasn't treason." The effort made him cough.

"Give them water," Iyon said impatiently. Ebreyu obeyed him, holding his cup to each man's lips in turn and allow-ing them each half.

It was hard to swallow, but the water gave Arris some relief. He tried to focus his cobwebbed thoughts into some-thing coherent to say to Iyon. "My . . . my lord, they weren't slaves. I bought their freedom. You remember Senna and his family, don't you? The Khalifate musicians? They were my friends, and they wanted to go home."

"You saved their lives, the morning after the attempt on the Emperor," Iyon said thoughtfully. "I remember. You risked Hareku's anger, but you insisted they could have nothing to do with the Ambassador's crime. And the young-er daughter, the composer . . . she is the one who fol-lowed you to the Citadel, who helped you spy for us there."

"Danae. Yes."

"My lord General, does it matter who they were?" Ebreyu said. "I was there when the Emperor told Arris not to take them out of the country. It was a direct order, and Arris admits he disobeyed it."

"I didn't want to disobey the Emperor. But I could not see the harm in letting them leave Deiran after so long." Arris tried to clear his raspy voice, and broke into coughing again.

"They will warn the Khalifate of the invasion," Ebreyu said. "You see no harm in that?"

"The Khalifate certainly knows of the invasion by now," Iyon said. "I have not killed everyone in this stretch of the Westrange foothills. Some of them escaped my raiding parties. I doubt that Arris's minstrels will do any real damage to our campaign."

A rap sounded on the doorframe of the tent, and two aides entered at Iyon's command to set out a supper for the two officers. Roasted meat, pork by the smell, and a dish of spiced potatoes and cheese. Arris tried not to look at it, telling himself he should be grateful for the water. But the smell made him feel faint.

Iyon did not begin to eat. "Terai," he said quietly. "You impressed me as a thinking man. Yet you went along with this foolish action."

Terai nodded, and spoke weakly. "My lord, Senna and his family were old friends of mine. If anything, the fault is more mine than the boy's."

Ebreyu sliced a juicy piece of meat and stuck it with the point of his knife. He held up the knife and took a bite of the pork. Arris could not help watching him, as a dog might watch, in hopeless longing. "My lord," Ebreyu said, "I say this respectfully, but your job here is not to judge the motive for their crime. They admit they did it. The Emperor said it would be treason, and treason calls for death. You have your duty."

Mildly, in a voice that Arris remembered meant Iyon was dangerously angry, the General said, "I recall saying to you that an officer should interpret his orders, his duty, based on circumstance. What is true for a lieutenant on patrol is far more true for a commander faced with this decision. You are not aware of all that bears on this case. Arris has been a loyal and very valuable operative for the Emperor and for me.''

''May I speak candidly, my lord?'' Ebreyu asked.

''As you will.''

''I believe that Arris has been your lover in the past. Will you let this cloud your judgement?''

Iyon looked at Arris with a distant expression in his eyes. ''There was no such relationship between us.'' At Ebreyu's apparent disbelief, he added, ''Oh, I took him to my bed on occasion. He was a very beautiful boy. It added to my pleasure that he hated me. Doubtless he still does. On my part, I have no great affection for him. But I respect his abilities, Lieutenant.'' He looked across the table, meeting Arris's eyes. ''I have made my decision, for good or ill. Arris, Terai, I offer you each a choice.''

Arris had begun to feel a desperate hope as the conversation went on, and now he did not know what to think. He feared Iyon was playing with them, and was about to offer them a choice between several ugly and painful methods of death.

''You stand convicted of treason,'' Iyon said. ''Your choice is this: to die as your crime demands, or to fight in the Deirani army under my orders.''

''General, this is outrageous,'' Ebreyu protested, getting to his feet and staring at Iyon. ''You said yourself they are guilty of treason.''

''Are you questioning my authority, Lieutenant?'' Iyon reminded Arris of the Emperor in the way he said this, and Arris remembered that the Emperor had asked Ebreyu much the same question, when the Lieutenant had protested sending an assassin after the Regents.

''It is a sentence of death in any case,'' Arris said, but he felt alive again.

''That depends on you and your skill at staying alive.'' Iyon smiled slightly. ''I intend to make good use of you. I can use an aide who understands the Shadowed Way, and I also need a good charioteer. If you have not forgotten all I taught you, you can serve me well.'' He glanced over at

Terai. "And you, Yaighan, I will place in my reconnaissance wing. I have no intention of sending you out on spying missions of your own, but you will be a great help in interpreting the information my people bring in. That is, if you choose the army."

"My lord General," Terai said in a dry, amused voice. "I am entirely at your command."

"And Arris?"

"Your servant," Arris said.

"I will protest this action to the Emperor when he comes to lead the troops," Ebreyu said stiffly.

Iyon's voice was icy. "You will not. You brought these men to me, and they are mine to dispose with as I decide. My authority is final in the field."

Ebreyu bowed, and turned to leave, picking up his cloak from the back of his chair.

"Ebreyu." The voice cut through the smoky air between them. "You will forget that Arris and Terai have ever been charged with any crime. You will work with them as you would with any men in my army, for the greater good of the Empire. That is a direct order, Lieutenant."

"Very good, sir." Ebreyu saluted and left without waiting to be dismissed.

General Iyon walked over to the bench where the two prisoners sat. He knelt beside Terai and began to undo his bonds. "Do not expect me to be lenient with you," he said. "If you try to desert, you'll be granted the traitor's death I could have given you tonight."

"That's understood, sir," Terai said.

Iyon frowned as he moved to the difficult knots on Arris's wrists. "I must meet with the captains of the Fengian garrison," he said. "I doubt I will be finished with them before morning. You are welcome to finish the supper Ebreyu left, and you can sleep here. You'll be assigned quarters tomorrow." He got to his feet and picked up his cloak.

Arris bit his lip against the pain of returning circulation, and he managed to speak. "We are . . . in your debt. Thank you."

"I didn't do it to please you," Iyon said. "You need not be grateful. I need your talents, as I said." He grinned. "And I began to wonder how the Emperor would react when he got here, if he discovered that I had put you to death. I have my career to think of, and the Princess Kakima's hand." He swept out the door with a flourish of his cloak, and it shut behind him. Arris and Terai were left on their unsteady legs, to stumble over to the table and start into the feast.

For five days after the arrival of the Fengian divisions, the army stayed in its hidden camp. Thirty miles south of the city Ummass, between two arms of the Westrange and beside a branch of the River Majeha, the camp was well situated. Iyon had not done much to fortify it. He did not plan to wait for the Khalifate army to come to him. He had twenty thousand soldiers now, half of them heavy cavalry, the rest light horse, infantry, and chariots. The divisions drilled on the high pastures each day, ready for the order to move out.

Raiding parties went out daily. Within a range of fifteen miles to the south and east, most of the inhabitants were gone. Their farms were sacked and burned, and the people who did not manage to flee were killed. Iyon had ordered that no captives were to be taken. He wanted the Khalifate to fear him.

As General Iyon's new aide, Arris stayed in the camp with the Commander. There was plenty of work for him to do, and he enjoyed some of it. Iyon led a group of scouts from his hill-fort garrison through Jai-Sohn training exercises for an hour or so each morning. He made Arris the teacher of twenty men who were learning the skills of infiltration of an enemy camp or town. The men were willing to learn how to move silently and unnoticed, how to scale walls and cling to rooftops, even how to kill sentries without arousing any alarm; but they refused to wear the short black sword of the Jai-Sohn, and Arris knew that they feared and despised him as a cutthroat assassin. General Iyon escaped their hatred only because he was also a regular soldier, and the Emperor's trusted man.

After the early morning work with the scouts, Iyon would inspect the troops from his chariot. The General had taught Arris to drive almost on a whim, years ago, and at the time Arris had not had the strength in his arms and chest to equal the balance and timing that came naturally to him. Now his body was more mature, and he found a new sense of control that he had not had before. He still remembered the wheel-feats Iyon had taught him, the acrobatic skills that some considered tricks beneath a warrior's dignity.

Iyon's previous charioteer, a proud young corporal named Mentes, spent three days with Arris to be certain he could handle the pair of flawlessly trained black horses. When he thought Arris was ready, he turned the animals over to his care. General Iyon promoted Mentes to sergeant and gave him command of a squadron of chariot-borne archers, and so he was not angry at Arris for taking his honored place as the Commander's driver.

Mentes and many others in the army had their own suspicions as to the General's reasons for bringing his new aide from Deiran. Arris knew what they thought: that he was Iyon's catamite as well as his student. The General never showed Arris affection, in public or in private, but the assumption was natural. Iyon's appetites were well known, and Arris had recovered his striking beauty after only a few days of rest. In the bare leather harness, kilt, and boots of a charioteer, his long hair unbound, Arris made a graceful picture as he leaned over the low shield-wall at the front of the General's chariot. Leaving Mentes to drill the other charioteers on the parade grounds, Arris drove Iyon on his morning tours of the camp, to hear the captains' reports and observe the men on the practice fields that had once been a farmer's land.

Arris cared little what people thought of him. He kept to himself as much as he could. Terai was busy with his new duties in the reconnaissance wing, under a coldly intelligent captain named Yehane. Terai knew the Khalifate lands well, and he spent hours with Yehane and with Iyon, going over maps and arguing about terrain for battles. Arris had provided many of the reports Yehane was working from, when he had been a spy at the Citadel. He had nothing more to add to them, and so he saw little of Terai.

Arris had no official rank beyond aide to the General, and officers and men alike could choose whether to treat him with courtesy or ignore his presence. The only man who actively hated him was Lieutenant Ebreyu. Ebreyu was responsible for the rumors of Arris's relationship with the General, and for the common knowledge in the camp that Arris had killed as a Jai-Sohn assassin. Arris did not understand the depth of the Lieutenant's bitterness, or how it could have arisen out of what had been between them on their journey to Khopei. But he avoided Ebreyu as much as he could, and did his best not to antagonize the young nobleman.

In the afternoons and evenings, Arris attended the General at his meetings with his officers, sometimes acting as a scribe, sometimes running errands for them. The work was not difficult. He was not unhappy. But he knew that it would not last like this: Iyon would soon plunge his full force into war, and Arris dreaded his first battle. He did not want to send any more souls to Aghlayeshkusa. But the alternative was a traitor's death himself, which he liked less. And he did not think it would be any better for him back in Khopei, or anywhere else. The gods could find him when they chose, and send their followers to kill him. At least in Iyon's camp no one had yet come after him with that fanatic's gleam in their eyes.

Arris had been assigned a bunk in a barracks of junior officers, most of whom were aides for captains and wing commanders. The barracks was a long, wood-framed tent, near the center of the officers' camp, convenient to the men they served. It must have seemed odd to the other young men that Arris slept when they did, and was never called to General Iyon's tent in the middle of the night, but they still persisted in believing him to be the General's lover. They were polite to him to his face. But they whispered ribald jokes to one another, and sometimes he overheard. Whenever he would enter the tent, they would fall silent as if guilty, whether they had been discussing him or the gloomy weather or the prospects of the raid tomorrow.

At midday on the fifth day after his arrival, Arris sat at his bunk, alone in the barracks. He was mending the heel on one of his chariot driving boots. It had a small crack in the leather, and Arris did not want it giving way in battle. The floor of the chariot was built with studs where the driver set the heels of his boots to brace himself. Those boots could be the difference between keeping your footing and losing the reins and your life.

It was a rare, clear day, and the central part of the camp was empty. The officers were out drilling their men, except for the captains of the Fengian garrison, who were leading raiding parties to the east. It had been quiet since Arris had come here, dismissed while General Iyon sought a few hours of sleep.

Iyon drove himself hard, up all night almost every night with his closest advisors, plotting the campaign. Arris suspected that Iyon was afraid. Not afraid of losing the war, but afraid of commanding some action that was not brilliant, not perfect. He had a reputation as a strategist that was based on his skill at putting down province uprisings in the distant parts of the Empire, and leading border raids into the Khalifate in the uneasy years that had led up to the invasion. Now he would be tested, and he desperately did not want to fail the Emperor.

A scream rose in the still, quiet air, rose like an eagle's shriek and then stopped. Arris threw down his work and sprang out the door. That was a death scream, he thought, glancing from side to side as he ran toward the sound. Guards were posted at the General's tent, and were scattered around the officers' camp, but they could not leave their places. They drew their swords, shouting for someone to investigate.

Arris heard more shouting, cries of pain and fury, and then the clash of steel, at the western edge of the camp below the sheltering hills. Other men were running there from all parts of the camp. They held lances and bare swords. Arris realized he had drawn his own short black sword, the Jai-Sohn blade Iyon had given him. He was running with it balanced loosely in his hand, ready to cut down whatever danger sprang into his path.

The earth was dust beneath his running feet, and dust was kicked up ahead of him into a cloud that stung his eyes. The battle sounds had ended almost as quickly as they had begun, and now there was only the confusion of shouting and running men. Arris saw Mentes, lithe and broad-shouldered, springing like a deer in his high-heeled driving boots. He hailed the charioteer, who swerved to run with him.

"What is it?" Arris panted.

"One man dead, at least," Mentes said grimly. "You heard the scream."

They ran together into the crowd that was gathering, and pushed to the fore past bigger men. A man was sobbing. He had a cut down the right side of his face that had severed an eye, and tears and blood ran down between his hands where he clutched his face. There were two men dead that Arris could see. One was a Deirani sentry with a crossbow bolt in his chest. His mouth was still open with the last of his scream. The other was blond and heavily muscled, with a stern, young face that reminded Arris of his brother Falcmet. He lay on the rocky ground at the bottom of the hill, curled around himself, still bleeding from half a dozen sword wounds, though he was dead.

Another blond man, this one bearded and older, crouched with his hands behind his head. A Deirani soldier held a spear to his neck. Crossbow bolts were stuck like a clerk's quills in the Khalifate man's belt, but Arris did not see his weapon.

"You! Iyon's boy!" A sergeant called out, waving to Arris with a bloody sword in his hand. "You speak their language, don't you?"

Arris sheathed his own black sword and walked forward. "Yes, sir. What happened?" Mentes followed at his heels, taking the opportunity to get closer to the scene.

"What does it look like?" The sergeant was enraged, and his peasant accent was hard to understand. "These two were skulking in the hills, and they shot Halkir. I heard him scream and came round the corner, and there were the pair of them running like wolves into the camp."

"Gods know what they meant to do," Mentes said wonderingly. "Only two of them, and in the middle of the day."

"A good time for such an attack, when no one expects them," Arris said. "And this part of the camp is mostly deserted at midday. They must have been watching yesterday at least to know that."

"That's what you need to ask him," the sergeant interrupted angrily. "What he was doing, what his orders were, who sent him."

Arris looked down at the prisoner, and the man's blue eyes met his, blue like shards of ice. "Who are you?" Arris asked in the Khalifate language. "Whose man?"

The prisoner blinked in the sunlight and did not answer. From the expression in his eyes, Arris thought that it would take a lot to make the man speak.

"Ask him if there are any more up there," said a man in the crowd nervously.

"Send someone for General Iyon," Arris said, feeling as weary as if he had been involved in the fighting himself. "He'll want to be present at this man's questioning."

The sergeant might have preferred to torture his prisoner where he was, but he saw the sense in Arris's words. He called for other spearmen, and three of them jerked the Khalifate man to his feet and prodded him away toward the center of the camp. The wounded Deirani man was led away by friends toward the healers' tents midway down the valley. Arris reluctantly followed the captured man. He had not yet found his duties as Iyon's aide very difficult, but he thought that the time had come.

CHAPTER
13

TERAI SAT with Captain Yehane at a table in the crowded tent. His face taut with barely controlled emotion, Terai bent over a piece of parchment with a quill pen. He was acting as a translating scribe, writing down the Khalifate man's screams in the equivalent Deirani when they were coherent at all. Arris stood at General Iyon's shoulder, sick with disgust and anger, repeating Iyon's endless, cold questions in the language of the man's screams.

Arris had seen Iyon work the knives himself once, when the old Khopei Overlord, Peroyu, had been accused of conspiring to assassinate the Emperor. This time, the General directed a thin, pop-eyed man named Duro who looked like a clerk and whose hands moved with unerring precision, cutting, pinching, burning, but keeping the prisoner alive and conscious. Corporal Berisi, who had been prepared to whip Arris at the hill-fort, acted as the torturer's assistant.

The Khalifate man talked, after his initial resistance was broken. There had been five men in his party, and they were not merely local peasants fighting back against their oppressors. They were the advance scouts of the Khalifate army, sent to investigate the unbelievable reports that Deiran had invaded at last.

After General Iyon had sent a page to order men to search the hills for the other three Khalifate spies, the ordeal continued. The bearded man spoke of the confusion in Trevena Province and the city of Ummass. Messages had been sent to the Citadel, and to the bureaucrats in

Khessard, but no one knew if they had been received. The last this man had heard, the Consulate noblemen had still been arguing over the election of a new Regent. The priest Karillos was favored by many, but the Regent Nievan's widow, the Lady Oella, led a strong faction against him. There were those who feared the power the Temple would gain if the Qadasiya high priest became the ruler of the Khalifate. And Karillos was not of the Ilkharani blood. There were various cousins, and even men of bastard lines of descent, who had a claim to rule for Prince Saresha.

Meanwhile, there was unrest in the provinces. The army had not been paid in a month. Local nobles had suddenly raised taxes with no authority from the central government. The army commanders were doing their best to respond to the Deirani threat, and troops were gathering in Trevena Province to march on the invaders, but none of the generals had any real authority to act. Their commissions had to be renewed by the new Regent before they could lawfully command troops in battle. The mass of the Khalifate army was in the Gharin Emirate, at the garrison at Khessard or at Rillath where the ships were being built to attack Deiran from the sea.

The account was pieced together bit by bit by General Iyon's relentless questions. The poor spy fell unconscious after a quarter of an hour, and could not be revived. Iyon had gotten the information he wanted, though, and he was quite pleased with it. He ordered the Khalifate man put to death then and there, an act of mercy under the circumstances.

With the screaming ended, Arris felt adrift in silence. The General spoke quietly to Captain Yehane, and glanced at Terai's scrawled notes. He ordered Terai to write them up into a coherent sequence and have them ready in an hour for a meeting of all the division and wing commanders. Arris was told to find Lieutenant Ebreyu, and between the two of them, they were to summon the commanders to meet outside the General's tent in one hour.

Arris caught Terai's eyes as he moved to obey his orders. The older Yaighan looked as if he had felt all the pain himself, and Arris almost expected to see blood seeping through Terai's clothing. He wondered if Terai had somehow been mentally open to the Khalifate man's suffering. The priests of Gama had that ability, but what good would it have done either Terai or the dead man? Or perhaps Terai had simply been unable to shut out the overwhelming agony. Either way, he looked utterly exhausted, drawn, gray, and old.

"Will you be all right?" Arris muttered, leaning over him as he passed the table.

Terai nodded, and waved him on. "The choice we made," he whispered in Yaighan, so low that even Arris was not certain of the words.

Lieutenant Ebreyu had command of the second wing of Iyon's elite light cavalry. Three hundred men and horses, they wheeled and danced as if windblown across the dusty field where they were drilling. Arris had taken a lively, fast bay gelding from the officers' stable, which had been the farmer's cattle barn. He galloped the horse up behind the wing's formation, as the front line of Ebreyu's men swept by a group of straw targets and skewered them with javelins.

"Lieutenant!" Arris shouted. He had to repeat his call several times before someone in the line noticed and pointed him out to their commander. Wearing only a leather uniform, with no helmet, Ebreyu was a dashing, romantic figure on his wild-eyed black horse. His hair blew freely in the wind, and Arris felt a fierce regret that they had only had four nights as lovers, before they somehow became enemies.

Ebreyu ordered one of his sergeants to take command of the drill, and pulled his horse expertly out of the formation. A few men turned their heads to watch him curiously, but the sergeant shouted for them to continue the exercise, and they obeyed.

"What is it?" the Lieutenant demanded, reining in his black horse with a flourish that startled Arris's gelding into laying its ears back and rearing a little off the ground.

"The General's orders," Arris said. "He wants a meeting of all division and wing commanders who can be found, one hour from now in front of his tent. You and I are supposed to tell them."

"I'm a wing commander myself," Ebreyu said, quick to take offense. "I'm not an errand boy."

Arris glared at him. "General Iyon told me to find you, and I've done that. You can take the southern part of the valley and I'll take the northern."

"What am I supposed to tell them about this meeting?"

"We captured a Khalifate spy, and he had a lot of information to give us. I think . . ." Arris hesitated. "I think we may be moving out soon. Two of the spies may have escaped. If they got away, their commanders will know where we are. And it sounds as if the Khalifate army is in no condition to face us yet."

"That's all speculation," Ebreyu said. "Your opinion."

"Just tell them we captured a spy," Arris said. He saluted, and turned his horse to gallop away toward the northern half of the valley. Glancing back, he saw Ebreyu wheeling toward the south. Why did he have to make even the simplest exchanges between them a matter of argument and insult? Ebreyu could not be polite even when they were both with the General, even after Iyon's orders the night Arris and Terai had been brought in.

Well, he could do nothing to change the Lieutenant's opinion of him, unless he changed his past, and who he was now. Arris shrugged off his irritation. He was glad for the fresh air, after the screams and the reek of blood in the interrogation tent. The horse was a pleasure to ride, eager and fast, with a smooth gait. He urged it over a bare hedge, and galloped toward the flat expanse where the charioteers were practicing with their teams.

The meeting of the officers lasted on into the evening. Arris stood behind General Iyon, in a line with the other aides. After hearing what the tortured spy had had to say, all agreed that the time had come to strike. The disagreement was as to where.

Some of the captains were for a siege of Ummass, to establish a base of operations near the Westrange roads that were the army's line of supply. Other officers argued that the Deirani army should strike at the heart of the Khalifate now, before their army could unite. They said that the time would never be better for an assault on the Citadel itself. With the nobles, the various candidates for Regent, and the Prince and the other Ilkharani killed, the Khalifate would be theirs.

Iyon listened with interest to all the proposed plans of action, and scrawled diagrams on pieces of parchment that made little sense to Arris. When all had had their say, he thanked them for their advice. "But I remind you," he said in his soft courtier's voice, "that a full one-third of our forces are still to join us. The Emperor himself will be leading them. I think you will agree that the prize of the Citadel should fall only by the Sacred One's own hand."

"But how long will it be before he arrives?" one of the eager captains demanded. "The Khalifate could have their Regent, and their army could be ready to face us, by the time the Emperor crosses the mountains."

"We should establish the siege of Ummass, and wait for him," said a middle-aged general sagely.

"Once again, that would give the Khalifate army time to form itself under leaders with authority from the Citadel." Iyon shook his head, smiling slightly. Arris thought that he had known what he would do from the beginning, that he had known while the spy was still screaming and Arris was trying to translate the cries into Deirani words. "I say we force them to meet us now, on our terms. Force them to march down into the plains south of Ummass, and meet us in pitched battle. We will defeat them decisively. From that point, we have all the time we need to take the Citadel and the other cities of the Khalifate."

Lieutenant Ebreyu spoke up, a little nervously, as he was one of the most junior officers among the wing commanders. "Another problem with taking the Citadel now, my lords, is that by avoiding this Khalifate army in Trevena Province, we will leave them to form up behind us, and cut off our lines of communication and supply. We might find ourselves besieged behind the Citadel walls in our turn."

"I wonder how we think to take the Citadel at all, Khalifate army or no," muttered the commander of one of the infantry division. "It is said to be completely invulnerable to siege."

The meeting degenerated into arguments over the practical problems of siegecraft, until Iyon told the commanders quietly that he had made up his mind. They would break camp tomorrow, and head for the fertile lands of the southern part of Trevena Province, cutting as wide a swathe of destruction as they could. The Khalifate army could not ignore them, and would have to come to meet them. They would destroy them.

Iyon dismissed the commanders to gather their troops and give the orders to break camp. He retired to his tent, as cheerful as Arris had seen him in all the years he had known him. The young officers' aides went to follow their commanders, leaving Arris and Terai in front of the General's tent with the door guards.

Terai walked a little distance away with Arris. His face was still lined from the afternoon's experience, and Arris meant to ask him why he had suffered so from watching the spy's torture. But Terai spoke first. "An interesting man, your General. A man to accomplish what he sets out to do."

Arris shrugged. "Perhaps."

"And he is only the hound to your Emperor Hareku. We may have allied ourselves to the winning side in this affair."

"I would rather be allied to no one."

"There are things the Yaighan can learn from these men, Hareku and Iyon. If the Millennium is ever launched, the Goddess freed, we will need a strong general for our Yearking."

Arris turned on him and spoke in a voice that was low and filled with fury. "Is *that* why you think I'm here? To learn something I'll need to know as Yearking?"

"The Goddess rarely acts without a reason." Terai seemed unaffected by his anger, but he spoke quietly to keep from being overheard by any nearby soldiers.

"The Goddess has no hand in any of this," Arris said. "She is trapped on another plane of the world, inside the Temple with the body of her Lady to keep her company."

"She is trapped, as you say," Terai said with a cold look in his dark eyes. "But I wonder if you can do anything that is not a part of the role you were born to fill.''

"Don't speak to me of destiny again. I won't listen.''

"It matters little whether you listen or not. The pattern is there without your knowing it.''

Arris could not let himself believe that. All that he had done to escape the Goddess could not have been a part of her plan. "You're wrong. I am free of her, and I wish I were free of you. Leave me alone, Terai.''

"As you will.'' Terai turned and walked away from him without argument. He obeyed Arris's wishes sometimes as if Arris were a prince, or the Yearking. Arris watched him go, still angrier because Terai had not responded to his anger. Finally he stalked away to the stables to tend his chariot team. He would have to drive them tomorrow when the camp became an army on the march. He thrust Terai's words from his mind as he groomed the horses and checked over their harness.

They marched out a few hours after dawn. Leaving a single division of one thousand men to hold the hill camp and guard the stores of supplies, General Iyon led his troops along narrow farm roads away from the foothills toward the east. Like a black snake jeweled with bright banners and painted chariots, the army of nineteen thousand coiled and twisted in the dust through the ravaged land. The sun shone on pike blades and enameled helmets, and on the faces of men who shared a fierce eagerness for the first real battle in the long-delayed war.

Arris squinted in the sunlight, his whole body jarred with the vibrations of the chariot, his arms and shoulders already tense from holding two spirited warhorses to a jog-trot. General Iyon stood behind him in the warrior's place. Most of his officers had chosen to ride horseback, but Iyon knew he made an impressive figure leading the column in the chariot. He wore the same black ringmail and leather as his soldiers, but with a red cloak and a red plume in his helmet to be easily seen in battle. He held onto one of the warrior's straps with a light grip, his other hand resting on his leg. He swayed with the motion of the chariot, as well balanced as an acrobat, his expression supremely confident.

Iyon was uninterested in conversation. Arris did not try to talk to him. He concentrated on controlling his team, and watched the land to right and left of the track in a kind of bleak fascination. Mile after mile of ruined land passed by; blackened pastures, burnt orchards, farmsteads reduced to ash and a few timbers, or piles of collapsed turf. Though he knew that the scouts would report any movement, Arris half expected to see a Khalifate force come shouting down from behind a grove of dead trees. If the captured Khalifate scout had told the truth, there should be nothing to fear. But there was a large garrison at the city of Ummass, no more than a day and a half to the north. Surely they had heard by now that a brutal enemy laid waste to their lands. And the earth might echo farther than Ummass with the tramp of the Deirani men and beasts.

Two divisions from Khopei, under General Iyon's personal command, led the column with two thousand heavy cavalry, horses and riders, and one thousand chariots with a team and two men apiece. These men were veterans of province uprisings and border raids, well trained and well paid, intensely loyal to their commander. Behind the Khopei divisions came the levies that had been training at the border hill-fort, some career soldiers and some recent volunteers, six thousand men balanced in a division each of cavalry and infantry. Lieutenant Ebreyu's horsemen were among them. Many of these soldiers were men with families. They were determined to win land and position for themselves in the war.

Behind the infantry division, in the protected center of the column, came the trains of pack mules, the supply wagons, a herd of captured cattle, and an attendant array of cooks, grooms, engineers, and carpenters. General Iyon might have a reputation as a daring man in battle, but he was not reckless when it came to the necessities to support his troops. The army had been living off the land, and meant to continue to do so, but they carried five days of food for men and horses nonetheless.

Behind the last of the supply wagons rode General Luo,

a forty-year-old warrior from the western plains. He led four thousand light horsemen, archers, and javelin slingers from the plains tribes. The plainsmen were herders, and occasionally raiders, on the high plateaus of the far western Empire. Some of Iyon's early campaigns had been against them. They held themselves aloof from the Sapphire Palace, but they were a part of the Empire, and they were eager to share in its expansion. Their gods were a fierce lot that demanded blood sacrifice, akin to the Crimson Goddess and equally condemned by the more civilized religions of Deiran. Arris did not fear an arrow in the back from one of the warriors' short horn bows; the Brothers Ylla would not be able to recruit assassins among Luo's people.

Behind Luo's troops marched the eastern city garrisons, two thousand men, a mixture of conscripts and professional soldiers that General Iyon considered his weakest division. Mostly infantry, trained by a few months of drill in farmers' fields, the conscripts could wield spears well enough, and they were kept in a semblance of disciplined order through fear of their officers. They marched beneath city banners; Arris had recognized those of Buval and Guelan.

Holding the rear guard was the heavy cavalry of the Fengian garrison, three thousand men in independent squadrons of fifty each. The soldiers of Feng were elite troops, loyal first to the Emperor, then to their squadron sergeants. Only the best young men and the fiercest warhorses were accepted into their ranks, and no soldier who had served in any other division was ever allowed to join them. General Iyon had begun his career at the Fengian garrison. He prized them highly, and deferred to the opinions of the garrison captain, Rais, more than to any other of his officers.

Arris was careful of Captain Rais, remembering that the man had wanted to kill him when he and Terai had been captured on the Westrange road. Lieutenant Ebreyu had ridden with him, and Rais knew that Arris was an accused traitor. The Captain had not spoken against Iyon's judgment in the case, but Arris sometimes felt the man's cool eyes on him, watchful for any suspicious act.

The sunlight made stark shadows in the clefts of the rolling hills, and the winter grass of the pastures was brown where it had not been charred by raiders. All was quiet except for the steady steps of soldiers and horses, the creaking of chariot wheels and leather, the occasional call of all clear that was passed from sergeant to sergeant down the long, winding column.

Arris could not share in the anticipation that the army felt. He could not desert, at peril of his life, but he rode toward a greater betrayal. He might hate the Khalifate and its gods, but each battle won would be a step closer to the Citadel, where Saresha waited. A Deirani victory would cost the Prince his kingdom and his life. Arris found himself hoping that he drove his chariot toward defeat so final that it would send the Deirani back over the Westrange in harried flight, not to invade again for at least another generation.

The first day passed without incident, and the army camped at dusk. Spread over the heights of three flat-topped hills, the campfires made lines of smoke like cobwebs against the night sky. A sacked village, the third they had passed, nestled silent and dark in the valley below the hills. They had come twenty-eight miles that day, and tomorrow would find them in farmland beyond the range of their earlier foraging raids.

Arris's hands shook at the end of weak-muscled arms by the end of the day's long journey. He was not in condition to drive a chariot for eight hours with little rest. He spent an hour before dinner watering, feeding, and grooming his team, then he left the horses picketed and went to rejoin General Iyon in the Khopei divisions' camp.

The General sat cross-legged on the ground before a large fire, alone except for Terai and two guards who stood a few paces distant. Both men were deep in conversation, eating from a roasted chicken while they scratched and poked at the earth with their knives. Arris answered the guards' challenge, and Iyon and Terai looked up at him.

"Arris." Terai seemed unusually cheerful. "Come, have

a look at this. You know the lay of the land here as well as I do."

The map he had drawn in the dirt was hard to see in the firelight, but Arris could make out the shapes of hills and the sweeping curve of the River Majeha where it met the Khessi and doubled back on itself to the south. Iyon stuck his knife into the earth at a point just above the river forks, and glanced up at Arris, his face lean and handsome in the shadows. His lips curved into a near smile.

"There." He rocked the hilt of the knife with two fingers, and orange light reflected from the blade. "I think we'll meet them there."

Arris crouched beside him to look at the rough-drawn map, as if it would reveal new details to a sharper gaze. "I've ridden through there with the Khalifate Prince's Companions. I remember grassy hills, and some dense stands of forest. There are marshes nearer the river."

Iyon nodded. "But here, where the knife point touches, Terai says there are broad meadows, high enough to be firm ground."

"And the hills are on the western side," Terai said. "Nothing but fields and meadows to the east and north, and the rivers to the south. A town ten miles north, but too small to have fortifications."

"The Khalifate army will have nothing to hold to, no place to establish a good position. We'll command the heights." Iyon broke the back of the fowl's carcass and handed half of what was left to Arris. "If we fight well, we can drive them south into the marshes, drown them in the Khessi. And follow them another fifty miles to the Citadel, if we like."

"You'd leave the Ummassid garrison at your back, and the Emperor yet to arrive," Terai reminded him.

Iyon pulled a stick from the fire and stared at its glowing end. "I know. Still, it would be a great deed, to plunge straight for their heart and end the war in a matter of a few weeks." He laughed softly, and waved the burning stick at Arris. "Go on, get to bed. I don't need you for anything. You look like one of the walking dead."

Arris would have been interested in hearing more of the

General's battle plans, but he could not argue with Iyon's observation. He saluted and left the two men there. He heard them laugh at something as he walked away. Terai seemed to be enjoying himself. Arris supposed he had no reason not to. Terai would not be expected to fight in the battle, and he had no qualms about its outcome; he had been working against the Khalifate for thirty years for what it had taken from the Yaighan people.

Terai was still the Goddess's servant, Arris had decided. Arris knew him too well to believe he had really changed the convictions of a lifetime for the sake of friendship. Terai had as much as admitted it yesterday, with his talk of patterns being fulfilled. Arris no longer resented him for it, but he was resolved not to trust Terai too far.

The Deirani aides had spread their blanket rolls near the fires of the commanders, but few of them were sleeping yet. They sat together and spoke of women they had known, of their families and the places where they had grown up, of their eagerness for the battle. Most were frightened, Arris guessed. Few of the noble youths had ever gone along on any raids, and they had no experience of warfare back in Deiran. They had their weapons training, and what they had read and heard from other soldiers. But Arris doubted that any of them had ever killed a man. In that, at least, he was a veteran.

Arris burrowed into his blankets with his cloak on top of him. It was cold on the hilltop, away from the fires. The sun had warmed the day enough to almost make him forget it was winter. The nervous boasting of the young soldiers was as meaningless as the wind, and the ground where Arris lay was cushioned by dry meadow grass and free of stones. He ate his piece of chicken, and was soon asleep.

CHAPTER
14

ARRIS WOKE, wide-eyed, out of a dream of burning temples. He heard footsteps approaching, softly rustling in the dry grass of the hilltop. Though it might be a sentry, Arris feared another assassin from the Brothers Ylla. He reached out of his blanket roll with his right hand and grasped the hilt of his sword where it lay on the ground beside him. The short black blade made no sound as he slipped it from its sheath. It was a Jai-Sohn weapon, meant for silent killing. Sooner or later, Arris thought, the Khalifate gods would send a Jai-Sohn after him, and he would be killed.

He lay on his back, holding the sword against his cloak, where it did not show even as a faint outline in the starlight. The air was cold, and he could see his breath. Around him, the officers' aides slept muffled in their blankets. A hundred sentries were posted around the perimeter of the hilltops, and outriders circled in the quiet valley. No one had seen a need to keep watch here in the center of the camp.

A shadowy figure moved toward him, blocking out the stars in the night sky. Arris sat up slowly, noiselessly, freeing both arms and lifting his weapon. He saw a gleam of teeth, a smile, and then he heard a whisper that was almost unvoiced.

"You're awake. Good. Put on your cloak and come with me."

It was Iyon. Arris sheathed his sword, still moving soundlessly. He folded down his blankets, and pulled on his boots and his cloak, buckling the black sword onto its harness so that it rested between his shoulder blades. Glancing around at the sleeping aides, he saw one glint of half-opened eyes watching. Finally, the confirmation they had needed for what they believed about Arris and the General. Arris scowled and followed Iyon back toward the small camp tent that had been pitched for the Commander.

There was a sentry posted at the front of the tent, but Iyon touched Arris on the shoulder and motioned him to go around to the back. Arris shrugged, and dropped into a crouch, moving as Iyon had taught him, scarcely rippling the grasses. In a few heartbeats he knelt at the back flap of the General's tent. He heard Iyon dismiss the sentry, saying that he might as well sleep, there was no danger tonight.

When the man had gone, Iyon untied the flap and let Arris in. The tent was not tall enough for a man to stand upright. Iyon's bed had not been slept in yet. Beside it on the floor of thick felt a sheaf of parchment had been weighted down with stones, and a shrouded candle gave just enough light to see what was drawn on the top sheet. It was a diagram of the southern wall of the Citadel, with close-written notes on everything from sentry patterns to the age of the mortar that held the stones in place. Arris had sent it to Iyon a year ago, smuggling it out of the Citadel on a pleasure trip to Qadasiya. He had left it with the old Yaighan woman Ruena to pass along the network of Deirani sympathizers to the border.

Iyon sat down cross-legged in front of the diagrams as Arris closed the tent flap and tied it loosely to keep the wind from lifting it. "You couldn't sleep?" Arris asked, sitting across from Iyon. He felt the man's dark eyes on him like heat against his skin, and the tent felt far too small and close. He was annoyed at his own nervousness. It was almost five years since the last time Arris had trembled before the General, waiting for the pain and humiliation that would give Iyon pleasure. He had been a boy then, and a slave.

"I've been looking at these. The rumors of the Citadel do not exaggerate. It will be near impossible to take it by assault." He frowned, leaning over the drawing. His smooth black hair shone in the faint light, and his face reminded Arris of a cat's, narrow and beautiful, keeping its secrets. "But I can do it if any man can. I would like to take it now, and let the Emperor ride south to see his banners already flying from the towers."

"You told the division commanders that would be disloyal."

"Yet the decision is mine, and it might even please him."

Arris shook his head, thinking how strange the young aides would find this conversation. The General was speaking to him like an equal, and the bed was unused. It seemed strange to Arris, too. "I think he would be angered. This is a personal war with him. The Khalifate army he could leave to you, but the Ilkharani and their Citadel he'll want to take himself. He still remembers that assassin."

Iyon raised one eyebrow, and his lips quirked slightly. "You and I both know that the Ilkharani never sent that Jai-Sohn girl. It was the Overlord Peroyu's own initiative. The man was no martyr, to hold his secrets to the grave. He would have confessed under torture if he had been in league with the Khalifate."

Arris stared at him. "You knew that then? You put the Khalifate Ambassador to the question, and had all his companions slain, and his body drawn and quartered on the city gate of Khopei with Peroyu's."

"By the Emperor's command," Iyon said.

"But you never told him you thought the Ambassador was innocent." Arris had faced Hareku's anger himself that morning, and had convinced him to spare the lives of Senna and his family among the Ambassador's party.

"He did not want to hear it." Iyon seemed vaguely amused. "You think you know the Emperor well, don't you, Arris? You shared his bed, and most of his secrets. But there are parts of him you never saw, or never admitted to seeing. He has wanted this war since I first knew him." Iyon drew his knees up to his chest and clasped his hands around them, silent for a moment. "I have had his trust for fifteen years. And for the first two of those years,

I had more than that." He looked up at Arris almost in challenge. "I was a nobleman's son, and he wanted it kept quiet. I don't think anyone ever suspected. I used his favor to get my assignment to the Feng garrison, and my promotions came through quickly. People assumed it was because of my family name."

Arris could only stare at him. He had never guessed that Hareku and Iyon might have once been lovers. Now he understood the way Iyon always spoke with the Emperor; respectfully, but without the deference or the caution of the other courtiers. It was not difficult in the darkness of the tent to see the face of the boy Iyon must have been, a flawless face that would have shamed any in the harem. A face much like Arris's at the age of fifteen; and at thirty, Arris might well look like Iyon did now. If he managed to live that long. The thought was strangely chilling.

The General rubbed his eyes fiercely with the back of his hand. "I don't know why I told you that," he muttered. "Too long without sleep. You won't repeat it to anyone, do you understand?"

Arris nodded warily. "Yes, sir."

"There are people it would hurt, after all this time. The Princess Kakima, for one. I mean to marry her. I don't want her to know I was once her father's lover."

"I've told her worse things about you," Arris said, immediately regretting the words. He habitually spoke with the General the same way Iyon did with the Emperor. At least when they were alone, it was impossible to be deferential to a man he knew so intimately. It was a risky way to act, with Iyon.

"And so she probably thinks I will tie her up, and beat her, and force her to do countless unpleasant things." He looked ruefully at Arris. "Do you know, I cannot imagine that sort of night with Kakima. She is so little, so fragile, I'd be afraid of breaking her." He ran a hand through his short-cropped hair, and lowered his gaze to the Citadel drawing and the guttering candle. "We . . . were discussing whether I should lead my troops to take the Citadel."

"Whether the Emperor would be pleased, or angry,"

Arris said, relieved that Iyon chose to force a turn in the conversation.

"Yes. It may be a useless argument. If I were to attempt it, Hareku would probably arrive with his army to find me still encamped in the forest, unable to even cross the moat . . ." The General paused. "Unless . . . unless we can plan another way to bring down those walls, besides direct assault. Infiltration would be better than rams, and enough Jai-Sohn in the Citadel could take out sentries and open gates in one moonless night's work."

"That's what we're training the scouts to do? They can't learn enough in the time we have." Iyon was a good Jai-Sohn master, and Arris his best student, but no one could create a Black Sword in a matter of a few weeks.

"All they have to do is get inside the walls, and kill as many as possible, as silently as they can." Iyon's voice was cold. "They need not get back out alive, and that is the hardest part of the Shadowed Way."

"I will not lead men on such a mission."

"You had no such moral qualms when you murdered the Regents. Such actions are necessary in war."

"I did not want to be a part of your war," Arris said bitterly.

"Then desert to the Khalifate army," said Iyon with scorn. "And face trial for your crimes. There are only two sides, Arris. Choose this one, and you can at least fight with honor."

"I will fight," Arris said, getting to his feet to leave. He had to bend almost double in the low tent. "But I will not lead a suicide mission."

"I would expect you to find a way back out of the Citadel alive." The General did not seem angry. "We'll speak of this again. In the meantime, I want you to think about this question. How could the scouts get inside, and where should they attack to best effect? I'll expect a report in a few days." He cupped his hands and blew out his candle, so that no one passing by would see Arris's silhouette as he crept out of the tent. "Good night."

The next day the army began to march through land where

no raiders had gone. The people had heard of their coming, though, and the farms and villages were abandoned. It was useless to try to set fire to the silent buildings, since the intermittent rain that darkened the day would put out the flames before much damage could be done. Outriders went through each house and barn to be sure they were empty of people and animals, but the column marched on down the easterly roads.

Terai rode in the ranks of mounted officers, a few rows back. Arris had not spoken with him since he had been so angry two days ago. Tonight, he thought, he would seek Terai out and camp with him. The Yaighan might be the Goddess's man, but he was his friend as well. And his company would be preferable to the unfriendly glares of the young officers' aides. This morning one of them had asked Arris outright if he had served the General well last night.

The gray morning did not clear, and it was raining steadily in the early afternoon when the outriders rode back to the column. They reported a large town ahead, stuffed to the walls with refugees from the countryside, and guarding the bridge across the River Majeha. It was the best place to cross the river for miles, and the river had to be crossed to reach the forks where Iyon meant to wait for the Khalifate army.

Iyon ordered the column to halt. The command was relayed back over the mile and a half of marching men. They stopped where they were, and waited in the rain. Iyon and his officers gathered at the front of the army.

"We can take the town," said Captain Ganiz, the commander of one of the Khopei divisions. He was a burly man a little older than Iyon, with a broad face pocked by some childhood disease. He belonged to a noble city family related to Ebreyu's, but he was uncomfortable at court and was rarely seen at the Sapphire Palace. "We should put them all to the sword."

"Yes, and let a few escape to spread terror through the land," the reconnaissance commander Yehane said.

"How many people are in the town?" Iyon turned to Terai. "Do you know anything about this place?"

At the back of the clump of officers, Terai held his horse's reins and leaned against the animal's shoulder. "It's probably a town called Oroci," he said. "Ten thousand inhabitants, and I'd guess another three or five thousand refugees. There will be a small garrison of troops, no more than a few hundred."

General Iyon shook his head. "The assault might last only a few hours, but it would take days to ferret them all out of their houses and hiding places. No. We won't sack the town. But I want to control it. The bridge, and the stores of food they'll have. We'll frighten them into a surrender. Relay these orders." He paused for only a moment. "Supply wagons and noncombatants are to stay here, guarded by Captain Riman's conscript infantry. All other divisions will draw up in battle formation on the western side of town. Chariots front and center, cavalry on the wings, infantry behind the chariots."

One of the aides asked, "Which divisions on which wings, Commander?"

Iyon shrugged. "The captains can choose. There isn't going to be a battle." The aides saluted him and rode off with the orders. Iyon turned to the nearest officers. "Captain Ganiz, Captain Yehane, spread the word to all the troops. When they let us into the town there will be no looting. They'll give us what we need without it. I'm going to give them guarantees of safety, and some gold for their lord and his friends. Who knows; I may even be able to buy their loyalty." He laughed as he climbed into the chariot behind Arris.

The hills had been growing less all day, and now as Arris drove over the next rise he could see the flatlands that spread along the riverbanks. Tangled, leafless trees grew in clumps in the valley and along the broad, silvery band of the Majeha. The town that Terai had called Oroci was a pretty little place, with walls of smooth stone, whitewashed houses, and red and blue tiled roofs. Surrounded by rich farmland, with a few acres of forest across the river that must be part of the lord's estate, Oroci looked completely peaceful.

"It would be a shame to see it destroyed," Arris said

over his shoulder as he urged his team to a fast trot on the valley slope. "The Emperor needs something to rule over when he commands the Khalifate."

General Iyon's red cloak blew out behind him in the rain, and he looked as confident as if he were getting ready to inspect his troops in the camp. "Yet they must fear us, if we're to control them. They must fear me. I have to be ruthless, so that by the time the Emperor takes the throne they will be grateful to him for bringing peace." He grinned suddenly. "Your horses are about to run away with us."

Arris turned quickly and took control just as the eager animals broke into a matched canter. The chariot teams were bred for speed and strength, for an overwhelming impact in a short charge. The slow pace and long hours of the march made the horses tired and frustrated. They tossed their heads and broke their stride raggedly, jolting the chariot and its riders off balance. Arris felt a hand on his back as Iyon steadied himself from falling forward.

The road was well kept, and even at a trot the chariot was moving quickly. Behind it, the army had begun to spread out away from the road, forming into wide ranks instead of the extended lines of the marching column. They would be upon the town gates soon at this pace.

"If I had the time, I would put it to the sword," Iyon said quietly. "But the Khalifate army may be moving south by now. We will be waiting for them, rested and eager for battle. If I let my troops loose in there today, the edge of their spirit would be dulled, and they would be burdened with plunder. I do not spare Oroci out of mercy."

"That motive did not enter my mind," Arris said with a slight smile.

Defiant and frightened men crowded the walls of the riverside town, watching as the heralds they had sent came riding back from their meeting with the Deirani General. The heralds had stammered out a demand from their Lord Jasid that the invading army leave his domain at once. General Iyon had answered them seriously and respectfully, and Arris had translated his words with the same expression. He had said that he meant no harm to the people of Oroci, and if they would agree to supply his troops with safe passage across the river, and as much grain, vegetables, and livestock as could be spared, he would consider them as neutral allies and leave them in peace. Obviously very relieved, the heralds had said that they could not speak for their lord, but they would urge him to agree to these quite reasonable terms.

In the end, the nervous Lord Jasid came out to meet with General Iyon himself. With the exchange of solemn vows, and a gift of five hundred gold pieces to Jasid for his trouble and the supplies he was to provide, the order was given to open the gate of the town and let the Deirani army pass through. The supply wagons and Captain Ramin's infantry were sent for, and they took up their usual place in the center of the column.

In triumphant procession Arris drove the General at the head of the divisions. They moved slowly through the narrow, rain-slick streets of the Khalifate town. The people stared from rooftops and windows. Iyon's troops stared back at them, marveling at the pale, blond inhabitants in their turbans and heavy robes, and the women whose eyes showed above thick veils. There were peasant refugees in the town square and in the small, forested parks, and those watched the Deirani in fear and hatred.

Lord Jasid dispatched his garrison of Khalifate soldiers—unarmed, out of courtesy to the invaders—throughout the city to gather the stores and animals Iyon had requested. New wagons were added to the supply ranks, and laden mules fell in with the pack trains.

Just before the Majeha bridge stood the beautiful Temple of Oroci, a dome between two minarets, set in a garden with a low wrought-iron fence dividing it from the street. Gold-robed priests had gathered in the forecourt to watch the Deirani pass. Most of the younger novices and the priests' slaves pressed up against the fence to stare.

Lord Jasid, who had chosen to ride beside General Iyon's chariot, indicated the Temple with a wave of one hand. "Would the noble Deirani lord pay homage to the gods of my people?" he asked, his voice so blandly courteous that Arris could scarcely detect the tension behind it.

"He asks if you'd like to visit their Temple," Arris translated, not slowing the pace of the team. He had no wish to linger near a house of the Brothers Ylla.

Iyon shrugged, and smiled. He seemed to be enjoying the occasion. "Why not? Doubtless they'll have a shrine in Khopei before the year is out. This will be part of the Empire, and their gods will join ours." He waved to his standard-bearer, who rode just behind them. The Emperor's flag dipped in the signal for a halt.

Though he would have liked to disobey, Arris flicked the horses' reins once to warn them, then leaned back and brought them to a precise stop. They shivered a little in the rain, and flicked one another with their long tails.

Iyon put a hand on Arris's shoulder and said, "Pull them around and bring me up to the Temple gates. I'll let one of the priests bless me, and we'll be on our way again."

Arris urged the team into a prancing half circle, his face a mask that hid the shrinking he felt inside. All of a sudden, inevitably, an agile young novice vaulted the fence with a bare scimitar in his hands, and ran for the chariot. The horses snapped their teeth and kicked at him, but he dodged them and came straight toward Arris. His eyes were glazed with a familiar madness.

The Khalifate lord of the city jerked his horse out of the madman's way. The chariot blocked the aim of archers or javelin throwers. Arris turned to Iyon and said, "Take the reins." He handed them back before the General could protest.

Arris sprang to the shield-wall of the chariot, balancing with his boot heels hooked over the rim. His short black sword whispered out of its sheath into his hand, in time to meet the novice's slashing attack. Arris parried the scimitar down and kicked the gold-robed Khalifate youth in the face. No more than sixteen years old, the novice staggered back a step, lowering his guard. "When will your gods stop sending fools to kill me," Arris said savagely in the Khalifate language as he threw his Jai-Sohn sword into the novice's chest. He jumped down from the chariot after his weapon.

The blond youth fell with a stunned expression on his face, and the other priests and novices and slaves who had clustered at the fence fell back with cries of horror. Six cavalrymen of Captain Ganiz's troops spurred their mounts to leap over the iron fence. Their javelins found quick targets, and their swords flashed to either side as they galloped their horses into the Temple gardens. Arris heard Captain Ganiz shout that more of the priests might be armed, and for fifty more men to follow.

The Khalifate people who had been watching the procession ran into houses and alleyways, and Deirani soldiers began to follow, but General Iyon raised one arm with a great shout. "No! Only the priests!" The men's commanders called them back.

Lord Jasid had gone very white with fear, but he did not flee. He quieted his rearing horse and called, "General Iyon, you cannot hold my people responsible for one mad priest!"

Arris put a foot on the dead boy's chest and pulled his short sword out, while he repeated the Khalifate lord's words in the Deirani language for Iyon. The screams and the useless, garbled prayers of the priests sounded all through the gardens and inside the desecrated Temple, along with the angry shouts of the attacking Deirani. Arris turned his back on them and climbed up into the chariot.

General Iyon did not immediately hand him the reins again. He looked at Arris for a long moment, and spoke quietly. "It is a pity that the only people with courage in this place are the priests. You saved my life."

The novice probably had not even noticed General Iyon's presence in the chariot. He had seen only Arris, and his gods had told him to kill their enemy. Arris looked away from the warmth in Iyon's eyes, embarrassed. "He probably had never picked up a sword before in his life."

"Still, I thank you." Iyon turned sideways to let Arris pass him and take the team again. Arris held onto the reins tightly, staring at the horses' rumps ahead of him. He was trembling. Another soul sent to feed Aghlayeshkusa, and hundreds on their way to the Khalifate paradise, and he did not know how he could have prevented it. It was the darkness that followed him. If he had not been here, the Deirani army might have passed through Oroci without harming anyone.

"Your balance looked good on the shield-wall," Iyon said in his dry teacher's voice. "You could have held it in battle at a gallop. But if you had tried that kick with the chariot in motion you'd have landed on your head, or been spitted on someone's pike." He put a hand on Arris's shoulder again, and squeezed lightly. Then he raised his voice. "Captain Ganiz! Have your men fall in when they are finished. Let's move."

"What does he say?" called Lord Jasid in a quavering voice.

Arris glanced back at Iyon. "He wonders what you said." He trotted the chariot team around again and headed them for the front of the column.

"Tell him I am disappointed in his town," Iyon said with a thin smile, "but that only the priests will pay for their treachery. He need not fear. We seek only justice."

Arris repeated the words to the Khalifate lord, who urged his horse alongside the chariot. "Your justice is . . . harsh," Jasid said, looking sick from the slaughter. "But . . . I am sure it is . . . justified. I trust that you will keep your promise, and go in peace. None of your people has been harmed, after all. It was a regrettable incident."

"I am satisfied," General Iyon said as Arris translated. They led the Deirani army across the bridge of the Majeha and through the western part of the divided town. The people at that end stood on the ramparts of the walls to watch them go, no doubt immensely relieved that they still lived, and thinking the price not too great.

CHAPTER
15

THE BANNERS FLEW over the Deirani camp that night, illuminated by the countless campfires. They had ridden through inhabited country since they had crossed the Majeha, and had bypassed villages and small towns without disturbing them, and also without attempting to hide their presence. By now a hundred messengers would be riding from farms and villages, riding north and east to find the Khalifate army and beg them to come defend the people. That was what Iyon wanted. By midday tomorrow he would be at the site he had chosen for his battle. Tonight the army camped on the top of a bluff with the river at their backs a hundred feet below. It was not really a strong position, but they did not expect attack. There were sentries at intervals along a five-mile radius around the camp, on the wild chance that the Khalifate army might be much closer than they thought.

Carrying his blanket roll and gear, Arris finally found Terai in the scouts' camp, in earnest conversation with a plainsman sergeant about the best ways to spy out densely inhabited country. Terai thought the scouts should go on foot anywhere near farm buildings or villages or lords' manors. But he should have argued it with someone else; none of the western tribesmen would be parted from their horses.

Terai saw Arris, and nodded slightly. Arris found an open space some distance from the scouts' fires, and began clearing rocks from a flat spot for his blankets. When Terai still did not break off his conversation to join him,

Arris lay down with his hands behind his head and stared up at the clouded black sky. The moon was almost full, but the moving clouds across it cut it into fantastic shapes. These moonlit nights were the Goddess's most powerful time. Arris felt that she could see him as he lay there, and he felt almost guilty for defying her. He remembered how the Horned God had been unable to believe that Arris could refuse to do the Goddess's will.

"You're all right?" Terai was a dense shadow in the moonlight as he set his own blankets down and began to unroll them. "You weren't hurt in that attack this afternoon?"

Arris shook his head. "No."

"I couldn't see from where I was, but someone said you killed him almost at the first exchange. They thought he was trying to assassinate General Iyon. Do you think that's possible? I didn't feel any foreboding, any sense of danger at all, beyond the tension of riding through the hostile town." Terai sat down cross-legged and drank from a waterskin.

"He wasn't looking at Iyon. He was looking at me. He was another one of them, Terai. I saw his eyes."

"They will succeed sooner or later. You know that." Terai spoke simply, not trying to convince Arris of anything. "I can't protect you. I couldn't even have warned you about this one. I didn't feel anything. The priest was probably shielded."

"If he had power, he should have attacked me that way, not with a sword. He was just swinging blindly. It was like killing a child, a beginning student." Arris scowled up at the moonlit sky.

"If the sword was poisoned, he would only have needed to scratch you with one of those wild swings." Terai spoke in a voice so low Arris could scarcely hear it. "They'll kill you next time, or the time after that. You can't go on like this, Arris. Come with me, back to Gama."

"No!" Arris sat upright, facing him.

"Keep your voice quiet," Terai said, barely whispering. "You aren't escaping from anything, and you know it. The only way is to face what you have to do. Free the Goddess."

Arris laughed, quietly. "I meant to apologize to you tonight. I was sorry I got angry with you. But I will never go back there, Terai."

"I'm leaving," the older man said flatly. "I'm going back to Gama, to do what I can there. If you won't go with me, maybe I can find some other way to set the Goddess free of her Temple."

"They won't let you just come back," Arris said in scorn. "They'll kill you. You helped Saresha escape; you helped me escape. The only way they'd let you back is if you brought me with you, and I won't go. And what about your destiny, the things you said that night in the Westrange? You said you were supposed to stay with me."

"I was wrong. The Lossiran came to me last night in a dream."

"To you?" Arris stared at him.

"You renounced your power, but I never did. The Vulture can still speak to me. The Yaighan were ready for war, the Lossiran said, before the disaster on Winter Festival night. Now they have no vision at all, and half a dozen factions are fighting for control. With no Lady and no Yearking, they have no one to guide them. No one can speak with the Goddess, or get through the world-gate to the Temple at all. The power they built up over the centuries to give to the Goddess at the Millennium is circling in on itself like a maelstrom, and all the Yaighan will be destroyed by it if nothing is done to prevent it. They need a leader."

Arris felt ashamed, but it was not enough to make him want to go with Terai. "Then I hope you can help them," he said seriously.

"But you won't go back."

"To be Yearking? No."

"That's what our people need. Only the Yearking can lead them, and free the Goddess."

"Then offer yourself as Yearking," Arris said in frustration. "Rehoman wanted you before. She might take you again."

"It may come to that," Terai said, apparently serious.

Arris shook his head in disbelief. He lay back down

again and glared up at the moon. "Why do you care so much, Terai? Why is it so important? The Goddess is dark, and bloody, and cruel, no better than the Brothers Ylla, and probably worse. Why do you have to bring her back into the world? Why do you have to serve her above everything else? And don't tell me it's your destiny."

"You don't understand at all." Terai was not angry; he sounded sad. "She is the heart, Arris, the soul of this world. I was born to her service. So were you." He lay down in his rough bed, and was silent for a long time. Later, he said, "I'll leave during the battle. Find some dark-haired corpse and mutilate the face, and say you found me dead. That way no one will accuse you of helping me escape."

Arris spoke sleepily. "I'm . . . sorry I can't understand, or do what you want. I'll miss you, Terai."

"We'll meet again," Terai said. "If you survive."

Two days later Arris waited in his chariot with General Iyon, in the morning shadows of a green cleft between two rocky hills. The rest of the chariot division was crowded behind them, too close together for the horses or the drivers' nerves. The Deirani army was set back behind ridges, along the sides of steep defiles, between the arms of the jagged hills two miles north of the river forks where the Majeha and the Khessi met. Only the Fengian heavy cavalry under Captain Rais waited at the edge of the high meadows where they could easily be seen.

They had reached Iyon's chosen battleground yesterday, and reports had come at dawn of the Khalifate army approaching from the north. General Iyon sent Captain Ganiz with five hundred Khopei horsemen to find the enemy, attack them, and lure them to follow an apparent retreat. That was two hours ago. Scouts had come riding in ten minutes ago with reports that they had sighted Ganiz's men galloping toward the meadow with part of the Khalifate troops in immediate pursuit. The rest of the enemy was not far behind.

Arris had driven over the meadows for hours already in formation with the other chariots. A few ditches had been filled in, and one farmer's stone fence had been dismantled and moved to a defensive line halfway up the central hill. But in general the land was flat and did not hinder the chariots.

Terai had ridden off with a squadron of scouts, headed north toward the enemy. Arris did not think he would see his friend again, not for some time at least. The scouts would fight in some engagement, and Terai would vanish, or feign death so they would leave him behind. Then he would be on his way back to Gama. Arris had no doubt that he would get there, but he was not likely to accomplish much. Arris did not think the priestesses, the priests, or even the soldiers Terai had helped train would follow a man they would see as a traitor to the Goddess and his people.

It was a cool day, and the mist was thick on the meadows. The cavalry and infantry who were deployed on the hills would have a clearer view when their time came to enter the battle. General Iyon would rely on his best troops to protect him, and on his messengers to keep him informed about the overall battle, but Iyon was not the kind of commander who liked to wait and watch from some safe vantage point.

Iyon was armed with a Jai-Sohn short sword and a long cavalry sword, and twenty javelins were set like quills around the shield-walls of his chariot. In his black armor and red cloak, he looked fierce and handsome, and his confidence inspired his men to a tense, controlled eagerness that even Arris felt.

One of Yehane's scouts rode to Iyon's chariot on a small, agile messenger's horse. "Lieutenant Ebreyu reports that he's well hidden, sir, below the river bluffs. His horsemen will be ready for any of the enemy who try to get out that way."

Iyon nodded, holding onto the chariot as Arris calmed the restive horses. "He isn't happy with that assignment," Iyon said. "But he is my least experienced commander, and there will be other battles where he can lead the charges he dreams of."

Arris wished he was with Ebreyu's squadron, or anywhere but driving the Commander's chariot. The drivers were the most vulnerable of any in battle, and they were early targets of enemy pikemen; Arris wore only his leather harness and kilt, along with bronze guards for his fore-arms, a small breastplate, and a round iron cap. To wear full armor would hurt both balance and agility, and a more elaborate helmet would hinder vision.

Another messenger rode up with a report from General Luo, whose plainsmen were deployed on two northern hilltops. He wanted to charge as soon as the enemy was in sight, and throw their vanguard into confusion. Iyon curtly refused permission, and ordered the messenger back to Luo to tell him to charge when he received his orders, and no sooner.

A shout went up from the Fengian cavalry in the meadow. One of their standard-bearers rode by the cut where the chariots waited, and dipped his raven banner to tell Iyon that the riders had been sighted. They would be coming down the narrow strip of farmland at the north end of the meadow, between the hills and the marshes. The right wheel of Arris's chariot was jostled by a neighboring team that trotted forward restlessly while the driver leaned back, trying to pull them in. All along the line, the creaking of wheels and the whinnying of horses could be heard. Squad-ron sergeants barked orders to hold formation. Arris saw Mentes standing with his team under perfect control; they were a pair of matched bays, their heads and tails high in expectation.

Iyon called to his standard-bearer to be ready to signal the line to move. He sent the messengers back to the cen-tral command post, where Captain Yehane stood on a plat-form of timber and stone atop the highest of the stony hills.

"Now it begins," said the General quietly. He nodded to his standard-bearer. The Emperor's blue hawk banner swung back and forth, and a horn sounded from one of the hills. Arris leaned forward and let go the tight hold he had over the team. The two black horses trotted a few steps, then felt the reins flick over their backs and moved smoothly into a lope that drew the chariot behind them without a jolt. They drove out of the shadowed gap into the meadow.

The cool mist was like a light rain against Arris's face in the wind created by the chariot's speed. His knees were bent, absorbing the bouncing of the wooden wheels over the meadow grass. He could not see far ahead of his horses. The rest of the chariots rumbled behind him and General Iyon, and they formed into a line five ranks deep that stretched almost all the way across the southern end of the open land. Mentes led his squadron in front of Iyon's chariot, and Arris found himself in the middle of the division instead of in the front as they halted again.

The horsemen of the Fengian garrison were now on the left wing of the chariots. They broke their ranks in the center, forming a crescent, to allow Captain Ganiz's retreating riders to gallop through to the fortified hills. Then they closed up again to face the enemy.

The Khalifate cavalry had stopped at the upper end of the meadow when they saw that it was a trap. They waited there in disciplined ranks, judging from the still, limp banners Arris could see above the layer of mist. He did not have to be able to see the soldiers to know how they appeared. They would be a bright contrast to the Deirani troops, wearing gold cloth turbans over steel caps, and blue and gold surcoats over their mail. Curved scimitars would hang from their wide belts, and they would carry long lances. Arris had seen squadrons of Khalifate cavalry on parade at the Citadel and in Khessard, and the Prince's Companions were a cavalry wing of the army, in theory. The Companions would take the field if Saresha was directly threatened. Arris hoped none of them was here today.

The chariot ranks shifted to allow a messenger to pass on his horse. A young plainsman scout drew rein beside Iyon's chariot and spoke breathlessly. "From Captain Yehane, my lord. The enemy army is gathering into a battle formation. More men are arriving all the time. But so far we can see four divisions of infantry, two of cavalry, and a few hundred chariots. Ten thousand men, at a guess in this fog."

"I want the infantry to fall in behind us," Iyon said, seeming pleased with the report. "Riman's men and the

Khopei footsoldiers. General Luo is to hold himself ready for a charge. The rest of the cavalry stay in reserve. Fall back now, or you'll be caught in the first melee.''

The plainsman saluted him and turned his horse to go back. Arris watched him race through the chariot ranks toward the central hill. ''What if the Khalifate army had retreated when they saw us here?'' he asked. ''Or what if they hadn't followed Ganiz's lure?''

''We would have taken the battle to them,'' Iyon said. ''If Yehane's estimate is right, we outnumber them.''

''This can't be all of the Khalifate army from Trevena Province and Ummass,'' Arris said.

The General shrugged. ''They probably underestimated our numbers. Or some of their generals refused to come against us without authority from the Citadel.'' He smiled brilliantly, and took hold of both the warrior's straps at the sides of the chariot. ''We'll show them their mistake. For the Sacred Emperor and Deiran!'' he shouted.

Drivers and warriors sent up a yell that would have terrified horses that were not trained for war, as the front ranks pounded into a full galloping charge and the body of the chariot lines followed. Arris only had to ease the reins a little for his team to leap ahead, their long legs stretching over the winter grass, not seeming to touch the ground. The chariot seemed to be flying on smooth stretches, but Arris felt the vibrations all through his body to his fingertips when the land was even slightly rough. His short Jai-Sohn sword bounced in its sheath on his back. He carried a knife in a wrist sheath to cut the harness with if one of the horses went down, and to cut himself free of the reins he had wrapped around his hands. The two chariots ahead of him seemed little protection as they approached the firm line of the Khalifate vanguard. Arris would have liked to pray for the favor of some god or goddess in the battle, but he did not think any would listen to him.

The first shock of meeting was borne by five hundred riders of the Fengian cavalry, who met the enemy lance to lance to break the line for the chariots. The noise of the battle being joined spread out through the mist all across the meadow; it did not blend into one massive roar, as Arris would have expected. Instead, he could hear each of the hundreds of individual cries of pain, shouts of rage, the clash of swords like dancers' cymbals, and the unearthly screams of wounded and dying horses. For a few minutes that seemed very long, there were only the engulfing sounds ahead and the rush of the chariot across the grass. The reins in Arris's hands seemed alive, moving forward and back with the horses' heads as they ran. Then suddenly the reins were loose as the team broke their stride to keep from running into the rear of the chariot in front of them. The first rank had slowed as the Deirani archers began to shoot from behind their drivers. Then the weight and momentum of their charge flung them into a widening gap in the Khalifate forces.

Arris could see the enemy now, as individual Khalifate riders forced their way into the slim space between chariots to slash with their scimitars at drivers and soldiers. Horses reared in their traces to lash out with hooves and teeth at the enemy animals. Men who were thrown from their saddles were trampled. The archers drew arrow after arrow from their belts and sent the long shafts against the blue and gold soldiers of the enemy. Chariot drivers shouted and cursed and did their best to guide their teams around to the right and along the Khalifate vanguard. Arris saw two drivers slain near him, and horses stumbling into enemy lances and falling, taking their partners with them and throwing drivers and soldiers from their chariots.

A blond rider forced his way through to attack General Iyon. Arris turned the chariot expertly away from him to allow Iyon to fight from the rear. He could not watch them; he was trying to watch everything else, his path and the enemies ahead and the other Deirani chariots crowding against him from both sides. But he felt the thud of weight falling into the chariot, and glanced over his shoulder to see Iyon pull out a javelin and kick the dead body of his attacker to the ground. The riderless horse ran maddened beside them, bucking and kicking, its eyes rimmed with white, its ears flat.

"Pull back!" Iyon shouted in Arris's ear. "We're too far inside their lines."

There were no open spaces in which to turn around. Arris pulled the reins up short and brought his team almost to a stop. The black horses fought him, wanting to run, but he managed to force them into a slow turn to the right. Two more enemy soldiers came against them, but javelins from other chariots knocked them out of their saddles. At last Arris was able to drive back toward the south. The Khalifate ranks made way for the General. Behind the chariots, the infantry soldiers were running into the battle. Iyon shouted encouragement to them as Arris drove him through. Men saluted him with pikes and spears, some of them smiling like idiots.

The fighting spilled down into the meadow all around them. A flank section of Khalifate cavalry had come around to stop the chariot's advance, and now the two armies were mixed together so that divisions and formations could no longer be seen. The grass was being churned into the dark earth beneath horses' hooves and chariot wheels and the bodies of the fallen. A slung javelin passed within inches of Arris's head and nearly grazed off his horse. He leaned farther over the shield-wall and urged the team on faster to get the General out of immediate danger.

From the northernmost hill red banners streamed down as General Luo's light horsemen made their attack. The high-pitched war cries of the plains tribesmen rose over the battle sounds, so sharp that they seemed likely to pierce the mist and clear it away. General Iyon shouted to Arris to turn and halt so he could see what was happening.

In the rear ranks of the advancing Deirani infantry, Arris stopped the horses and gave them some lead on the reins to stretch their necks. They were winded from the charge and the fighting, and their flanks pulsed in and out with their rapid breathing. There was a sheen of sweat on their black coats despite the coolness of the morning.

Several messenger riders had come through the infantry ranks looking for the General. Now they converged on the chariot. Iyon wrapped his red cloak around himself tighter against the mist and listened to their reports. Arris rubbed his tight, aching arms and shoulders with his blistered hands. One of the horses was twisting its head around, trying to bite at its left side. With the reins in one hand, Arris vaulted over the side to the ground. A raw scratch ran along the black's lower belly, where Arris had not been able to see it from above. It was bleeding, but it was not deep enough to be dangerous. Arris stroked the horse's neck and murmured reassuringly to it, all he could do for it now.

The battle grew more and more confused. Arris drove General Iyon from one side to the other along the southern edge of the fighting, and watched fresh troops ordered in and wounded men helped into the hills by comrades. Yehane's reports from the hilltop platform indicated that the Deirani army was making great inroads into the Khalifate ranks, but despite their losses the enemy troops did not retreat. Iyon was losing men, too, and he still had not committed all his troops to the battle.

A small squadron of Khalifate cavalry punched a way through to the rear, fighting through Khopei footsoldiers toward the red-cloaked General. For a desperate time Arris and Iyon both were defending themselves with their swords against enemies who crowded against the shield-walls of the chariot. Arris was wounded slightly in his upper right arm by one man who leapt onto the side of the chariot, but a Deirani infantryman dragged the soldier off and killed him. The horses screamed and reared. Arris thought that the team would surely be killed unless he cut their traces and let them loose, but then a group of Deirani horsemen rode up and engaged the Khalifate soldiers.

Iyon was bleeding from a cut on his scalp. His helmet had been knocked off his head. He shouted to Arris to fall back well behind the lines. They drove into the shadow of the hills, below where Yehane was stationed. Iyon was about to order the rest of his troops into action when five riders appeared at the far southern end of the meadows above the river bluffs. Lieutenant Ebreyu was one of them, galloping his horse at a killing pace. Iyon unclasped his red cloak and waved it over his head. The Lieutenant saw him and wheeled his men over to the chariot.

"My lord," Ebreyu said, saluting. His hair was damp from the mist, waving around his face under his helmet.

"What are you doing here, Lieutenant? You're supposed to be guarding the river." Iyon looked weary and grim as he wiped at his forehead, smearing the trickling blood.

"We've sighted more Khalifate troops, my lord," Ebreyu said almost reluctantly.

"What?"

"Across the river. A lot of them. Maybe another army."

"On the south side of the Khessi?" Iyon swore softly. "I told Yehane myself that we didn't need any scouts there. That was a mistake. They must have come up from the south, maybe even from the Citadel. The northern troops would have no reason to make the river crossing, only to have to cross back again. Have they seen your men, Ebreyu?"

"I think so, sir. We're only hidden from the northern side by the bluffs." The Lieutenant paused, rubbing his horse's neck as the animal puffed from its run. "Should we pull back into the hills?"

"No. Stay where you are and watch them. See if you can make out their numbers." The General looked away, back toward the clamor of the battle. "So that's why they won't give way. Go back to your command, Lieutenant. Arris, drive us back into the hills. I want a look from Yehane's platform."

As the five riders turned back, Arris urged his weary team to a trot along a rocky upward path. It was midday now, and as they climbed the pale sun dispersed the mist. They reached a steep ditch that had been dug to fortify the hilltop, and stopped there while soldiers ran up to take the team and the chariot back to the camp. Then Arris and Iyon climbed the steep slope together to the top of the hill.

CHAPTER
16

AFTER THREE LONG HOURS of fighting, the Khalifate troops retreated with heavy losses. General Iyon did not harry the enemy retreat, but let them pull back to a point ten miles to the north in the forest marshes, followed only by scouts along the ridgetops. The Khalifate army to the south was larger than the one he had engaged today. The river would slow them, and any crossing would be an opportunity for Iyon, but still the Deirani were between two forces. Iyon was not too proud to be cautious.

He regrouped his men in the hills and set them to strengthening the fortifications, felling trees and erecting a palisade on the highest hill above the newly dug ditches and banks of soft earth. Arris and the other charioteers were set to other labor. They led their teams over the trampled ground of the meadows, while conscript infantry soldiers piled the bodies of the dead into the chariots to carry them to the pyres. The Khalifate dead were stripped of weapons, but they left them their ornaments and clothes, stacking the bodies in rows at the northern end of the meadow for their people to claim when the Deirani had left the field.

With a cloth around his nose and mouth against the smoke, unable to avoid the smells of blood and death, Arris tried to keep his black horses calm as he led them back and forth over the battleground. The tired animals were trained to the chaos of war, but they were frightened and sickened by its aftermath. Arris felt much the same. He had never seen anything like this before. Vultures and ravens clustered where the chariots had not yet gone, and they only fluttered a few yards away when soldiers came to take the bodies on which they had been feeding.

Arris thought he saw the Lossiran more than once. He did not have the power to see more than a black, winged shadow hunched where the dead were thickest, and it vanished if he looked again, but he was certain he felt the cold presence of the Mother of Vultures. Perhaps some of the Khalifate warriors had been secret followers of the Goddess, and the Lossiran had come for their souls. Arris had not killed anyone in the fighting today. He had sent no souls to Aghlayeshkusa in the Gods' Realm. He had wounded a few of the horsemen who had attacked the General's chariot, but they had been slain by others.

Some soldiers were found to be wounded. Those who could not live much longer were given a merciful knife in the heart. The rest were borne back to the hill camp, where the healers could tend them. Iyon had commanded that wounded Khalifate soldiers not be killed. He wanted captives to question about the army on the other side of the river.

When all the bodies were piled and counted, Arris and the rest of the drivers were allowed to return to the camp, leaving the long business of tending the pyres to the weary conscript soldiers. Arris unharnessed his team, watering and feeding them, cleaning and salving their scratches. Neither horse was much hurt, but both were exhausted. He left them on the picket line with their heads hanging low.

The camp spread over the central hilltop and down into two narrow, stony valleys between two nearby hills. The palisade was being erected by men who had fought in the battle. The Khopei cavalry, who had been in reserve, were being kept fresh in case the Khalifate army attempted to cross the river. Arris passed through the sentry lines around the palisade, seeing the bruised, grimy faces of the soldiers at work. Some of the men complained, but most of them understood the necessity. Just a few more hours, and the camp would be almost as well fortified as the border hill-fort had been. Then they could rest.

His black armor still clean but his eyes bloodshot, Captain Yehane stopped Arris as they passed one another. "Your friend Terai seems to have vanished. His scouts separated in the woods, and when they came back together he was missing."

"Maybe he lost his way," Arris suggested.

"General Iyon didn't want him sent on patrols, but I trusted him. Did he go over to the enemy?" Yehane demanded.

"No. He's wanted in the Khalifate as a Deirani spy."

"Then he has deserted."

"It's more likely he was captured and killed." Arris did not really believe that. Terai would make it to Gama, he was sure.

"If you knew he planned to desert, and told no one, you could be hung in his place." Yehane looked at him coolly. "If I were you I would be careful to seem very loyal to the General."

"Thank you for the warning." Arris bowed to him and turned away in the direction of Iyon's tent.

A stained bandage on his head, the General sat in front of his tent with the other captains and General Luo. The standards of all the divisions hung on poles beside the tent, with the Emperor's blue hawk flying highest. By now the General would have been told the count of casualties: fifteen hundred of his men, and seven hundred horses including thirty chariot teams. The Khalifate army had lost more than four thousand men. It was a victory, Arris supposed, but it was not the decisive one Iyon had wanted.

The commanders were arguing whether they should withdraw back to the Westrange and await the Emperor with the rest of the Deirani army, or continue what they had begun. While Arris stood there listening, Iyon did not speak in favor of either prospect, but Arris was certain he did not want to withdraw. The General saw him after a moment, and waved him away.

"I don't need you. Go get some rest while you have the opportunity."

Arris bowed deeply and went to find some food, and get the cut on his right arm cleaned and bandaged. After that, he found the place where he and Terai had camped the

night before, at the edge of the hilltop just within the
newly erected wooden palisade. Terai's blanket roll and
gear were still there, neatly wrapped and weighted down
with stones. He could not have taken them on his scouting
mission. Tired and sick at heart, Arris spread out his own
blankets and lay down alone.

That evening, envoys swam their horses across the river
from the Khalifate army that was camped near the southern
bank. Lieutenant Ebreyu escorted them courteously to the
hilltop stronghold, and Arris was called to interpret for
General Iyon. He knew both men by sight from the Citadel, aging members of the minor nobility with some relation to the royal family. They were very stiff and correct in
their sodden tunics and splashed turbans, and Arris could
not tell if they recognized him.

General Iyon met them in his tent, with only Arris and
Ebreyu present. He offered each man a welcome cup of
Deirani wine, which they solemnly drained. Arris translated the words of the older envoy. "I am Lord Bel jen
Graith, advisor to the Holy Regent Karillos. I drink the
health of the Sacred Emperor of Deiran, and assure him of
our great respect and admiration, and our desire that the
gods will favor him in administrating his distant Empire."

So the high priest had convinced them to name him
Regent. General Iyon responded gravely, but Arris could
tell that he was amused. "And I in turn salute the Crown
Prince of the Khalifate, and pray that the Regent Karillos
will consider what is best for His Highness's people, and
will choose not to prolong this war. Surrender quickly to
us, and you will have peace."

The other envoy was less calm. "We are a peace-loving
people, my lord General. But we will not therefore submit
to invaders."

Lord jen Graith crossed his arms and nodded. "This
adventure you have undertaken will bring you no further.
The Holy Regent will consider it the ill-advised attempt of
an ambitious general, not supported by the Emperor of
Deiran and with no blame resting on him. We will allow
you to withdraw back over the Westrange, and will send a

party of envoys to negotiate the reparations you must make for the devastation you have caused.''

"Those are your terms?" Iyon shook his head and laughed softly, something Arris did not have to translate.

"We are here to warn you that the Holy Regent of the Khalifate will declare war against the Deirani Empire unless you depart our lands." Arris remembered the younger envoy's name. He was Fanil j'Aran, an intelligent member of the noble council and one of the Prince's supporters.

"The Sacred Emperor Hareku has already declared war against the Khalifate," Iyon said. "We are ready to face a committed enemy, my lords. Go back and tell your commander that I will not retreat after a victory. Tell him I suggest that he surrender or prepare for another battle."

The Khalifate envoys bowed and left the tent. Lieutenant Ebreyu followed them to escort them back to the river. As they walked away, Arris heard j'Aran say, "He is scarcely a reasonable man."

"Would a reasonable man invade another country with no provocation but old enmity and ambition?" countered jen Graith. "Yet I think he has overreached himself, coming this far so quickly . . ." He was out of earshot now, walking quickly out of the Deirani camp to where their horses waited.

"They think you are ambitious and unreasonable," Arris reported, turning around to see Iyon sit down wearily at his table.

"And they are overcautious and as slow as creeping ice." Iyon unrolled a map of the region and drew circles on it with one finger. "When they do act, they will try to overwhelm us with sheer numbers and finish us in one battle. I'm beginning to think we may have achieved a true victory today. Do you suppose that all their troops from the Citadel and Qadasiya are in the army south of us?"

"Probably most of them."

"They think they have us trapped here. Yet they can't get close enough to really see what we're doing. If they can believe we're hiding in these hills behind our fortifications . . ." Iyon grinned, tracing a definite line on the map. "My men can travel lightly if necessary. No supply wagons, no chariots. We'll slip out of here and sweep around to the west and south, crossing the river thirty or forty miles below their position. We can be encamped in front of the Citadel before their commander realizes we're gone." He looked up at Arris, pleased with himself. "Give me a reason why that would not work."

Arris sat down across from him and spoke uneasily. "How did this Citadel army know we were here at all? We've seen no signs of Khalifate scouts, and we had outriders watching for them. I know this man Karillos, their new Regent. He's capable of knowing our plans before any reconnaissance tells them to him. He has his gods' favor, power that I've seen."

His eyebrows raised, Iyon leaned back in his chair. "I remember your friend Terai saying something to that effect. I don't fear magical power, and I won't base my strategy on the possibility that Karillos can guess what I'll do next."

"That's your decision, my lord. But there's another thing I should tell you. As long as I'm with your army, the Khalifate is more likely to know where we are. Believe whatever you like. But the Khalifate gods, the gods Karillos serves, keep trying to kill me. The novice priest in Oroci meant to assassinate me, not you. They'll find me along the route to the Citadel, and then Karillos will know what you're attempting."

"That," Iyon said, "is nonsense. Superstitious nonsense. Slaves' talk. You disappoint me, Arris." He was curious, though. "Why do you believe the Khalifate gods are trying to kill you? Because you murdered the Regents? Were Nievan and Maenad Ilkharani the gods' favorites?"

"I have told you the truth." Arris met Iyon's eyes steadily. "The more I try to explain, the more fantastic you'll think it is."

The General smiled slightly. "You say that Karillos will track the army's movements by you. On the chance that that's true, I won't send you with the troops." His face sharpened with new eagerness. "I won't even go myself, not right away. I'll ask to meet with this Karillos, and make him come to talk to me. You'll be there as my interpreter and my driver. He'll have no reason to suspect that I'd send my army away under the command of Captain Yehane, with only a token force to guard this hill.''

"That's very dangerous," Arris said. "I tell you you can't underestimate Karillos."

"He'll see what he expects to see, magic power or no. You shouldn't underestimate me either, Arris. Now go get my commanders. We'll argue about this all night, but they'll see that my plan will work. Go on. And don't mention anything to them about magic or gods, understand?" He watched thoughtfully as Arris bowed and left the tent.

Arris had not expected him to believe what he said, but Iyon had almost taken him seriously. The thought of meeting with Karillos as Iyon's aide terrified Arris, enough to make him think of deserting and trying to find Terai. But he would be watched, now that the older man had vanished. And Arris did not really want to go to Gama, even if he did escape Iyon's army. Nowhere in the Khalifate was safe. Deiran would be dangerous if he was a deserter. He could see no choice but to stay with the General and hope for the best.

General Iyon did not have to suggest a meeting with Karillos. The next morning, with one of the Fengian divisions already gone in secret toward the west and south, the Khalifate envoys reappeared to say that their Holy Regent would like to speak personally with the Deirani commander. It amused Iyon to set up the terms of the meeting: on neutral ground, which meant the middle of the river; on a raft which would be tethered there, to which each commander would be rowed by one man. The envoys j'Aran and jen Graith would be held as hostages on the Deirani side, and Iyon would send two noble-born officers across to the Khalifate bank.

Karillos agreed to those terms, and by early afternoon the raft was in place, built on the southern bank and moored by Deirani soldiers with ropes against the current. Lieutenant Ebreyu and Sergeant Mentes volunteered to cross the river as hostages for their General's safety. In

their chariot, Arris and General Iyon waited on the Deirani
bank until the two Khalifate envoys had swum their horses
over and Ebreyu and Mentes had arrived on the other side.

The Khessi was wide and deep near the place where it
joined the Majeha, and the current was steady but not
treacherous. Under a clouded sky, with a light wind blowing, the water was silvery gray. Thick stands of trees and
tangled bushes crowded both banks, beneath high bluffs on
the northern side and gentler slopes on the southern. Lieutenant Ebreyu's squadron of light horsemen had drawn up
in formation on the bank beneath the trees, and there was
an equal number of Khalifate soldiers across the quarter-
mile distance. Arris got down from the chariot after General Iyon, shivering a little in the cool air. He wore his
charioteer's harness, kilt, and boots, with a short cape over
his shoulders that was not very warm.

The hostages on each side were made to kneel on the
bank with swords at their throats. Arris could see Karillos
and his attendant stepping into their small boat; the new
Regent still wore the gold robes of a high priest, and his
short blond hair and clean-shaven face made him easy to
identify. He had a younger man with him, dressed in a
blue and gold soldier's uniform with no helmet or sword
belt. Arris thought that if Terai were here, the Yaighan
would doubtless warn him against going anywhere near
Karillos. Arris knew the danger without sensing it with
power. But he did not expect an attack, not here. Karillos
followed the Five Gods, whose main concern was law and
honor. There were ancient laws that dealt with such con-
ferences of enemy leaders.

Fully half of Iyon's army would be gone from the hill
camp by tonight, traveling in the shadowed, narrow valleys toward the west before they crossed the river many
miles away. The General was in a cheerful mood as he
climbed into the rowboat and took his seat. Arris followed
him in, taking up the oars with his face toward the Deirani
bank. The boat had been found only a few miles upstream,
abandoned by some farmer at the arrival of the invading
army. The Deirani soldiers came to attention and saluted

their General on a signal from their standard-bearer, meaning that Karillos had left the bank on the other side.

Arris waited for Iyon's soft command, and dipped the oars into the cold, gray water. He rowed a little upstream of the ropes that moored the raft to trees at the edge; if he could not hold the boat against the current, the ropes would catch them. But he was strong in the arms and shoulders, and the boat moved smoothly through the water on a straight path.

After a few minutes they bumped against the raft, and Iyon tied the boat to it. The raft was sturdy, a flat platform twenty feet square, made of heavy logs. Karillos and his companion were already climbing onto it. It swayed only a little with their weight. General Iyon stood up in his boat and stepped out onto the raft, balanced and graceful. Arris followed him and stood at his right shoulder.

The two commanders gazed at one another stubbornly, each waiting for the other to speak first. Arris was struck by the likeness between them. Both men were thirty years old, lean and tall, and both had a driven intensity about them, the look of a genius or a fanatic. Iyon was blackhaired, arrogantly handsome in his black uniform and red cloak. Karillos had blond hair and pale skin and ice-blue eyes, in the gold robes of a priest of the sun. If there was a difference in their ambition, it was that Karillos worked from an utter conviction that he was morally right, while Iyon believed only in the right of arms. To Arris, Iyon's way was cleaner.

At last, the young soldier with Karillos broke the silence. "I present the Holy Regent of the Khalifate, the High Priest Karillos of the Qadasiya Temple, holding this land in trust for the Crown Prince Saresha Ilkharani and the Five Brothers Ylla."

Arris matched his formality. "The noble General Iyon of the House Idari, Commander of the Armies of the Empire of Deiran, under the authority of the Sacred Emperor Hareku." Then he translated the aide's words for Iyon.

"Regent," Iyon said with a very slight bow.

"General." Karillos held himself very straight.

"You asked for a meeting. I assume you wish to discuss the terms of surrender I have offered." Iyon made no such assumption, but he looked supremely confident as Arris relayed what he had said.

"No," the high priest said with a note of irony.

"I can think of no other reason why we should be here today," Iyon said, as if he had not been going to suggest such a meeting himself.

"Indeed. I doubt that you can imagine why we are here." Karillos looked for the first time at Arris, a look that might have seemed natural to others, but that struck Arris like a blow. He glanced away quickly from those pale blue eyes to keep from being trapped by them. The raw power of the priest was explosive, stronger than he remembered, perhaps stronger than it had been before. The soldiers behind him on the shore, the hostages with swords to their throats, were no protection at all, and Arris did not have any way to protect himself.

"What did he say?" Iyon demanded, glaring at Arris in his turn. His hand was at his side where his sword hilt should be. He had sensed some threat, but he did not know its meaning.

"Tell the General," Karillos said, "that we understand one another. We will fight this war he has brought us. We will defend the land of the Five Gods with power and the sword."

Arris translated, his voice unsteady, and then he added, "My lord, we must go back."

"And we accept the offering he has given us, of the criminal who murdered Nievan and Maenad Ilkharani."

Iyon understood the names at least. He put a hand on Arris's shoulder and took a breath to speak.

Light blinded Arris suddenly, as the sun pierced the clouds with rays so bright they burned. Arris felt Karillos's hatred attack him, white-hot, through the last remnants of shields he had. He lunged toward the side of the raft, but the young Khalifate soldier tripped him and flung himself on top of him. The man's touch burned. The gods' power was in him, too. Arris writhed and struggled to get free, trapped in a net of light.

Iyon lunged for Karillos with a knife he had hidden in his sleeve, but a crescent of fire sprang up on the raft between them, and the searing heat drove Iyon back to the edge with an arm flung up over his face. Arris was on Karillos's side of the fire. He heard shouts of fury from the Deirani shore, and two bubbling shrieks that must be the hostages being killed. All was quiet on the Khalifate bank of the gray river.

Arris could not break the hold of his enemy. He felt a needle-thin dagger at this throat, and heard Karillos say in poor Deirani, "I vowed you would be unharmed, General. Go." Iyon had no choice; the fire had driven him back into his boat, and he cut its burning rope with his knife and pushed away.

"Give me my charioteer," Iyon shouted. "Arris!"

The blade at Arris's neck cut him slightly. It was sharp enough to slit his throat with terrible ease. Karillos knelt down beside him in his gold robe, fire reflecting from his pale face. He untied his belt of five cords and bound Arris's hands behind him, then his feet. The flames did not advance onto their part of the raft. The knife was put away. Arris struggled against the bonds, but they were tight. Karillos stood up.

"Bring him," he said to his companion. The younger man did not bother to pick Arris up, but dragged him by the feet over to the boat and dumped him in the bottom. The boards were shipping a couple of inches of water, and Arris turned onto his side to keep his face clear. At the mercy of his greatest enemy, he was rowed to shore.

CHAPTER
17

THE BOAT WENT AGROUND at the riverbank. Karillos stepped out, and the other man untied the bindings around Arris's ankles and hauled him to his feet. He pushed Arris out of the boat, and Arris barely managed to keep from falling face first on the rocky shore. The Khalifate soldiers on their horses stared at him. Arris did not recognize any of the pale faces. The young soldier shoved him from behind, and he walked up the slope at Karillos's heels.

The two Deirani hostages had not been killed. Ebreyu and Mentes had been put back on their horses. They were led to the water at Karillos's nod. "Oath-breaker!" Mentes shouted in Deirani. "You would send us back, as if you had done nothing?" Karillos showed no sign of understanding the words, or of anger.

Mentes spurred his horse into the river, and Ebreyu followed for a short distance, but then he turned and cried out to Arris, "Run!"

To die quickly now, or slowly under torture; that was the choice that raced through Arris's mind. He ducked the reaching hands of the soldier behind him, and kicked to the side of the man's knee. The soldier fell as Arris ran with his head down as fast as he could toward the water.

"Stop him!" Karillos yelled.

Arrows sang past Arris's ears and struck in the ground around him as he ran. Mentes was hit in the back and fell with a splash into the river. Ebreyu crouched over his horse's neck as the animal floundered out into the deep water. Arris felt a moment of wild hope that he could reach the river and swim to Ebreyu, but then an arrow struck the back of his right leg. The muscle seized up around the fiery pain, and he fell full length on the river-bank a few yards from the water.

Khalifate soldiers reached him and stood with javelins poised, but Karillos called out that they were not to kill him. Arris raised his head to watch Ebreyu, halfway across the river now. Some of the Deirani soldiers on the other bank had ridden into the water, but they were turned back by their officers. General Iyon did not dare begin a battle now, with half his troops gone in secret. Arris could not hope to be rescued. Mentes had lost his life for him, and Ebreyu had risked his; that was more than he could have expected.

Arris bit his lip against a cry as one of the soldiers picked him up and set him on his feet. The wounded leg would not support him. The arrow was embedded against the bone, protruding from the large muscle at the back of his thigh. Blood ran down his leg into his boot. The pain claimed his whole body, making it hard to breathe, hard to see.

The sun still shone brightly, making Karillos's pale hair glow like textured gold. The high priest said, "You can't escape. Not this time." He turned to his men. "Keep watch on the Deirani. Corporal Hasi, put the prisoner on your horse and come with me back to camp."

The Khalifate camp was five miles south of the river. Slung over the horse's back, his head and feet hanging to either side and the arrow still in his leg, Arris saw the camp only as flashes of color and movement. It seemed to be very large, and it was on high ground, though not as steep and easily fortified as the hills where the Deirani had their camp. Soldiers and horses passed by him on the path, and he recognized different uniforms but could not remember the divisions they represented. The backbone of the horse cut into his stomach, and the right side of his face was bruised and raw from bouncing and rubbing against the animal's shoulder. Corporal Hasi, who had been the man with Karillos in the boat, sat behind him on the

overloaded horse with one indifferent hand on Arris's back
to keep him from falling.

Arris would have been glad to retreat into a haze of
pain, even unconsciousness, but instead he remained fully
awake. All his senses seemed to be heightened by the
throbbing, harsh shaft of pain in his leg. He could smell
his own blood and the horse's animal musk, and he could
pick out every word of the soldiers he passed in the camp.
The Khalifate language sounded harsh to him, barbaric,
after speaking Deirani for a few weeks. The soldiers spoke
of the battle yesterday between their northern forces and
General Iyon's army, bragging that as soon as they were
allowed to attack the Deirani they would finish them all.

Arris heard his name quietly in some conversations as
he passed. Men who knew told men who did not that he
was Arris j'Areyta, the spy who had murdered the Regents. One man remembered that Areyta had been the
traitor general who killed the old Khalif, Rasul Ilkharani.
Another asked if he was not the brother of Falcmet and
Husayn j'Areyta, of the Prince's Companions. Yes, he
was told, but the two brothers were loyal, everyone knew.
That man had heard Falcmet himself calling for his younger brother's death.

Corporal Hasi pulled Arris down from the horse and
carried him into a tent. Two other men took Arris's boots
off his feet, and locked iron shackles around his wrists and
ankles. Only a few inches of chain separated the cuffs.
The leg irons were attached to a heavy wooden post. The
men had not spoken at all, and now they left Arris alone.
He lay on his left side on the bare earth that was the tent
floor. The flow of blood from his wounded leg had slowed,
but the pain had only grown worse from the arrowhead
still pressing against bone. He gazed at the canvas door
flap, where the unseasonal sunshine was still bright through
the slit opening, and waited without much hope for whatever was going to happen next.

After some time had passed, an old man in a healer's
pale green robe was admitted by the guards outside the
tent. He carried a satchel, which he set on the ground in
front of Arris's face. He knelt down with the careful

movements of a man whose joints pained him, and touched Arris gently on the shoulder.

"The Regent allowed me in here only on the promise that I would not give you anything to numb the pain. It is your choice. I can merely cut the shaft of the arrow, leaving the head and some of the wood in your leg, to cause inevitable rot. Or I can go in and remove it all. It would hurt very much, but you would have a chance of healing."

Arris shook his head. "Karillos won't give me time to heal, or the time to die of an infection from this wound. Do whatever you want." His voice was strained and breathless.

The old man looked troubled. "I . . . serve the gods through healing," he said finally. "I must do what I can to prevent death. If the choice is mine, I would choose to remove the arrow."

Arris closed his eyes. "As you will." He faced worse pain than a surgeon's knife, he knew. The only way he could see to avoid torture was to appeal to Saresha for a quick death. Surely the Prince would grant him that for what was left of their friendship.

The old man turned him onto his stomach and began to work, giving Arris a thick roll of leather to bite down on. It took a long time, and Arris kept from screaming after the first shock of the knife. The arrow came out, and with it a chip of bone. The ground was wet with blood, and the healer's robe and hands were smeared with it by the time he finished. He washed the wound and bandaged Arris's leg with tight linen strips. Then he whispered a short blessing in the name of Kerami Ylla, and left the tent.

Drained of strength, nauseated and fighting tears, Arris was in no condition to face the Holy Regent Karillos when the priest swept into the tent in his bright gold robe. Power and light radiated from the man, no longer attacking, but meant to inspire awe and fear. Arris did fear Karillos, but he had seen the Horned God in his own woods, and this slender blond priest did not deserve his awe.

"You'll be taken back to the Citadel," Karillos said,

looking down at Arris in disgust. "Your harlot Goddess cannot save you from the Black Masks of the dungeon."

"You are very sure of my sentence," Arris said hoarsely.

"You have already been tried by proxy. I have sentenced you to the slow death you deserve as a traitor and a regicide."

"The men I killed were not kings."

"They were of royal blood. And you would have killed the Crown Prince with your foul sorceries, if the gods had not been outraged enough to intervene." Karillos folded his arms in his sleeves. Arris hated the pious, superior look on the man's face. "The gods themselves command your death. I am their humble servant."

"I'll appeal to the Prince," Arris said fiercely.

"This does not concern him. He will not be told you were captured until you are dead at last, when your hold of witchcraft over him will be broken." The Regent turned to go. "You will not see me again. I have a war to conduct and a kingdom to rule, by the grace of the sun." He lifted the tent flap and was gone.

There would be no trial. Arris's hope to beg for a merciful death was useless. Saresha would not know he was even in the dungeons. What had Karillos meant about the "hold of witchcraft" he had over the Prince? Perhaps Saresha had protested the sentence of torture that Karillos had proclaimed in the proxy trial. Arris was warmed by the thought, even knowing what he had to face.

Soon after Karillos left, Arris fell into a shallow, pain-filled sleep. He woke at intervals, but he was sleeping when another man came into the tent at dusk. Some little sound woke Arris; the scuff of a boot sole in the earth, an indrawn breath. He opened his eyes, blinking to try to focus them. A tall, broad-shouldered young man stood there staring down at him. He had shoulder-length blond hair and deeply tanned skin, and there was a hint of the Yaighan in his features. A look of their mother.

"Husayn," Arris said dully.

"The gods damn you, little brother," Husayn said in a quiet voice. "Why did you let them take you?" He was wearing a cavalry uniform, with the striped tunic of the Prince's Companions beneath his blue and gold surcoat. There was a raw cut on one side of his face, and a bandage on his left knee. He wore his sword belt, but both scimitar and knife sheaths were empty. A lieutenant's insignia glittered on his collar.

Arris pushed himself up on his elbows. "Were you in the battle yesterday? I didn't see you."

"I saw you. Driving the Deirani commander's chariot." Husayn's blue eyes kept darting away, then returning reluctantly to Arris.

"I was conscripted. I wouldn't have chosen to fight on either side in this war."

"No, I'm sure you wouldn't. Killing unarmed men from behind is more your style." Husayn did not sound angry, only very tired. "It doesn't matter, Arris."

"How did you get here? You were with the northern part of the army." Arris was able to sit up a little, leaning against the post where his feet were chained.

"Half of us, half the survivors, circled around to the east through the forest and then crossed the river downstream."

Arris could not keep from laughing. It was a strange sound in his hoarse voice. "Oh," he said, "oh, well done."

"What's funny about it?" Husayn said, puzzled. "Anyway, it was Falcmet's idea. He's been made captain of one of the Trevena Province divisions. The Yaighan don't want us as their ambassadors anymore after what happened at Gama, so we had to do something. And after what you did, Karillos has forbidden us both to go anywhere near Saresha."

Arris nodded. He had known he would hurt his brothers somehow. He had hurt everyone else he loved in the Citadel. "I'm sorry about that, Husayn. But you're still wearing a Companion's tunic."

"Aye. The Prince won't dismiss us from the Companions, even though Karillos wanted it. But he can't keep us with him."

They were silent for a moment. The pain of Arris's wound made it hard to think, hard to say what he wanted.

He heard the clinking of armor outside, and his guards and several new voices began to speak. He guessed it was the soldiers who were going to take him to the Citadel.

"Is Falcmet in this camp?" he asked finally.

Husayn was embarrassed. "He wouldn't come. He's still furious with you."

"You don't seem to be," Arris said, meeting his brother's eyes and trapping them with his own.

In a low voice and in Yaighan, Husayn said, "I was at first. But you did avenge our father. And you saved Sasha, in the end. You're my brother. I can't hate you."

"They're going to kill me, Husayn."

"I know."

"There's no one else to help. I don't have any power to fight Karillos. If you can't help me escape . . ." Arris swallowed hard and went on. ". . . you could keep me from dying the way our father did. Kill me yourself, quickly and honorably."

Husayn said in a bleak voice, "Mother would say that a brother's blood is the heaviest debt of the soul. I couldn't kill you, Arris. I . . . did have a dagger hidden in my boot. They searched me outside and took it away. I was going to give it to you. There's nothing else I can do."

"There's something," Arris whispered. "Get word to Sasha. Karillos isn't going to tell him I was captured until I'm dead."

An infantry lieutenant came into the tent, followed by two privates. He looked hard at Husayn. "What were you talking about in that unbelievers' language, j'Areyta?"

Husayn saluted him and said mildly, "We were praying together, Sedeven. Would you deny a man the solace of his gods?"

The officer's mouth quirked in distaste, but he seemed satisfied. "All right. You have to go now, we're to take him."

Husayn bent over to embrace Arris. There were unshed tears in both their eyes. He straightened. "I'll tell our friend," Husayn said in the Khalifate language. He turned and left the tent without looking back.

·   ·   ·

Once again, Arris found himself in the back of a covered cart. Night fell soon, and Arris continued in cycles of sleep that brought no rest and wakefulness that was only misery. Five soldiers rode ahead of the cart, two drove it, and three more rode at the rear with the drivers' warhorses on leads. Arris longed for those horses, more than he could remember ever wanting anything before. He wanted to be on the back of one, unbound, galloping away from this procession of his executioners. He imagined how the horse would outdistance pursuit, leaping ravines that baffled the lesser animals that followed. He did not know where he would ride; he could think of nowhere safe. Perhaps he would become a hermit in the mountains. A little stone cabin overlooking the desolate cliffs of the Deadly Horns, gazing out over the Endless Sea . . . it was a delightful prospect.

He knew that it was useless to think of escape. He was in chains, and wounded. He could not even make an attempt in hope that the guards would kill him. They would only shoot to wound him again, and he would reach the Citadel in more pain than he felt now. And despite what he had said to Husayn, and his fear of torture, Arris did not want to die. He would not try to take his own life. Though he knew it was irrational, he almost believed what Terai had said once, that he could not be killed, that he was still protected by the Goddess. If that was true, Rehoman would have to manage a miracle to get him out of this.

Morning came, and the sun shone through the cracks between the boards of the cart's roof and sides. Arris watched the narrow beams of dusty light, like long fingers reaching toward him, and thought of the Brothers Ylla. He had never set out to become the enemy of the Five Gods. When he had been a child, he had watched his father pray to them. The Lord Areyta had been devoted to Sygathi Ylla, the Truthsayer, above the others. Arris had seen Sygathi appear to his priest Karillos when the god had commanded Arris be killed after the battle at the Temple. He had been beautiful, as all the Khalifate gods were, though stern and cold in his judgment.

Myrdethreshi the Warrior, Kerami the Lover, Ogliatu

the Eldest Brother, and Verchaki of the Night were the others in the Mythos. They ruled a religion based on moral laws and unquestioning obedience. The Yaighan saw the Khalifate religion as a cruel and confining deception, that ignored the wild magic of the Goddess and was frightened of the strength of women. Arris could never have worshiped the Brothers Ylla as he had once worshiped the Goddess. But he had never meant to work against them. He had wanted revenge on the Ilkharani family for what they had done to Areyta. That had little to do with their religion.

The Brothers Ylla did not fear him for what he had done, but for what he might do if he chose to go back to the Goddess. Arris wished he could speak with them as he had spoken with the Horned One, to try to convince them he would never do what they feared. To free the Goddess would mean becoming Yearking. He would not accept that role. If the gods were as powerful as they seemed, they should be able to read his thoughts and know he was no danger to them.

It was too late now to do anything to save himself, Arris thought as he lay alone in the dusty cart. Karillos had won. Arris hoped that General Iyon would destroy the Regent's army, and that the Deirani would take the Khalifate as part of their Empire. Arris would be dead by then, but he would rest easier in the ghost world if he was avenged.

The journey ended at last in the afternoon of the second day. The cart rolled through the main gates of the huge, ancient fortress that was the Ilkharani Citadel. Weak from hunger and blood loss, unable to walk for his wounded leg, Arris was carried down into the dungeons. He had been there before, when he and Terai had rescued a prisoner for Saresha. He remembered the long, sloping corridors, and the ladder that led through a vertical stone tunnel into the lower levels where the cells and the torture rooms were hidden. He was thrown into a small, bare cell on a floor of time-worn stones. The heavy oak door shut him into utter darkness, muffling the sounds of his guards speaking to the prison warden. After a few moments the

men left the narrow corridor of cells, and it was silent
except for Arris's breathing and the beating of his heart.

Hours passed, and he did not know if it was evening or
morning when the Black Masks came for him. There were
three of them, big men whose faces were hidden by sculp-
tured cloth masks that fit closely over their features, with
large eye holes and openings at the nostrils and over the
mouth. Their clothes were simply cut, short robes and
trousers of archaic design. Each of them bore the smell of
blood and smoke and sweat that pervaded the dungeon.

Arris had had some idea of being brave and arrogant,
but he was too terrified. He begged them to spare him; he
claimed that the Prince was his friend and they would lose
their heads when he found out; he said that he would pay
them well to set him free in secret and say they had killed
him. They ignored his words as he might have ignored the
yapping of a little dog.

His boots, cloak, and driver's harness were removed,
leaving him clad only in his kilt. The men forced him to
walk between them past the bank of cells. He heard the
moans of other prisoners, and cries for mercy, and wild
claims that they had been framed and were innocent. The
Black Masks led him limping through the circular room in
the center of the level. Arris wondered if it was the place
where he had killed a prison guard when he had rescued
General Fallayan. A heavy stone door was set behind the
ladder that led upward to freedom. That was where the
Black Masks took him.

Arris could not have put names to half the instruments
and racks he saw. He was almost relieved when he was
tied to a simple whipping post; at least he knew what to
expect. He had seen men whipped before. Some had
screamed and some had been silent. Arris screamed, when
the first lash hit. The whip had a metal tip that cut across
his back and around his rib cage. The pain was red and
rending, and each time he thought he had steeled himself
for the next blow he was shocked by its ferocity.

One of the Black Masks asked him questions at intervals. He was a condemned traitor and assassin, but he also

was a prisoner of war, and they wanted to know about the Deirani army and its plans. Arris knew very well that they would not stop hurting him, no matter what he told them. He found it simple to keep from answering the questions. All he did was scream.

The pain became constant after a time, and Arris could not tell when each lash hit. Colors were exploding in his head, red and orange and the Goddess's crimson. He stopped making any sound, lacking the strength, no longer even really frightened. He drifted in and out of consciousness. At one point the Black Masks did something with a hot iron against his stomach that brought him back to a vague awareness, but that did not last long.

He did know when they cut him down, but he awoke back in his cell with the feeling that many hours had passed. The blood on his back had made the stones dark and sticky where he lay. He tried to stand up, but the darkness spun around him and he fell. He lay there trying to remember what had happened. He had lost something, something precious and terribly important. He wept a little when he realized that it was his wing tattoos.

CHAPTER
18

ON THE SECOND DAY they beat him with rods. On the third day they broke his arms, carefully placing weights and then slamming them down with a great hammer so the bones snapped precisely. The forearms, then the upper arms; it took several hours, since Arris had to be brought back to full consciousness after each blow. They no longer asked him any questions. He begged them for mercy in Yaighan, which they did not understand.

That night in his cell he could not sleep. He lapped at some of the water they had left for him, but he did not eat any of the thin soup. The Black Masks had been commanded to give him a slow death. He thought it might be a kind of triumph to die before they meant for him to. Besides that, he was too sick to eat. The loss of blood from his mangled arms and the effort to fight the pain left him feeling like a swimmer in a rough ocean who could not come to shore.

Arris waited out the hours until the torturers came for him again. He was delirious by that time, and saw faces overlaying their masks. They were the faces of ordinary men, some kind and compassionate, some marked with bizarre lines of cruelty like a street artist's depiction of a villain from the Mythos. They crowded around him, making him walk to the torture room with his swollen arms stiff at his sides. When they got there, they hung Arris from the ceiling by his wrists. His feet did not touch the floor, and they attached weights to his ankles.

It was a new kind of pain, that started bearably but then

grew with each moment. His screams were weak and hoarse, but no less heartfelt for that. He felt the broken bones in his arms set themselves into a straight line, and begin to pull apart slowly, as did the sockets of his shoulders and hips and the joints of his knees. Arris could not stay there and feel what was happening to him. He remembered how it had felt when the daimon and the Horned God had summoned him to the Gods' Realm. Now he tried to leave his body of his own will.

It seemed to him that he had succeeded. He saw the daimon's face turn toward him in the darkness. It looked as it had years ago in a cellar in Gama, with an oversize hero's features, vaguely misshapen eyes, and a wide mouth with stained teeth. "Help me," Arris said in his mind. "Take my soul now. Don't let me die like this. It hurts . . ."

Aghlayeshkusa did not answer. It turned its head slightly, and became a lop-eared dog Arris had had as a young child. It licked his face, but its tongue was a searing fire against his cheek. Arris opened his eyes and smelled burnt flesh. One of the Black Masks held a red-hot metal rod in a pair of tongs. Arris was still in the torture room, and they would not let him leave. The brand on his left cheek hurt so much that he wept. Stretched out as he was, he did not have the breath to sob, but the tears spilled over his face. He had not left his body at all, he knew. He had no power to do something like that. The daimon he had seen had been only a hallucination, like the faces over the masks.

Now he saw another vision, he thought. The smoky light of the torches reflected off burnished golden hair as a young man suddenly thrust open the door of the underground room. It looked like Saresha Ilkharani, the Crown Prince, in a dark red tunic and high boots, like a messenger from the sun. He was nineteen years old, short and wide-shouldered, with golden skin the color of his hair, and eyes the warm blue of a summer lake. Arris wondered why his fevered brain would imagine Sasha here, with his hair cut like that over his ears. It had been past his shoulders when Arris had seen him last.

"Your Highness," said one of the Black Masks, step-

ping away from Arris. "The Regent Karillos . . . would
not want you here."

"The outer guards would have tried to stop me, if they
hadn't been called to defend the Citadel from invaders,"
the Prince said. He was out of breath and his voice was
unsteady. "The Deirani got men inside the walls somehow. They killed sentries, opened a gate . . . the palace is
a battleground, and Karillos's army is still miles away to
the north."

"This is true?" asked another of the torturers, clearly
suspicious. But Arris could hear, and surely the rest of
them could as well. The corridors above them rang with
shouts and the bright clash of swordplay, echoing down
through the ladder hole and through the open door. Iyon's
Jai-Sohn scouts had managed it, without Arris to lead
them. The Deirani were in the Citadel.

"Go!" Saresha shouted. "Fight them. They'll surely
kill us all unless we can drive them out again. No soldiers
can be spared the battle."

He was not old enough to have the throne, but his voice
was commanding. The Black Masks drew their swords and
ran from the room. Arris wondered if they would take their
masks off to fight. He was beginning to think that this was
no delirium.

The Prince shut the door behind them and ran to Arris.
He unfastened the weights that were attached to Arris's leg
irons, and let them drop to the floor. "Oh, gods, Arris,"
Saresha said, his voice choked. "I never thought they'd
take you. I thought you really were a witch, after what
happened in the Temple, the creature you summoned to
help us."

His words faded in and out as Arris tried to listen. He
could not possibly speak to answer. It was too late, whatever Sasha was trying to do. Arris did not think he could
live more than a day or so, even without any further
torture. The pain that he felt was not only from his broken
arms and torn muscles, but deeper, radiating out from
inside his chest and abdomen. He had lost too much blood,
and he thought he was probably bleeding inwardly as well.
Still, he was filled with love for the beautiful Prince. He

tried to smile as Saresha stood on a table to reach his bound wrists.

"I thought you were more powerful than Karillos. He swears you used magic to escape him in the Dark Hills." The Prince caught Arris around the waist as he fell forward, and eased him down onto the tabletop.

"Guard the Prince!" The shout sounded from the central room of the prison level. There was a cry of agony and shouts in two languages.

"The fool," Saresha whispered. "Now they know I'm here." Arris realized that the Prince was frightened, even terrified. He had reason to be. The Deirani would kill him when they found him, to finish the task Arris had begun destroying the Ilkharani line. Arris could picture the blood slowly staining the Prince's dark red tunic, scarcely noticeable except for the sudden paleness of Saresha's skin as he died of a brutal sword thrust. What a waste of beauty, what a crime, for them both to die here. They had been the favored of the gods, meant to fill glorious destinies.

There was a heavy thump against the door, and then three Deirani soldiers opened it and stepped over the body of the last Black Mask. Arris saw that the man's mask had been partly torn away, but he could not see his face. Sasha knelt on the table, holding Arris tightly against him. Arris felt the Prince's trembling. One of the Deirani glanced at Arris, a look of shock and pity, but they all held bloody swords as they advanced on Saresha.

"Call your gods," Arris said, making an urgent effort to speak. "Myrdethreshi . . ."

"Kerami, Verchaki, Sygathi, Ogliatu," Sasha completed the chant on a rush of breath. "Help me, if ever you loved me, help me . . ."

A maelstrom of power, light and darkness flashing, a spinning, endless fall. Sasha's arms around him were all Arris could feel. That, and the Prince's terror, worse than the fear of facing death. Sasha did not know what he was facing. Arris did not wonder that he could sense his friend's thoughts; they were touching, in a place where there was nothing but that touch, no sight or hearing or even pain. Arris reassured Sasha with his mind. *You're all right. I love you.* He guessed where they were going, and supposed that they must have left their bodies behind to die there in the underground dungeon of the Citadel. But that did not matter. They still lived, somehow they still lived, and the Five Brothers of the sun had answered their Prince's despairing call.

Arris had been mistaken about leaving his body behind. He knew he had arrived in the Gods' Realm, because of the peculiar thinness of the air that his exhausted, aching lungs tried to breathe. All the pain of his tortures had returned to him in full measure, seeming greater because he had not expected to have to feel it again. He opened his eyes to see where he and Saresha had been drawn.

The Five Brothers Ylla stood before them, huge and radiantly powerful in a domed chamber ten times their height. Light sparkled from the curved walls in myriad reflections, rainbow shafts that gathered around the standing gods. The building seemed to be made of tiny faceted jewels like insects' eyes. The Brothers did not wear the armor Arris had seen at the Temple of Rehoman. They were dressed in nearly transparent robes of gossamer weave, nothing like the elaborately embroidered and brocaded gowns and turbans that were granted them in paintings.

The Prince still knelt at Arris's back, holding him upright with his embrace. Arris squinted against the light that surrounded them. He was hurting too much to be awed or frightened by his glorious enemies. The floor beneath him was a kind of mosaic tile, and he was dripping blood onto it. He was like a cracked egg, he thought, with the shell broken and the life trickling out.

One of the gods spoke, striking a pose like a declaiming orator. He had a stern face that did not seem young, though it was unlined. Arris recognized him as Sygathi Ylla, the Truthsayer, the god who had demanded his death before. "You are safe, Saresha Ilkharani. We heard your call. We have brought you to the Realm of the Gods."

"I found Arris," the Prince said in a small voice. "Then they were coming at me with swords . . ."

"You need not fear." This god was bearded, and his

voice was low and grave. Ogliatu, Arris guessed, the Elder Brother, who was also sometimes called the father of the other four. "You will find peace here, child."

"You saved me. I wouldn't have thought . . ." Saresha did sound like a child, gaping at marvels. Arris reminded himself that the Prince had seen little magic in his life. "I am in your debt."

"You are to command our priests one day, as Khalif." Sygathi said with a glance down at Arris. His eyes were colorless gray, like smudge mirrors. "Then we will depend upon you to see that we are not forgotten in the world. That is the only price for what we have done."

"Then . . . you'll send me back," Saresha said.

"Eventually. When the danger is past." A gentle, beautiful face, and a seductive voice: Kerami. "While you are here you will want for nothing. You are a prince. You need only name what you desire."

"I . . . am honored," Saresha said. "What of Arris? You brought him here with me. Can you heal him?"

There was a short silence among the gods. The air hummed quietly, in the way Arris remembered from the forest of the Horned One. "He is a creature of the Crimson Goddess," Kerami said. "Our enemy. He has been your enemy, Prince."

"He will not die here," said Ogliatu. "No one can die here. He can continue forever as he is."

"No," Saresha said. Arris felt a spreading horror at the thought. Immortality, within a broken and bleeding body, every breath a struggle—faced with that prospect, Karillos's sentence seemed merciful.

"You would forget about him soon enough, my Prince," said Sygathi Ylla. "You need never see him again."

"No," Saresha said again. "I don't care what he's done."

"As long as we have him here . . ." said one who stood a little behind the others, narrow-faced and bony. Arris guessed he was Verchaki of the Night, a god he had sometimes prayed to as a child. "He can do no harm in this realm. He'd have to return to his world to free Rehoman from her prison. He could not return without our help, and that we will never give. He is no threat to us here."

"You said I should say what I desired. I want you to heal Arris, if you can. You must have the power to do it. I don't know what he's done to you, to make you hate him so."

"He murdered your uncles," Sygathi said. "He almost murdered you on the altar of the Bloody Goddess."

"He is my friend, in spite of all that."

"So be it," Ogliatu spoke slowly, with an archaic accent. "But understand he may never return to your world."

"If that is your condition for helping him . . ."

"It is no condition, but a truth. We will never send him back."

There were other gods, Arris thought, and other powers that might think differently. He would find a way. If the Brothers Ylla agreed to heal his tortured body, if he was granted the life he had thought was over, he would travel over the whole Gods' Realm to search for a way to return to his world. For now, he let Saresha believe what the Five Brothers told him.

"Very well," the Prince said. "I want you to heal him, and I understand that he will have to stay here."

The biggest of the gods strode forward, and Arris was lifted in huge, muscular arms. Myrdethreshi the Warrior was a familiar figure. The daimon Aghlayeshkusa had matched his face almost exactly the last time, maybe even refining it a little. The real Myrdethreshi Ylla was almost brutally handsome. Arris remembered the Mythos tale, "Myrdethreshi and the Whore," that was told to Khalifate children as a lesson in morality. As he recalled, it ended with the god killing the unfortunate woman and making her skin into a sacred drum. The laws of the sun-gods were strict where women's virtue was concerned. Arris did not think they were any less violent and cruel than the Goddess Rehoman. They only went about it in a different way.

"Would your Goddess want you like this, with your beauty in tatters?" the god whispered to Arris now as he carried him into a smaller chamber and laid him on a soft, gold-draped couch. "I could heal you so that you bore no scars, but then you might forget the great mercy we showed you. Better that you remember and be grateful.''

He touched Arris on the cheek, and the burned place there was seared anew, a vertical band from cheekbone to jaw. Then the pain went out of it, and Myrdethreshi drew his hands down over Arris's back and arms, his chest and stomach, his hips and legs. Bones knit together. Tendons and muscles rejoined, bleeding stopped, and injured organs resumed their normal function. When it was done, the god smiled almost gently and passed a hand down over Arris's face, closing his eyes.

''Sleep,'' he said. ''Later will be time enough to plan your schemes against us. Sleep, child of darkness.''

Arris scarcely heard his words, so quickly did the spell of sleep draw over him. He had not slept deeply since he had been wounded at the riverbank, and the last few nights not at all. His body had been healed, but his exhausted mind needed peace. He descended into a tunnel of silence and was still.

Birdsong and soft light filled the room when Arris woke, and he supposed that it was morning, although there was no sun to rise or set in the Gods' Realm. He was alone, lying uncovered on a couch in a small alcove. A window was set like the pearl in a shell on one of the curving, jeweled walls. Through it came the sounds of the birds and the perfumed green smell of a garden. Arris sat up slowly, cautiously. He felt light-headed, but there was no pain, only a stiffness in his joints as he got to his feet.

Someone had brought a mirror into the room. It stood by the couch, as tall as Arris, glowing with its own light. Arris remembered that he had not been able to see his reflection in the stream the first time he had come here. He moved in front of the mirror and gazed into it. Its surface was milky white, and it swirled like river mist as he watched. In a few moments it resolved itself into his reflection, but the image was insubstantial, wavering, produced by magic, not natural law.

Myrdethreshi had healed him, but the scars remained, as the god had promised. Arris lifted a hand to the left side of his face and touched the puckered white burn mark. He turned and looked over his shoulder at the elaborate tracery of whiplash scars on his back. In them, he could see a pattern much like the wing tatoos they had destroyed. The Black Masks had certainly not intended that. The new design held a twisted kind of power, bought with blood and pain, and Arris's heart beat faster as he looked at it.

There were ugly, raised scars on his arms where the bones had been broken, and he could feel the thickened tissue in the sockets of his shoulders and hips, and in his knees. It would take a punishing regimen of dancer's training to regain his former agility; it might never return. Arris looked at himself for a long time. His face was still handsome, but the burn scar and the memory of pain around his mouth and eyes had destroyed his once-perfect beauty.

Strangely, he did not feel bitter at the loss. He would face Karillos someday and repay the priest for his pain, but he thought that Karillos had unknowingly done him a favor. Surely the Goddess would not want him like this. Almost cheerful, he left the room to search for Saresha.

He had thought to find the huge, domed chamber outside his room, but instead there was an airy colonnade of roofed pillars that opened into the garden Arris had smelled when he awoke. Living trees in winter colors shaded brown lawns, where tame deer and peacocks wandered, and birds sang spring songs despite the season. Two fountains sprayed mist into the air. Saresha sat on the bench of one, frowning up at a sculpted willow with branches that dripped curtains of water.

Arris remembered the Prince holding him last night, as fierce and protective as a lover, and he felt suddenly shy. "Good morning," he ventured, walking slowly across the lawn to the fountain.

"Arris!" Saresha's bright hair had its own glow in this world, without the sun to spark it. He sprang to his feet with a wide smile. "You're all right?"

"Yes. Where are they?"

"I don't know. They left me here last night, and I've been alone since then. Myrdethreshi said he had healed you, against his better judgment." The Prince looked embarrassed. "And he said I was their honored guest, but you were still an enemy. He did not want you here when he returned."

Arris nodded. He knew he would get no more help from the Brothers Ylla, and help was what he needed. "I'll go. Maybe Aghlayeshkusa can find a way to get me back to my own world."

"Who?"

"A daimon. He's helped me in the past."

Saresha looked down at the cobbled path that ran around the fountain's base. He kicked a stone loose with his foot. It rolled a few paces away, then turned and rolled back into its place of its own volition. "I was right. You really are a witch. You did summon that thing in the Temple, the monster."

"That was Aghlayeshkusa. He doesn't look like that now." Arris smiled slightly. "But I don't think you'd like him much in any case."

"Karillos thinks you're little better than a daimon yourself," Saresha said. "That you're evil."

"What do you think?" Arris looked at him directly, and the Prince's blue eyes did not flinch away.

"I . . . don't know what evil is. You murdered my uncles, but I saw what they did to the Lord Areyta years ago. They made me watch it. I believed he was guilty, but still, it was horrible. I think my uncle Maenad was the one who really killed my father the Khalif. I began to think that a few years after it happened. And yet I still loved my uncle. You killed him, and Nievan, who had a wife and sons."

"All I wanted was revenge," Arris said. He sat down by the fountain and drank from it with cupped hands. "I never thought about what would happen when it was over, or who it would really hurt."

"You betrayed me, too. I almost died on that altar," Saresha said. "I trusted you. You were one of my Companions. Not only that, but my closest friend. I hated you then. And then . . . you saved my life. You fought your Goddess for my sake, and betrayed your own people."

Arris's voice sounded rough when he spoke again.

"You've saved my life twice after that, Sasha. So where does that leave us?"

Saresha laughed softly, and took Arris's hands to lift him to his feet. "With only each other to rely on. Karillos is probably right about you, but it doesn't matter. It doesn't matter what you did to my family, what you almost did to me. In the end I could trust you. You've always been my only real friend."

Arris embraced the Prince on impulse, then immediately pulled away, afraid Saresha would be offended. But the other man hugged him back, warm and strong, and held him tight for a long moment. Confused but happy when Sasha let him go, Arris thought that this should be enough for anyone. "I'd . . . better go," he muttered. "Your gods don't want to find me here, and I don't want to see them again either."

"I'm coming with you," the Prince announced. "The Brothers Ylla want to keep me safe, but I want to go back to our world as much as you do. My kingdom is at war. The Citadel must have fallen. Find us a way to get back there, and help me win my throne."

Arris looked at him in wonder. He felt almost disoriented. He had been running for so long, with nothing ahead of him to strive for, no new destiny to replace the one he had rejected. "We may not be able to find a way back . . ."

"We won't if we stand around here getting splashed by the fountain." Sasha put an arm around Arris's shoulders. "Come. Let's find this daimon friend of yours." They walked out of the garden of the Five Brothers with the glow of the Gods' Realm in their faces, casting no shadows.